THE YEARS BETWEEN US

VANIA RHEAULT

❀ Created with Vellum

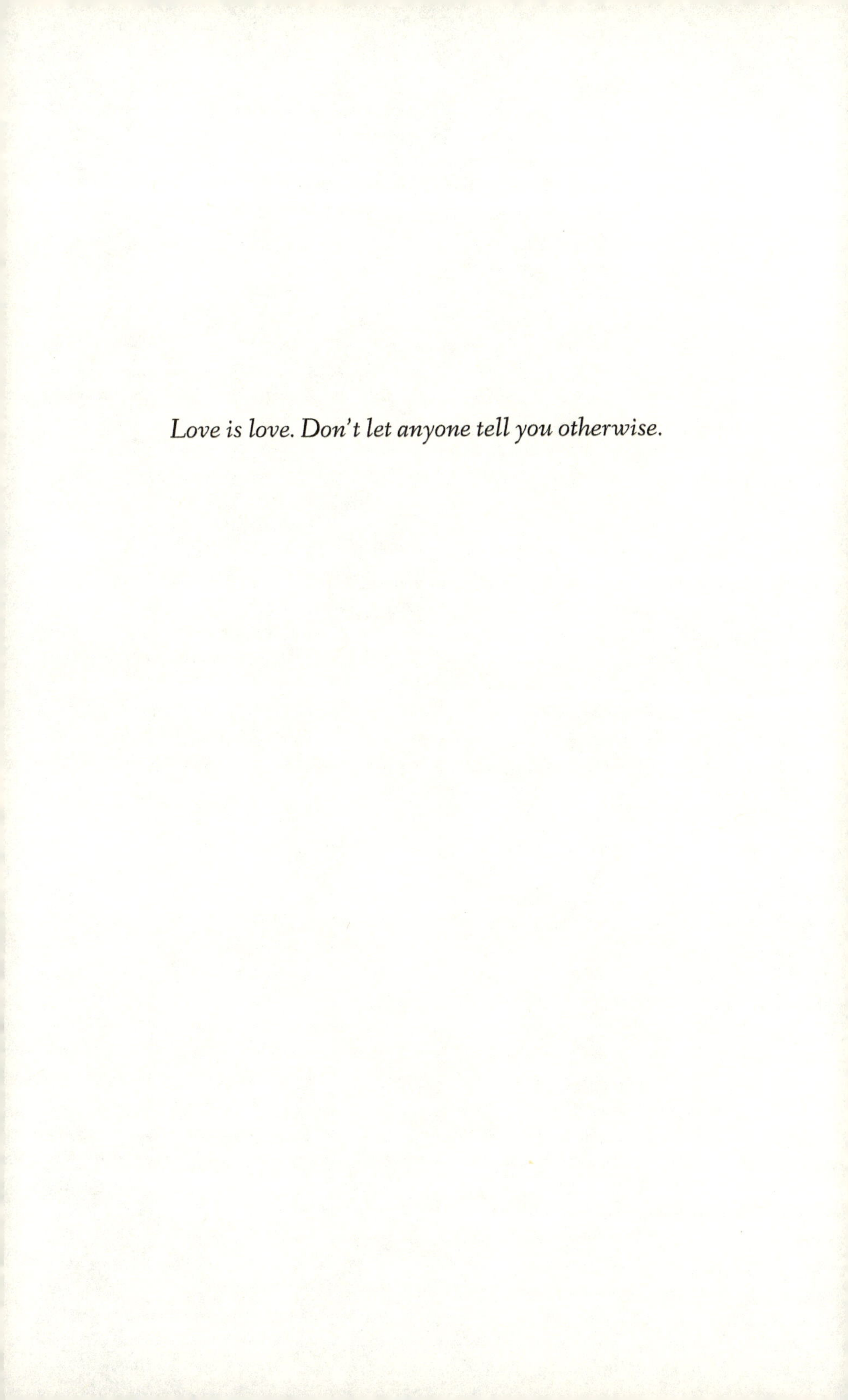

Love is love. Don't let anyone tell you otherwise.

You are cordially invited to a showing by

Zia Bishop

October 5th, 2019 | 7:30 PM

Post 15
1213 Jefferson Avenue
Lake Kenosha, Minnesota

Black Tie, *s'il vous plaît*
Masquerade Ball to follow
Harborview Hotel

CHAPTER ONE

Matthew Harcourt gratefully took a glass of champagne from a waitress wearing a plain black dress and a single strand of fake pearls. Indifference covered her face, almost crossing the line into boredom. He didn't blame her. He wouldn't have attended this party either, but the only daughter of his business partner and best friend had graduated high school, and despite the mind-numbing conversations murmuring around him, he wouldn't have missed it for the world.

At eighteen, Zia Bishop fluttered barefoot around the room, wearing a creamy, frothy dress, her flame-red hair billowing behind her in a storm of curls.

Perched on the arm of a chair in the corner of the room and sipping champagne, he watched her float from one group of guests to the next. She acknowledged congratulations and discreetly accepted envelopes that would contain lavishly written checks as if she'd been awarded the Nobel Prize rather than simply finishing twelve years of school. To her credit, she'd graduated Valedictorian, which hadn't surprised him in the least, and the Bishops wouldn't have done anything less to celebrate their daughter's success.

Neither would he, had he been in any position to do so.

But he wasn't.

Zia caught him staring, and she squeezed an older woman's ample arm then stepped tentatively in his direction.

Her smile could have rivaled the sun, but her gaze shot past his shoulder and a cloud moved across her face.

"She's grown into quite the young lady." A woman appeared at his elbow, and he grimaced into his empty champagne flute. He needed more. Lots more.

"Chloe," he said, "you're looking lovely." She didn't, not in his opinion, though most people would consider her beautiful. He preferred a more natural approach, but over the past few years Chloe Bishop had set her sights on him and she hadn't taken the hint that the more she did to herself the more determined he became to avoid her.

She rested her hand on the back of his neck. "Thank you," she purred. "I've been visiting a new spa and going a tad lighter with my hair color. I shouldn't be spilling my secrets, but I know you won't tell."

Zia's smile disappeared and she turned toward her mother who called to her.

"No, I don't suppose I'm interested enough to say anything," he muttered, hunching his shoulders in a subtle attempt to discourage Chloe's touch as well as in disappointment Zia walked away.

The slight barb went over Chloe's head. "How are things at the office? Is my brother going easy on you?"

He scoffed. "I'm surprised you care."

"I don't, not really. Raymond gives me my allowance, and that's all I need. Of course, the more successful you are, the more money he's able to give me."

"Yes, I'm well aware of your penchant to avoid working."

Her fingernails raked over his skin. "I'm simply dreadful in the workplace, Matthew. No one would hire me even if I wanted to find a job."

"I'm sure you have a skill inside you, somewhere. Possibly. Sylvia does just fine," he needled. Chloe hated being compared to her sister-in-law.

She bristled. "Sylvia wouldn't have done half as well without her father's money."

"You have Raymond's. He's told me several times he would help you do anything you like. Sylvia built her decorating business from the ground up. Her father may have given her the start-up cash, but she made it work using her tenacity and grit." *Not to mention the brains between her ears.*

"I've no use for that." Chloe paused. "I'm thinking of getting married again. I want to fall in love. Perhaps I could find a man who would write me love letters. I think that would be so romantic."

"The mail is unreliable, and stamps are too expensive," Matthew said, apprehension shivering through him. He hated talking to Chloe, and her touch grated on his nerves. "Sexting seems to be more your style. Aren't you on Snapchat?"

"I do plenty of that kind of thing," Chloe said, her fingers brushing his jaw, "but I want someone to love me."

Fighting the urge to knock her hand away, he said, "When you find him, he'll be a lucky man." He couldn't stand the woman's grating presence for one more second. "Goodnight, Chloe. I'm going to find Zia and tell her goodbye."

"You're leaving already?" Chloe pouted. "Raymond planned fireworks."

"I'm sure they won't be any different than any of the others I've seen. Have a nice evening." Matthew set his empty champagne glass on a small table, the surface littered with knickknacks.

"Matthew," she said, crowding him into the corner and running a fingernail down the lapel of his black suit. "What if I come over later? Please?"

He hated saying no. She'd bitch to Ray who would complain over coffee before their first meeting Monday morning. Raymond wouldn't have liked anything better than if he took Chloe off his hands. Ray could stop giving his sister the massive allowance she lived on between marriages and let him foot the bill for all the meaningless garbage she loved to buy.

"Not tonight. I have early meetings tomorrow. Another time." He patted her shoulder, for lack of anything better, because he certainly wasn't going to kiss her, despite the faux kiss-kiss thing that had suddenly become so popular.

"I'll take you up on that," she said.

I'm sure you'll try.

He dodged Zia's guests who wanted to talk. He avoided Raymond, not in the mood to listen to another speech about Chloe's fine qualities—as there were many—and searched the house for Zia, even going up to her bedroom to no avail.

Sylvia caught him with his hand on the doorknob, and heat stained his cheeks.

"Matthew, what are you doing up here?"

"Looking for Zia. I'm going home."

"Oh, she's in the maze getting a bit of air. Raymond's having the fireworks lit soon. You're sure you want to miss them?"

"Zia doesn't need an old fuddy-duddy like me around to enjoy the fireworks."

She straightened his tie and smiled. "Zia doesn't see you that way, and you know it. Come down. You didn't have cake, and you can bring Zia a glass of punch. Matilda spiked it with champagne, and I have to say, it's better for it."

He followed Sylvia downstairs and she shoved a dessert plate and punch cup into his hands.

"Here, take these. You know where to go."

"What are you doing?" he murmured, narrowing his eyes.

Sylvia lifted a flute of champagne to her lips that were curling into a smile. "I have no idea what you're talking about."

"Mmm-hmmm. Goodnight, Sylvia."

"Goodnight, Matthew."

Zia sat on a secret bench inside a maze made of thick hedges in her parents' monstrous backyard. As far as she knew, she'd been the only one in years who could find the dead end, and she often ran there to seek solace. No matter how long or loud someone called for her to come inside, she only returned to the house on her terms. Usually after a crying jag, and usually about Matthew.

She hated seeing her aunt's hands on him.

She hated more he didn't seem to mind.

Not that she could say anything. Aimee, her best friend since second grade, told her she couldn't win a grownup's game. That was three years ago, but she felt no more equipped to play now than she had back then.

Running away because Chloe the Tramp had been touching Matthew wasn't very adult, proving Aimee's point.

She heard a rustling behind the hedge and wiped her cheeks.

"Zia," Matthew said, walking around the corner, holding a cake plate in one hand and a glass of punch in the other.

Zia swallowed and tried to smooth her tangle of curls. He was completely out of her league. Rich and sexy as sin.

"How did you find me?"

"I can always find you, Little Star." He sat down next to her.

"Stop calling me that," she snapped. It'd been his nickname for her for as long as she could remember. As a child, she'd beam, a tiara sitting precariously on her head, and spin pirouettes wearing her pink tutu wanting to make him laugh.

She didn't want Matthew to see a child when he looked at her. She wanted him to see her as a woman. Someone who could compete against her aunt.

It was a wasted wish.

"What's wrong?" he asked, handing her the punch. Hurt tinged his voice, and she looked away, ashamed.

"Nothing," she muttered. She swished the pink punch in the cup, wishing he'd thought to bring her a flute of champagne.

Matthew set the piece of untouched cake beside him on the bench. Twisting sideways to face her, he said, "You've always been able to talk to me, Little . . . Zia. Why can't you now?"

Tears pricked her eyes. She hadn't meant what she said. She still wanted him to call her his Little Star. She loved it, and now he stopped because she was being a brat.

She dropped the punch glass onto the ground and leaned into him, needing his arms around her.

He complied, and she inhaled his scent, a scent that hadn't changed in all her life.

Her mother had shown her pictures of Matthew holding her as a baby. As a toddler, pressing her chubby hands to his cheeks. As a kindergartner, then first grade, second. In fourth grade, her father had told her he needed to go out of town on a business trip and they'd have to miss the father/daughter dance. Matthew escorted her instead, and years later, looking through the photos, she'd found one of them dancing. She stared into his eyes, and he into hers, and a lightning bolt had told her what she already knew.

She loved Matthew Harcourt.

Even if he was old enough to be her father.

The hopelessness of it all made her sob into his chest, and he rubbed slow circles on her bare back, his hand warm.

Her skin tingled and her nipples hardened.

She lifted her head, and his features wavered through her tears. Fairy lights decorating the maze cast just enough light and Matthew's blue eyes glowed.

Zia pressed her body into his. "Please, Matthew," she whispered, though she had no idea what she was begging for.

He cradled her face in his hands and wiped her tears away with the pads of his thumbs. She thought it was the most romantic thing in the world. She leaned in, closer, and he tilted his head, his breath floating over her skin.

"This isn't right," he whispered, but he covered her lips with his.

A dam of need broke inside her. Finally. Finally, after years of yearning, after years of hoping, Matthew was kissing her. She wrapped her arms around his neck and pulled him closer.

He did the same, and without breaking their kiss, she scrambled into his lap.

His cock hardened beneath her, and though she'd never had sex before, she knew what it meant, and she wanted to cry in relief.

Matthew felt the same way about her.

She opened her mouth in invitation, and he complied, slipping his tongue between her teeth.

Moaning, she threaded her fingers through his hair. He tasted of champagne and a spicy flavor that belonged only to Matthew.

"Zia," he gasped, tearing his mouth away from hers, "we can't do this."

With a ragged breath, she buried her face in his neck, brushing her lips against his hot skin. "Why? I'm eighteen. I can make my own choices."

"You don't know what you're asking," he said, but he skimmed his fingers up her bare leg. He stopped, his hand near the apex of her thighs.

She stilled.

Panties damp, a pressure tightened between her legs in a way she'd never felt before.

To encourage him, she shifted, giving his hand more room.

"I know what I want," she whispered. "Please, Matthew." A sob of desperation clogged her throat. "I need you to touch me."

"Zia, look at me," he murmured.

She didn't want to, afraid of what she'd see in his eyes. Disdain. Disgust. Loathing he succumbed to a girl her age.

Reluctantly, she lifted her head off his shoulder and met his eyes. She straightened her spine, preparing for his letdown. That he could never be with someone like her. Too young, too immature. That he wanted, needed, someone like her aunt. Who knew what she was doing. In bed and out.

"You can feel I want you," he said and chuckled, a rueful sound rumbling from the depth of his chest. "How could I not?"

He ran a hand over her curls, his fingertips grazing her shoulder. "You're so exquisite. Your name settles in my soul like a smoldering ember, like the feelings for you I've been trying to extinguish."

She forgot to breathe. She'd never heard anyone say something so beautiful. Her eyes watered with the simple joy of the moment.

He continued, rubbing a thumb over her lips. "But if you're going to give yourself to me, we'll do it right. You deserve more than a stone bench and a hundred people only fifty feet away."

"What do you mean? I don't understand." Hope flared in her heart.

"If you're going to let me have you, we'll do it in my bed."

"Yes. God, yes. But how . . ."

"You'll need to stay and watch the fireworks. Tell your parents you're sleeping over at Aimee's. No one can know. You know what people will say."

She didn't, but she nodded. If they loved each other, how could anyone say anything bad? She was eighteen and could do what she liked. It wasn't anyone's business whom she slept with, but if that's the way Matthew wanted it, then that's the way it would be.

He pushed a kiss to her mouth, and she melted in his arms.

Just another hour and she could give herself to him completely, the way she'd wanted to for so long.

Matthew stole one more kiss before nudging her off his lap. What he planned to do was wrong. He knew it. But the sweetness of her mouth, the look in her eyes that said she wanted him, the heat radiating from between her legs . . .

This would be consensual.

And reciprocated.

Maybe a stronger man could turn her away. Maybe a smarter man would choose Chloe and all she had to offer, but he wanted nothing more than to sample the flame, the heat of this woman in his arms.

He loved her, but that didn't make it right.

He knew what people would say.

Zia had agreed, but she didn't know what he meant. She'd agree to whatever he wanted her to, so long as he brought her home.

He'd need to protect her. Encouraging her to lie broke his heart, but they wouldn't be able to spend the night together if she told anyone the truth. He wanted to spend the night with her. He didn't want to kick her out of his bed and have her sneak home like a used-up whore.

As he led her out of the maze, she tried to hold his hand.

He jerked away. "No."

"I'm sorry," she mumbled.

He tightened his hands into fists to stop himself from wrapping his arms around her. "No, I am. But you'll have to play by my rules if you want this." He tucked her against the hedge near the opening of the maze. Out of sight of the other guests, he cupped her breast through the thin material of her dress. "Please say you do."

"More than anything." She sighed and pressed into his hand.

"Good." He kissed the tip of her nose.

Hiding how Zia made him feel proved difficult. He greeted guests and made small talk. She remained in his periphery, and he tried to keep his cool.

"Are you all right?" Sylvia asked, stepping across the grass, barefoot, like her daughter.

Zia's guests milled about the yard waiting for the fireworks to begin. A light breeze graced the Minnesota spring evening and stars twinkled in a clear sky, giving the fireworks a lovely backdrop.

"You seem out of sorts," she continued, tugging a wrap tighter around her shoulders. "Did you find Zia?"

"I did," Matthew said and swallowed, wishing he had a drink to calm his nerves. He nodded in Zia's direction. She'd joined a group of her friends, her skin glinting like gold in the torch lights dispersed around the yard to keep the mosquitoes at bay. "The cake isn't sitting well with me, and I'm going home. I've told Zia goodbye."

The lies weighed heavy on his conscience. His friendship with Sylvia meant the world to him.

He should walk away. From Zia, from Sylvia. From Bridgewater Financial. Ask Raymond to buy him out and walk away.

He'd already caused so much damage.

She frowned in concern. "Okay. Chloe saw you go into the maze and was asking about you. Be careful."

"Thanks for the heads up."

He lived in the same neighborhood, and five minutes later, he turned into his driveway, greatly relieved he'd been able to avoid anyone who wanted to trap him in last-minute conversation.

Huge evergreens, pines, and spruces dotted his expansive yard, as well as a man-made pond where several ducks and geese had made their homes. An older neighborhood, Raymond Bishop would never have chosen a house in the quiet community, but Sylvia had fallen in love with the charm and architecture of the house she and Raymond purchased before Zia's birth. Both Raymond and Sylvia had insisted he live near them, and rootless, he didn't have a reason to disagree.

His house was smaller than the Bishop's, but that suited him. He'd never married and hadn't any children. At forty-three, he was considered one of Lake Kenosha's most eligible bachelors.

He didn't think about it, and when people asked why he was determined to remain single, he simply said he hadn't found the right woman.

It wasn't anyone's business but his own that he'd wanted to

marry, many years ago, but he hadn't fought for her in favor of a friendship.

He had few regrets, as it had worked out for everyone involved, and usually he thought nothing of it.

His day-to-day activities pleased him. Work, casual parties, meeting up with a friend for an early morning run. He was one of those rare people who didn't mind spending time alone, and he often sat reading long into the night, his only companion a glass of scotch or a strong cup of coffee.

He didn't turn on any lights as he walked through his living room, preferring the cocoon of silent darkness. The twinkling lights attached to his porch emitted more than enough to see by, and in the kitchen, he poured a drink in the shadows.

He drained it and loosened his tie.

Now would have been a good time to change the sheets, but he hadn't had a woman stay here for years. If he needed, or wanted, companionship, he'd take her to the Harborview. Women preferred the romance of the luxurious hotel, the thirtieth floor affording them a lovely view of the city's bright skyline, the room service and breakfast in bed.

He was then free to leave, and she could linger, do with her morning what she liked. He always left cab fare and directed the concierge to have flowers delivered later that morning thanking her for the splendid evening.

It wasn't that he was a son of a bitch. He was well-liked by everyone. He preferred a no-strings type existence, and keeping himself from tangling in Chloe's sticky web used up enough energy.

He hunted around his kitchen and was pleased to find the small stash of tea lights he'd needed when a thunderstorm last summer knocked out the power. He lit them in his bedroom upstairs, placing them on his nightstand, the headboard's alcove, and a few shelves of his armoire. He wanted to give Zia the most memorable of experiences.

He made his bed, untangling the sheets and bedspread. She wouldn't object to the scent of his cologne on her pillow.

Downstairs, he poured another drink and settled to wait, his erection pulsing against his abdomen.

He'd almost come when Zia had wiggled into his lap. If he was smart, he'd give himself a handjob to take the edge off. He couldn't be rough and he sure as hell didn't want to scare her, but he didn't want to dilute the evening. In a futile attempt to loosen up, he sipped his drink, inhaling and exhaling in a steady rhythm.

Zia's innocence enthralled him. Captivated him. Charmed him.

He couldn't keep her.

He already knew that, and he didn't need anyone to tell him so.

But tonight, he would take what she offered.

Headlights cut into the darkness of his front lawn, and he stiffened.

Someone timidly knocked on his door and he tried to relax, but his shoulders tensed when a car's engine faded.

Zia stood on his front porch wearing her cream dress, her height aided by a pair of heels she'd slipped onto her feet. Her red hair blazed in the streetlight, and she carried a small valise. "I had Aimee drop me off. I hope that was okay."

"Can she keep a secret?" he asked, hating himself for it. He wasn't cut out to have a clandestine love affair.

"She thinks it's romantic . . . and so do I." She leaned toward him, tilting her head, wanting a kiss.

He groaned, tempted, always temped, but he said, holding the door open, "Come inside. You're hardly wearing anything and you'll catch a chill."

"You like it," she teased, toeing off her heels.

"I do," he admitted. "Too much." He wanted to carry her upstairs and have his way with her, but she deserved better than that. Just as she deserved better than a stone bench.

"Would you like—" He was going to offer her a glass of wine, but he pursed his lips.

It didn't seem right she wasn't old enough to drink, but old enough to sleep with him.

"I have Perrier," he finished lamely.

"I wouldn't mind," she said, peering out his French doors. "Do you have the lemon?"

"Yes, I do."

She'd been in his house millions of times, of course, and he'd often babysat her there, as well, a disturbing picture he pushed away as he pulled the bright green Perrier bottle out of the fridge.

His hand shaking, he poured the fizzy water into a tumbler.

Zia ambled around the living room, looking at the knick-knacks and photos, her fingers lingering over one of him and Sylvia, Zia as a toddler in his arms, grinning into the camera.

Had Raymond taken the picture? Matthew had forgotten who'd made them look like the family they weren't.

Bile churned in his stomach, mixing with the champagne, but the nausea didn't stifle his erection and he throbbed.

"Here. Zia—"

"I'm not changing my mind." She sipped the sparkling water bubbling against the ice cubes. "I want this." She set the glass on the coffee table, the *clink* echoing through the room. "I've wanted it for a long time, Matthew."

"That doesn't make it right. I'm twenty-eight years older than you."

"Why does that make it wrong?"

Teasing him made her heart stop pounding. They'd always gotten along, they'd always had a chemistry that was more than only . . . "Friends" didn't sound right. He'd been her father's childhood friend first, then business partner. She'd heard enough stories to know Matthew had also known her mother when they were teenagers. Only, Matthew went away to school and her father and mother had stayed in Lake Kenosha and fell in love. When Matthew came home after graduation, he and her father started Bridgewater, and since then, everything was the way she'd always known it.

"Can we go upstairs?" she asked, sounding more confident than she felt. If she hesitated, even for a second, he'd bring her home, and she'd never have this chance again. She couldn't blow it.

Matthew kissed her palm. "If you're sure, Little Star."

"I am."

She followed him up the staircase, knowing where he'd take her. She had thousands of memories of playing in this house, and she had to wave them away, her little girl laugh echoing through the hallways. She was here as a woman, and she straightened her spine, determined to act like one. Matthew had his choice of women, and he'd chosen her.

She couldn't let him down.

"Oh, Matthew," she breathed, stepping into his suite. "You did this for me?"

"It wasn't that much," he muttered, shutting the door.

But it was. Candles flickered on every available surface, and he'd turned down the bed like at a hotel. He'd sprayed some kind of scent too, or maybe it was the candles. Vanilla, and the faint hint of his cologne she loved.

"Zia . . . my Little Star, sit down, please."

She swallowed. Surely he wouldn't have brought her up here to turn her away.

She sat on the decorative bench at the end of the bed, and he did as well. She hoped the dim light hid her freckles. She was hopelessly ashamed of them. Especially since her aunt made it a point every time Zia saw her to complain how childish they looked.

Matthew cupped her face between his palms, and she licked her lips.

Gorgeous. The man was simply gorgeous. Dark slashes, his eyebrows framed eyes boasting long, dark lashes. Strong, straight nose. Stubble along his jaw. And kind. Oh, so kind. Zia believed when someone was kind you could see it in their eyes, in their expression. Matthew would never, ever hurt her.

She knew that as deeply as she knew she'd one day be a famous artist.

"Zia. I want you to know I haven't had a woman in my bed for a long time. I . . . I don't mean any bed. This one. A woman in my room."

He was nervous.

Zia bit back a smile, suddenly feeling more in control. He was nervous.

Thank God.

She stood and stepped between his knees. "It's okay. You're a good-looking man. Sexy," she said, loosening the knot in his tie. "I don't blame any woman for wanting to be here, right where I am. My aunt wants you."

He laid a hand over hers. "I've never been with Chloe. I want you to know that. You wouldn't be standing where you are had I been with her, in any way."

"I'm glad." She didn't want to be her aunt's sloppy seconds.

She wanted Matthew all to herself.

She unbuttoned the top button of his dress shirt. She'd never undressed a man before.

"Now you."

"Now me, what?" she whispered, stepping closer, the edge of the bench biting into her legs.

"How many men have you been with? How many times have you given yourself to someone?"

She lifted her chin. If this was what would change his mind . . . she could lie. She could tell him . . . he called them men, but they were boys. The boys she'd gone to high school with only wanted to screw as many girls as they could before their parents shipped them off to college. She could tell Matthew she'd slept with all of them. Turn herself into a slut because that would make him feel better about sleeping with her. But she couldn't lie, and the truth slipped out of her mouth before she could stop it.

"None."

"I don't understand."

He tightened his hands around her wrists. She flinched but didn't cry out.

"Did you say none?" he asked, to make sure, because this beautiful creature standing in front of him couldn't have said she hadn't been with anyone. Smart, passionate, a glow so bright she could power the city with her smile alone, his Little Star couldn't still be a virgin.

"I've never slept with anyone. I've been saving myself for you."

He lowered his head into his hands. It had gone from bad to worse, from sinful desire to his own personal hell in a matter of seconds.

She knelt in front of him and moved his hands away from his face. He let her, caught in the radiance of her green eyes in the candles' flames. A witch. A siren. She was everything rolled into one woman, kneeling before him, holding out her virginity and asking him to take it.

"I want you to be my first." She kissed his palm as he'd done downstairs. "Please. You'll treat me better than anyone else would. You care about me, don't you, Matthew?"

"I do. Too much. Too much to do this with you. You shouldn't be here. You should be making out in a car at the park. You should be in a backseat, at the lake, letting some drunk guy grope you, the way teenagers are supposed to have sex for the first time." The scenarios chilled him.

Anger flashed across her face. "You want me to lose my virginity like that?" she whispered. "You want a guy forcing himself on me because he's had too much to drink and won't listen to me say no? You want a guy ramming his fingers inside me, and I can't stop him because we'd be at the lake and I'd have nowhere to run? Is that how you want my first time to be?"

He recoiled, unwilling to picture her in a situation like that. "You're twisting my words. Of course I don't want that. I want you to have fun. After a party, giddy, high on youth and promise. I want you to be with someone your own age."

"You mean stumbling around because I don't know what to do, and then after, embarrassed, a cop knocking on our window, telling us to go home. I l . . . ike you, Matthew, and you know what you're doing. Will you show me?"

She unbuttoned his shirt and slowly brushed kisses over his chest.

His breath hitched, her lips searing his skin.

"Are you sure? After you give yourself to me, you can't take it back. This memory will never fade. No one forgets the first time they make love."

She lifted her head, and the moment her eyes met his, he knew he spoke the truth. He loved Zia Bishop with all his heart, no matter how wrong it was, no matter that it would cast a shadow on the remaining years of his life. For he also knew this truth: they could never be together. Not in a way she would want. Not in the way a woman hoped when she gave herself to a man.

"Is that what this is? Love?"

He trailed his fingers down her cheek, his heart breaking she had to ask. "Yes. I love you. I've loved you as a baby, vowing to protect you as you lay in your cradle, only hours old. I've loved you as a toddler, a little girl playing princess, hair and magic wand waving. I've loved you as a young woman, only discovering who you are, what you would become. And I love you now, Zia. A woman coming into her own, her talents blooming. I've had the honor of seeing you through all those stages of your life, and my love for you grows stronger every day."

A tear dripped down her cheek. It shimmered, and he brushed it aside with his thumb.

"I'll only ask you one more time, Little Star. Are you giving yourself to me, tonight? Are you sure?"

CHAPTER TWO

And *always*, she thought, but bit the words back. "Yes. I wouldn't want to be with anyone else."

"Then stand, and let me see you."

Heart pounding, she rose to her feet, and so did he. Her artist's eye drank him in, and tomorrow she'd lock herself in her studio and capture the memory on canvas. She'd keep this night with her forever.

Gently, he turned her around and brushed her hair aside. He pressed his lips to her neck, and she shivered as he drew the zipper down.

He whispered kisses down her back, and goosebumps covered her skin. Heat pooled in her belly. He pushed the dress off her shoulders and it skimmed down her body and onto the floor.

Turning around, she said, "I know I don't look—"

"You're beautiful," he said, his voice hoarse.

She wished she'd worn lingerie a little more sophisticated than the cream lace bra and matching panties. They accentuated her virginal state.

She stood on her tiptoes and kissed him.

The longer he stood there and looked at her, the greater the chance of him saying this would be a big mistake.

He wrapped his arms around her and eased a hand through her curls. His scruff scratched at her cheeks as he tilted his head and slipped his tongue into her mouth, but she didn't care. It was the most romantic thing she'd ever done, and there was no way she'd complain about the burn against her skin.

Breaking the kiss, he stepped away. She wanted to cry out in disappointment, but he only undid the hooks of her bra and slid the straps over her arms. "God, you're magnificent," he mumbled. He captured her mouth again, and she leaned in, losing the last wisps of self-consciousness.

He trailed his kisses down her neck, bending to linger at her breasts. Her nipples puckered in anticipation.

Lowering farther, his tongue darted into her belly button, then he moved his mouth to the waistline of her panties, grabbed the lace between his teeth, and tugged lightly before letting go.

He looked up at her and met her eyes, and he slid her panties down her hips. She steadied herself with a hand to his shoulder as she stepped out of the material.

As he nuzzled her soft thatch of hair with his lips, Zia tipped her head back, enjoying the sensation of a man between her legs. She widened her stance, giving him access. "Like this?" she asked, wanting him inside her. Fingers, tongue, his cock, she yearned for him to fill her completely.

He kissed her thigh. "No. Have patience, Little Star. Undress me, please."

Of course. Her cheeks blazed.

Matthew stood in front her, his blue eyes sizzling, his five o'clock shadow covering a hardened jaw. His shirt hung open, his jacket perfectly tailored to his shoulders, the tie hanging around his neck an exact match to his eyes. He wore a black leather belt, the silver buckle shining, his dress pants crisp and unwrinkled. Though he'd taken off his dress shoes, he still wore black socks. Lean, not an ounce of fat on his body, her mouth watered.

She took his jacket off, her hands trembling, and laid it neatly across the back of a chair. Stealing a moment, she deeply inhaled. She wasn't nervous, but somehow, she knew that after tonight, her life would never be the same.

Zia slid the tie out from under his collar and let his dress shirt fall to the floor near her dress.

His abs were chiseled, his skin cast bronze.

Kissing his hard chest, she unbuckled his belt and unbuttoned his pants. As he'd done for her, she unzipped the zipper and skimmed his dress slacks over his ass, down rock-hard thighs.

He kicked them out of the way.

His erection strained his black briefs, and she reached out, pausing an inch over his cock.

Matthew held her hand and pressed it to him. He surged under her palm. "This is what you do to me. This is what I've hidden from you because you were too young. You're still too young, but you were right. I want to be the one to give you this."

She swallowed. His cock felt so big, and tonight, it would turn her into a woman.

Silence hung in the air, and it wasn't entirely comfortable.

"I want you to be the one, too," she whispered.

"Take my briefs off, Zia, and look at what I'm going to put inside you."

Her gaze flew to his. His eyes bore into hers, and she realized it then. He wasn't angry. He was trying to stay in control.

She wasn't naïve. She knew enough about sex to understand a man needed only a few seconds, and then it would be over.

Matthew had more respect for her than that. He loved her and would make her first time the way every young woman hoped it would be.

She tugged his briefs down and his erection sprang free of the material. "Can I touch you?"

"Yes, I'd like that very much."

Wrapping her hand around his hard length, she breathed in his musky scent. His skin was silky and smooth, the head of his penis slick. She'd never tasted cum before and she lowered her head, slightly sticking out her tongue.

"Not yet, sweetheart. I want to pleasure you first. This night is about you. Come here."

Matthew had overestimated his control, and her kneeling in front of him, his cock held gently in her hand, he'd almost come. And when she said she wanted to taste him . . .

Gripping her arm more roughly than he intended, he urged her to her feet. "Come to bed."

He searched for any fear, any hesitancy that would make him put his clothes back on and send her home. There was nothing but anticipation and want on her face, and she slipped between the sheets, her hair splayed over his pillow in a burning tangle.

He lay on his side and smoothed her hair away from her face. "This is important now. You need to tell me if I do something you don't like. It will probably hurt, but I'll try my best to keep that as minimal as possible, okay?"

"I know you won't hurt me."

The naked trust in her eyes shattered him. No one should ever trust someone as much as Zia trusted him.

It never ended well.

Words wouldn't matter now. Nothing he said would sound right. He kissed her, and he reveled in the feel of her lips. Years of watching her grow into a young woman he thought he'd never be allowed to touch pent up a desire he couldn't describe. Kissing her released that tension and replaced it with a new expectation. A new understanding that as he took, he would give and protect.

He sprinkled kisses over her collarbone and lingered at one of her breasts, teasing her sensitive nipple until it hardened under his tongue. He switched to her other nipple, and she arched her back, raking her fingers through his hair and murmuring his name in response.

Moving on, he kissed down past the valley of her belly, where once again he nosed the shining curls between her legs.

"Open up for me, sweetheart. Let me see you." She widened her slim thighs, and he choked. Her pink skin sparkled, dewy with arousal. "I want to touch you. You'll tell me if you're uncomfortable?"

"Matthew, please," she whimpered, tilting her hips.

Ever so slowly, he pushed a fingertip inside her, aware he could be the first thing to breach her body.

"Do you like this, sweetheart?"

"Yes. I want more, please," she whispered.

He nuzzled her clit with his tongue and pushed his finger deeper inside her. His cock ached in response to how wet she felt, her muscles clenching around his finger.

As he licked her, he drowned in her flavor and scent.

Nothing in the world could rival how she affected his senses.

"Matthew," Zia cried. "What's happening?"

"You're close to having an orgasm, and it will feel good. I promise. Let yourself go, Little Star. You're safe."

"No. I wanted to come while you're inside me," she protested, jerking her hips from his mouth. "I want to know how that feels."

"You will. We have all night, I promise. Come for me first," he said, wanting her pliant and languid when he pushed his cock inside her for the first time. "Relax."

He licked her clit and slowly pushed two fingers inside her, filling her.

She moaned.

Her clit grew under his tongue, and he knew it would only be a few more seconds before she fell to pieces. So slightly, he twisted his fingers, and she came under his mouth. He drowned in her heat, in her musk, the pleasure rolling through her.

He gave her a moment to catch her breath. As gently as he could, he slid his fingers from inside her, and her small whimpers scratched his heart. He covered her body with his. Tears glistened on her cheeks. "Zia. I hurt you, didn't I? I'm so sorry, sweetheart." He rested his forehead against her temple, her tears wetting the tip of his nose.

"No, no. That's not it. I love you so much, and for you to be the first to do that for me . . . it was beautiful. You didn't hurt me. But . . . be inside me now, please?"

She held his face between her hands and scrubbed his whiskers. His cock throbbed. He was more than ready to accept her invitation. "I need a condom," he said, reaching toward his nightstand.

"No, please. My . . . Mom put me on the pill." Her cheeks pinked. "For college. She wanted me to be prepared."

"You've been on it long enough that it's working? Zia, a baby right now wouldn't be good for you, for either of us. You have so much to look forward to. I should wear a condom."

"I've been on it for a couple of months now. Please. I want to feel you. You're my first. I don't have anything."

"I don't either, but . . ." God, he wanted to be inside her without a condom, but he was forty-three years old and didn't want a baby, either. It wasn't that he never wanted children, but he'd never met a woman he wanted to start a family with. Zia might be that woman, but the timing couldn't be worse. "I should still wear one. Accidents can happen. I love you, and this is one way a man protects the woman he loves. You can put it on, okay?"

He wouldn't add she should know how so she could keep herself safe at school.

She licked her lips. "Okay."

He ripped the foil packet open and wiggled the condom out. "It goes on like this," he said, positioning it over the tip of his cock, "and you roll it down."

Holding her hands, he helped her smooth down his cock, jerking every time her fingers touched his skin.

"You're so big," she said, clumsily rolling the latex to the base of his erection.

"Does it scare you?" he asked, praying the answer was no. He would stop if she said she didn't want to go further, but it would cost him and he didn't want to calculate how much. "To think of me inside you?"

Zia leaned toward him, her breath caressing his lips. "You said you wanted me when it wasn't right. It's the same for me. I've wanted this since before I understood what it meant. I knew if you were with me, like this, as close as two people could be to each other, I would finally feel whole. And I will."

She laid back against the pillow and widened her knees. "Please, Matthew. Make me yours."

Thank God she sounded more confident than she felt. She *did* want him inside her, so badly she felt consumed by it, but there was no doubt it would hurt. She had to think of the pain in a different way. Watching her aunt hang on Matthew hurt. Him turning her away because of their age difference hurt. Not having him would hurt more than feeling him move inside her.

She widened her legs and gripped the pillow from underneath. She needed to hide how frightened this made her, and she bit the inside of her cheek as the tip of his cock probed her opening.

It helped she'd already come. She knew she was wet and she focused on keeping her muscles loose.

"Will you kiss me?" she asked, hoping it would distract her.

"Of course, Little Star, I'll do whatever you ask."

He settled between her legs and gently pushed inside her. Her body accepted him as easily as her mouth accepted his tongue, and she wrapped her arms around his neck, angling her hips upward, helping herself take all of what he had to give her.

His cock filled her body, and his love filled her heart. She imagined her soul sparkling like stars, pinpricks of blinding light in a dark sky.

She found home in his arms, his eyes boring into hers.

He began to move back and forth.

Sweat covered his back, and the muscles in his arms corded as he kept himself from crushing her. She smoothed her hands over his skin, his perspiration and their desire mingling with the scent of the flickering candles.

She inhaled, committing the scents to memory. She'd always remember the night Matthew made her a woman. It was everything she hoped it would be.

"I love you, Zia," Matthew murmured. "I'm going to come."

"Yes, yes," she said, meeting his thrusts, hoping she was making him feel good, too.

His cock twitched inside her, and he groaned.

She almost laughed. He sounded so animal, so unlike the elegant man she'd given her heart to, but it thrilled her she could elicit such a response from him.

With a hand under her butt, he held her close. Her amusement turned into a shocked cry, his cocked buried so deep inside her the tip touched her center.

He shuddered, bracing himself over her. "I hurt you," he said, releasing his strong grip. "I'm sorry."

"No, I'm okay." She bit her lip and looked away. She had no experience with this. "I hope it was good for you."

"Hey, look at me," he said, his voice a husky growl.

Just then, she envied every woman who'd had the pleasure of hearing his voice in a darkened room after an evening of sex.

She met his eyes, the blue blazing like the hottest part of a fire.

Electric blue.

"What?"

"You were perfect. There's nothing I'd ask you to do differently. It was perfect."

He pressed his lips to hers, and she fell into his kiss, smoothing her hands over his shoulders, the sweat cooling on his skin.

"You're getting cold."

"So are you," he said, then kissed the tip of her nose.

She almost told him not to do that, that it reminded her of being a child and the time they used to spend together, but she didn't want to hurt his feelings like she had in the maze, and she forced a smile instead.

"This might hurt, sweetheart. I'm going to pull out, okay?"

"Yeah." She tensed, but he slid out of her in a warm gush that wasn't painful.

"Was that okay? Are you sore?" he asked, concerned.

"A little," she admitted. "I'm crampy."

"I was deep inside you, Little Star. That's natural, but you're not sore here," he asked, whispering his fingertips where his cock had just been.

She knew what he meant, and her skin didn't hurt. "No."

He brushed a kiss over her knee. "Good. I'll be right back." She burrowed into the blankets while he used the bathroom. Her future with him flashed in front her eyes. They'd get married, but they'd have a long engagement first. Maybe wait until she turned twenty-one so she could drink at the reception. She giggled.

She'd move into his house. He'd never had a woman live here, and it pleased her she'd be the only one.

She had plans to go to school in the fall, but those plans would change. She could go to art school here, in the city, instead of the Art Studio in California. Being an artist, a painter, had been her dream since she was a little girl, and being accepted into the Art Studio had been a wish come true. She'd let herself dream, plan her career, because she never thought in a million years that Matthew would return her feelings. But he had, he did, and she was willing to brush everything aside for him, to be the loving wife he needed.

"You look happy," he said, walking out of the bathroom and slipping into bed.

Immediately, she cuddled against his chest. "I am. I was thinking about what we'll do next. I'll move in here, and change schools. My parents will probably be mad, but after we get married, they'll see that you make me happy—" Matthew sat up, and her heart sank. "What is it?"

"Zia. I love you, you know I do, and tonight was incredible, but sweetheart, you're not thinking clearly."

She sat up too and skimmed her fingers over his lips. A sizzle traveled through her body, into her core. His lips had been between her legs, and she wanted them there again, his tongue, making her come. Feathering her fingers down his cheek, over his neck, skimming his nipple and going lower, she said, "I don't understand."

Matthew captured her hand in his and brought it up to his mouth, kissing the tips of her fingers. "People won't understand what we have. They'll call me a cradle robber, or worse."

Wiggling closer, she wrapped her arms around his neck. "I don't care what people say. I love you, and you said you love me, too. What else is there?"

Her green eyes glittered, her cheeks flushed. He'd never forget the sight for as long as he lived. Zia Bishop in his bed, sated, smiling, telling him she loved him, wanting to build a life with him.

Remorse stabbed him, and it was all he could do not to dress her, drive her home, and hide like a coward, tail tucked between his legs.

He'd taken her innocence, and he had nothing to offer in return. Nothing he *could* offer.

"There's a lot, but now isn't the time to talk about it. I didn't give you your graduation present. Do you want it now? Then we should sleep. It's late, and I'm an old man."

He tried to joke, tried to force joviality into his voice, but he failed miserably, and he knew it. She rested her head on his shoulder. "You aren't old. You could be thirty years older than me, forty, and I would still love you as much as I do right now. But yes, I want my present."

He walked to his dresser and lifted a long, thin box out the top drawer. Pink wrapping paper covered in little white hearts was taped around the box, white ribbon curling cheerfully.

"I was walking downtown on my lunch hour and saw this in a jewelry store window. I've hung on to it for a few months because I wanted to give it to you tonight." He cleared his throat. "Not that I thought we would be doing this, but I wanted you to have it on your graduation day. I've always wanted the best for you. I remember the evening you were born. Eyes so wide, skin like porcelain. Your mother let me hold you, such a fragile little thing, and from that second, you've held my heart in your hands. You've known," he said, sitting on the bed and holding out the box.

Zia wiped a tear off her cheek. "And you've known how I feel about you, too. How I've never trusted anyone as much as I trust you. How, when I look at you, I don't see a friend of my father's, but someone I can depend on, count on, when I can't turn to anyone else. Someone who understands my hopes and dreams. Never once have you told me what I want is silly. You've always had my heart, Matthew, and you've known it, too." She tilted her head, asking for a kiss. "Thank you for the present."

He brushed his fingers over her hair and whispered his lips against hers. "You haven't opened it yet."

She slipped the ribbon off and carefully peeled the tape from the paper. She opened the white box, revealing a rose gold necklace nestled inside. Engraved on a heart-shaped disk was the saying, "She believed she could, so she did," and 2019, the year of her graduation.

"It's beautiful. Put it on me, will you?" she asked, dangling the chain and pushing her hair aside. She turned around, exposing her back.

He indulged himself, lightly connecting her freckles with the tip of his finger.

"Hey, that tickles," she said, scooting away, laughing.

"Your skin is gorgeous. I can't help it." He fastened the necklace and placed a kiss at the base of her neck. "We should get some sleep."

She hid a yawn with her hand. "It's been a long day. Thank you for coming to my party. I know you hate doing things like that."

"I'll do anything you ask," he said, lying next to her and wrapping his arms around her.

He hated to think about what was to come.

In her immaturity and naiveté, Zia thought they could have something, but he knew the truth. People calling him filthy names would be only the beginning of a wretched life for both of them. He wanted her, there was no doubt about that, but he'd already taken her virginity. He couldn't steal her future. There was plenty of time to let her down gently, encourage her to go to school. Perhaps if she could leave thinking they could have a long distance relationship . . . Matthew sighed.

That would only lead her on, not help her understand that he wanted her to have more.

Zia cuddled closer, and he tightened his arms around her. "Goodnight, Little Star."

"Goodnight, Matthew. Thank you for everything."

"You're welcome."

He'd do anything to keep Zia from harm's way, even if that harm included himself.

One day at a time, he thought as he drifted to sleep.

Everything would be fine.

At least, he tried to tell himself that.

They slept late, indulged in some late morning lovemaking, and they sipped coffee while he made omelets. She hummed as she toasted bread wearing his wrinkled dress shirt. By the time Zia left his house, it was nearly noon. He kissed her on the porch, her hand down his pants caressing his hard cock, Aimee idling in his driveway looking everywhere but at them.

The whole scenario screamed danger, but he was helpless to do anything about it. She drew him to her, like a moth to a flame, a bee to a flower, all those pathetic clichés that were clichés because they were so fucking true. Now that he'd had a taste . . . if only she were ten years older. Five. Things would be much different.

Simpler.

Possible.

He expected her to text him constantly, but her silence surprised and relieved him. Not that he wasn't used to pushy women. That particular trait didn't seem to lessen as a woman aged. In fact, in his experience, if women wanted something, manners and etiquette went completely ignored the older and more desperate they became.

He enjoyed the days he had to himself, puttering around his house and doing the odd chore. He'd left the weekend open in case Zia or Sylvia and Raymond had other plans for her graduation, but the party seemed to be the main event as he hadn't been invited to join in any other activities.

It wasn't until he was settling in bed Sunday night that his phone chimed, and Zia talked him into going to lunch the next day. A small café downtown would suffice, as no one who knew them would think much of seeing them together. Only a change in body language would give them away, and he'd need to tell her to keep her hands to herself.

A ball of unease rolled around in his stomach.

He'd never been good at charades.

What he needed was advice and reassurance.

He texted Tucker McCarthy, an old friend. *You up for a run in the morning?*

Absolutely. Same time, same place?

He could always count on Tucker for a long run and conversation. The same time and place meant the ten-mile loop at the Silverwood Country Club. He used to golf there as well, before he came to the realization that the quiet sport bored him. After that, he refused to play, preferring other modes of networking. Raymond happily took over his tee times, saying using the golf course as an office was more than acceptable. That had been ten years ago and he didn't miss it, but the beautiful and serene eighteen-hole course made for a perfect run before work.

See you then.

Matthew set the alarm on his phone to wake him at six. He'd meet Tucker at seven and walk into the office by nine.

Being his own boss had a few perks.

Damn few, but he'd enjoy the ones he could.

Bedding his business partner's eighteen-year-old daughter was not one of them. The thought of what Raymond would do if he ever found out he'd slept with Zia kept him up late into the night, and when his alarm woke him, he felt like he hadn't slept at all.

Tucker was already stretching against the clubhouse when Matthew arrived, blurry-eyed, turning into the parking lot in a haze of fatigue and caffeine withdrawal. He needed coffee but forced himself to refrain. It would wake him up, yes, but he'd heard whipping his dick out and taking a piss on the eleventh hole was frowned upon. He knew firsthand running while he had to take a leak was a very uncomfortable experience.

"You look like shit," Tucker called, bouncing on his toes, bright and shining, probably because he'd gotten ten hours of sleep after fucking his smoking-hot wife.

Matthew had met Tucker at a crap bar downtown, both hitting on the same waitress. He'd eaten dinner that night at Raymond and Sylvia's, and hearing her announcement she was pregnant shoved him off his feet and onto his ass.

He drank to forget the baby growing inside her could have been his, if he hadn't gone to New York to go to school. But he had, and she'd moved on with Raymond.

Nursing a glass of scotch, he vowed to be Sylvia's best friend.

It had worked, too, too well.

He'd stayed good friends with the Bishops all these years, he and Raymond working sixteen-hour days to get Bridgewater Financial off the ground and helping carry furniture for Sylvia's interior design business when she couldn't afford to hire movers.

He'd been Zia's honorary uncle, her confidant. Raymond's stand-in when he was busy.

Matthew had watched her grow from a small tiny spark in his arms as an infant to the blazing inferno he'd ravished in his bed.

"I feel like shit," he said honestly, slamming his SUV's door shut. He secured a running belt around his waist, locked the truck, and tucked the key fob into one of the tiny pockets. He hid his eyes behind a pair of dark sport sunglasses, the sun's glare already shoving ice picks into his skull. "Let's go."

"You don't wanna stretch?"

"No. I need to get moving and wake up."

"Your call, buddy," Tucker said good-naturedly, jogging toward the path that would weave around the golf course.

There were golfers already on the range, and Matthew thanked God he wasn't one of them.

He started at an easy trot, Tucker running easily alongside him.

"How's Liza?" he asked, starting a benign conversation. He'd move on to Zia soon enough.

"Good. Excited. She's taking a girls' trip with some of her friends to Florida. They're renting a beach house for a week."

"It's going to be you and the kids, huh?" Tucker was the same age as him, but unlike Matthew, he'd had children years before and his son and daughter were a bit younger than Zia.

"We'll be okay. They're never home anyway. I have to remember to feed the dog, that's usually Liza's job. How'd Zia's party go? Sorry I couldn't be there to drink you through it. Chloe all over you like white on rice? Man, I don't know why you don't go after that."

"She'd eat me alive," he said, focusing on the sidewalk.

"But what a way to go." Tucker laughed.

"I like my dick attached to my body, thank you very much," he said, which only made Tucker laugh harder. He let a few minutes go by. "Hey . . . how young would you go?"

Tucker sucked in a breath. They'd picked up speed as Matthew's body loosened, and the physical exertion felt good. He hadn't realized how stressed he'd been since Zia left his house.

"You mean, like, a woman?"

"Yeah. Sex. How young?"

"Half your age plus seven. That's the magic formula."

He frowned. "I never heard that."

"You didn't learn that in college? What were you doing?"

"Studying. Going to class. You obviously weren't."

"No, apparently I was learning more useful things," Tucker shot back. "I'm forty-six, so twenty-three plus seven . . ."

"Thirty."

"I was getting there," Tucker said. "It's not even eight o'clock. Some of us are slower in the morning than others."

Matthew thought that between him and Tucker, Tucker had more brains.

"Why?" Tucker asked. "You get some puppy tail over the weekend?"

"Puppy tail?" He hated thinking of Zia like that. Derogatory.

"Was she any good? Who was it? How old is she? Tell me she's at least in her mid-twenties."

Suddenly, Matthew didn't think telling Tucker was a good idea. He'd approached Tucker as a friend, but that had been a mistake. Tucker's daughter was only two years younger than Zia. He wouldn't find any understanding here.

But, if he backed out now, Tucker would only be more determined to find out who she was. If Tucker ever happened to see him and Zia together, he'd know without a second's hesitancy. It's what made him one of the best detectives in the city.

"She's not exactly in her twenties," Matthew hedged.

"Early thirties? That's not bad. Doable. The thing is, you go younger, you gotta have stuff to talk about, right? You can't be fucking all the time. Too young, and what? You want to talk about Discord chats and what's happening on TikTok? My daughter's all about texting with her friends about how stupid boys are. Not a lot of stimulating conversation there, you know what I mean? At least if she's in her early thirties, you're more likely to have stuff in common. Movies. Plays. She'll know who the Beatles are, even if she doesn't listen to them. She could maybe name them, huh?"

Tucker had a point. He and Zia hadn't spoken much the night she'd stayed over. He tried to think of other times he'd spent with her and mostly she complained about school, or homework. Occasionally, she'd talk about her painting, her dreams of becoming a famous artist, and those were the conversations he liked best. When the passion for her art would glitter in her eyes.

"Dip your dick, but it's not good long-term. Who was it? Anyone I know?"

"Zia," he said reluctantly.

Tucker skidded to a stop and swiped the sunglasses off his face. "Are you out of your fucking mind? I should haul your ass in for statutory rape. You son of a bitch."

"Calm down, she's eighteen."

"Barely." Tucker started running again and he kept up, but over a mile went by before his friend said anything more.

"You know what people will say."

"I'm only worried about what one person will say," he bit out. "It wasn't until after that it occurred to me just who the fuck her father is."

"There goes office morale."

Matthew scoffed.

They ran half a mile in silence, and then he said, "If it makes it any better, I do love her. She wasn't puppy tail. And the feeling, for what it's worth, is mutual."

This time it was Tucker who scoffed. "You can't have a future together."

"Of course not. She was talking about staying here and getting married, but I'd never let her do that. She has tremendous talent. I'd never let her waste that on me. I . . . if she were older. Just five years older."

"Raymond doesn't know."

"No. If he did, I wouldn't be running with you. I'd be drawn and quartered."

"Yeah, I guess you're right. He'll find out, you know. Nothing like that can stay a secret."

"I asked her to keep it between us."

Tucker laughed. "You're forgetting I have a sixteen year old at home. Secret keepers they are not."

"She just has to keep it to herself until she goes to school. Then she'll be halfway across the country and she'll forget I exist."

"I bet you blew her out of the water, huh?" Tucker asked, smacking him on the arm, too hard. "Gave her a real man instead of the boys she fooled around with. Showed her how a real gentleman treats a lady. At least, I hope you did."

"Of course I did. I used protection and everything, *Dad*. But she had no one to compare me to. She was a virgin."

"I'll request bereavement time next week."

"What are you going to do that for?"

"So I can attend your funeral when this shit show blows up in your face."

If he'd been hoping Tucker would make him feel better, he'd been sorely mistaken.

They finished their run in silence, Tucker's disapproval hanging above him.

He skipped breakfast, made a pot of coffee, and stood under a hot shower, hoping to no avail the scalding water would rinse away what he'd done.

Monday morning Zia woke out of sorts. Graduation had come and gone. Normally she'd be up and getting dressed for school.

She'd thought about finding a summer job to give herself something to do, but her parents had been against it. While she attended school she'd have no time to work and there wasn't any point asking someone to hire her for only three months.

She texted Aimee, and she agreed to meet to have coffee and go shopping. She'd need the clothes anyway, though she promised her mother they'd have a girls-only weekend to shop for what she needed to start the next chapter of her life.

Zia arrived at Starbucks first and sat a table under the awning outside to wait. The spring breeze felt welcome after the dregs of winter.

She'd paint this summer. Capture Matthew on canvas. The light in his eyes, the serious slash of his brows. His black hair he let grow out until it curled around the collar of his dress shirt.

"Something, or should I say *someone*, put a smile on your face. I cannot wait to hear all the details!"

Aimee had brought her home Saturday afternoon, but she kept the details of her night with Matthew to herself. She hadn't wanted anything to spoil her memories. She held onto them all weekend, savoring them. Going so far as in the middle of the night to touch herself, thinking about Matthew's mouth where her fingers lingered.

She hadn't been as sore as she thought she'd be, and any discomfort she experienced was gone.

It was like it never happened.

She missed him terribly, and only the idea of being like other women made her leave him alone over the weekend. She'd attended enough events to know women clung to him, and letting him have his space was one way she could stand out.

Like Aimee said, she was playing a grownup's game and she had to learn the rules or she'd lose. She'd called last night and asked him to lunch. He'd sounded agreeable, and she knew she'd made the right choice.

"Let's get coffee first," she said, standing. "I was waiting for you."

Wearing a crossbody purse, her peasant top billowing in the breeze, her floral skirt fluttering around her ankles, she and Aimee walked down the sidewalk, peering into windows. She sipped on an Americano that had extra cream in it and fingered the necklace Matthew had given her, warmed by her skin.

She could be anything she wanted to be. She could do anything she wanted to do. She was Zia Bishop, of the Lake Kenosha Bishops, though that didn't mean anything except they had lots of money.

She could have anything she wanted, but she wanted Matthew.

Sleeping together didn't make them a couple, but Zia didn't know what would.

"You're quiet," Aimee said, gesturing her into a store that was more Aimee's style than hers. "You seemed happy Saturday. Did something happen?"

She stepped into the boutique, uninterested. Business suits and handbags.

"No, everything was great. He was such a gentleman, Aim." She sighed. "He ate me out."

Standing near a rack of pencil skirts, Aimee looked over her shoulder. "Wow."

"He knew what he was doing, for sure. And he's sooo big. I was afraid he wouldn't fit."

"Did it hurt?"

Aimee dated, but she hadn't done anything like sleeping with a man like Matthew.

"A little, but it was worth it. Sometimes I can't believe we made love. I've been in love with him for such a long time and he told me he loved me too. Showed me, so delicately. I couldn't have asked for a better first time. He lit candles, and the way he looked at me . . . it was everything I wanted."

Tears seeped into her voice, and her hand trembling, she sipped her coffee to wet her dry throat.

Aimee noticed and led her to a bench, shaking her head at a saleswoman who started walking across the floor to assist them. "If it was so good, then why are you about to cry?"

"I tried to talk to him, after, about . . ." She shrugged. "You know." He brushed me off."

"He didn't say anything?" Aimee asked, smoothing a curl off Zia's cheek.

"Mostly he said having a relationship would be hard. People would call him names."

"There's a big age difference between you," Aimee said tentatively.

"That doesn't matter to me."

"I know it doesn't, but you have to look at it from his point of view. He's your dad's age, and you're only eighteen. You're moving away to go to school in a couple of months. He's probably like every other man and doesn't want to get invested in something that won't work out."

"I told him I'd stay here. There are good art schools in the city."

"Would you be happy doing that? You were thrilled when the Art Studio accepted you."

"I'd do it for him."

"And that's probably exactly what he doesn't want. He's known you all your life. He's finger-painted with you, he's gone to all your art stuff at school. He knows how much the Art Studio means to you. When someone loves another person, they want to give them the world. He wants you to go to school, I bet."

"But I love him and I want to give him *me*. I'll learn to cook and we'll throw dinner parties and he can invite his friends."

Aimee arched an eyebrow. "Your dad?"

Zia set her coffee cup on the floor and hid her face in her hands. She sounded so stupid. Of course not her dad. She'd told Matthew her parents would be mad, but it would be worse than that. Her father would be absolutely livid if he found out she and Matthew slept together, and only God knew what her mother would say.

She couldn't do that to Matthew.

"There has to be a way we can be together."

"Zia, sometimes the right people meet at the wrong time. There's nothing anyone can do about it."

She shook her head, her large gold hoops swaying. "No. I love him and we'll make this work. I just found him. I can't lose him now."

Aimee didn't say anything, only smiled sympathetically, then continued browsing, keeping the opinions written so clearly on her face to herself.

She and Matthew were meant to be together.

The look in his eyes when he pushed inside her told her everything she needed to know.

CHAPTER THREE

Matthew's guilty conscience still hadn't eased, and he looked forward to his lunch with Zia to talk through their precarious, if not dangerous, situation. Asking her to keep their love affair a secret hurt him, but even though she was only eighteen, she had to see that them sleeping together would do nothing for his business relationship with her father, never mind their friendship.

He should have learned from his mistakes long ago, but he couldn't think clearly around the Bishop women.

It killed him to think it, but he could always deny anything Zia said. It would be his word against hers, and Raymond would believe him over his lovesick daughter.

Sinking into his chair behind his desk, he sighed. He'd never do that, and he felt like shit even entertaining the idea. She trusted him, and he had to behave as if he deserved it. He didn't though, otherwise he never would have touched her in the first place.

For the rest of the morning, he tried to focus on work. He and Raymond were debating where to open new branches of the bank. It was Raymond's idea to continually expand while he was content with the size of the company it presently was. He argued they didn't want to grow so large they lost the friendly, personalized service their banks offered their customers, but it was Raymond's nature to always want more. It was a small bone of contention between them.

Near lunchtime, Chloe walked unannounced into his office and he held in a sigh. He was hungry and eager to see Zia.

"Chloe, you're looking lovely on this sunny Monday morning," he said, standing and smoothing his tie. She loved the attention, loved the praise. Flattery was the way to this one's heart, but it was a double-edged sword. She hung around him to hear it, and he coddled her so she wouldn't cause trouble.

"Matthew," she said, gliding across the gray carpet. "I trust you had a good weekend."

"I did," he said cautiously. "Did you have a good time at Zia's party?"

"Oh, you know how it is," she said, sliding elegantly into a chair in front of his desk. "The usual men, the usual drab talk. Sylvia going on and on about her client list and how much she's going to miss Zia when she moves to go to school. I swear, the woman can't speak of anything else these days. She really needs to get out more."

Matthew reclaimed his seat and put his computer to sleep. He wouldn't be getting any more work done. Glancing quickly at his watch, he was relieved to see he still had half an hour before Zia stopped by. He suggested they walk to the café as he wanted the extra time with her. At least the two women wouldn't cross paths.

"She loves what she does," he said, defending Sylvia. "Perhaps you need to think of a hobby. It's never too late to go back to school."

"Well, I'm thinking about getting married," she said,

studying her nails.

"Yes, I do recall you saying something to that effect," he said, tapping a pen against his blotter. "I didn't know you were dating anyone."

"I'm not, but it isn't that difficult to find a man."

She met his eyes. Hazel, flecked with gold, but her eyes were anything but warm. They glittered like shards of broken glass. Sharp enough to make a person bleed.

"You certainly know where to look."

"I think I may have found one to my liking," she said, crossing her legs.

Thank God, he thought, grateful she'd finally leave him alone.

"Congratulations."

"Thank you." She paused. "I asked Sylvia if I could have a couple of the steamer trunks that were in their attic. I wanted them if she wasn't going to do anything with them. She said I could, and they arrived last week," she said, leaning forward.

Thankful the talk turned to something besides her next marriage, he relaxed. "Really?"

"I haven't spoken to her about it yet, but . . . I don't think she meant to send me one of them. If you're hiring movers, you need to be so careful they do their jobs correctly."

"Tell her you received one in error and she'll take care of it." Unobtrusively, he looked at his watch. Chloe had been in his office only ten minutes. It felt like a lifetime.

"You know my sense of curiosity, Matthew," she said, preening. "I had to see what was inside it first."

"I'm sure you did." He wouldn't say she had a sense of curiosity, more like a nose for gossip. The kind that hurt people.

"What I found was very interesting. Do you want to see? I brought them with me."

"I don't think it's any of my business what was inside, and

it's almost lunchtime. I trust you have a lunch date with your lucky man?"

Chloe slanted him a glance. "Oh, Matthew, I definitely think what was inside that trunk is your business, and I think, yes, after I tell you, I'll have a lunch date for many years to come."

"I don't understand," he said, a pit forming in his stomach.

She looked at him like an eagle eyed a mouse, calculating.

Waiting.

Slowly, she reached into the purse she'd dropped onto the floor and pulled out a thick stack of worn envelopes. They were different colors and sizes, some torn in haste to retrieve what was inside, some water-stained, from the rain, perhaps, some stained in other ways, maybe tears. A red tattered ribbon held them together.

Dropping them onto his desk, she smiled. "As I said, I'm sure Sylvia had no intention of sending over that particular trunk, but she did. Mistakes happen, don't they, Matthew?"

He didn't have to pick them up to know what they were. He'd burned his, many years ago, for this very reason.

Sylvia had been foolish enough to keep hers.

Fury burned through him, but it faded. How could he fault a woman who wanted to keep love close to her heart?

He'd loved Sylvia, all those years ago. When he'd been at school, homesick, they'd started writing, just as friends, but as the years went by, their relationship turned into something more.

Going to university in Lake Kenosha, Raymond had the advantage, and in the end, Sylvia had chosen him, letting Matthew down gently.

Over time, his feelings for her had faded from romantic love to that of pure friendship, and he knew things had turned out the way they were meant to be.

Matthew never begrudged Sylvia her choice, especially when Zia was born. He'd watched his Little Star grow into a beautiful woman, and if Sylvia hadn't married Raymond, Zia wouldn't be lighting this earth.

No way in hell he could resent Sylvia that.

Chloe tapped her fingernails on his desk, the clicking echoing through the silent office.

"I don't know what to say." He had nothing, no means to defend himself.

"Tell me Raymond knows that while he was courting Sylvia, she was receiving love letters from you . . . and, possibly, writing them? Hmm?"

She knew he couldn't tell her that. He hadn't had to tell Sylvia to stay quiet. It was the kind thing to do, not to flaunt it in Raymond's face. Ray got the girl, Matthew had stepped aside. He didn't pine for her, and he didn't hate Raymond for marrying her.

"You can't tell me that, because he doesn't know." Chloe slipped the satin between her fingers. "Does Zia?"

"No. Why would she know?" he whispered, suddenly aware of where this was going. Like being trapped on a roller-coaster mid-ride, there was no getting off, no matter how badly he wanted to throw up.

"Oh, I thought since you were sleeping with her, she'd know you and her mother had an affair twenty-three years ago. But then again, that doesn't seem like appropriate pillow talk, does it?"

"I have no idea what you're talking about." He swallowed around a lump in his throat the size of a boulder.

She feigned a look of surprise. "Oh, you mean, Saturday morning, when I took pictures of you kissing Zia goodbye on your porch while she had her hand down your pants, that it *wasn't* after a night of hot sex? You know, that girl wiggled her little ass into your bed and I've been trying to get there for years. How did she do it, exactly? Was it her virginity? Matthew, I know you're a virile man and you have needs, but I didn't think you were a pedophile."

"That's enough," he shouted, jumping viciously out of his chair, sweat and fear running down his back. "She's eighteen, and everything we did was with her consent."

Chloe smiled, smug and arrogant.

She caught him in her crosshairs, and in defeat, he sank into his chair. "What do you want?"

"Let's have a little review, shall we? Just to make sure we're both on the same page. You had an affair with the woman my brother married."

He narrowed his eyes. "That's not true."

"Now, now, I know they weren't married at the time. I read them. I know she had trouble deciding between the two of you, but still. Once you knew my brother was serious about her, you should have given up like the best friend you said you were. Yet, you wrote each other love letters until . . . the night of the wedding, if memory serves." She *tsked*. "Cheating on your fiancé like that. What would Raymond say? To you? To her?" She widened her eyes, a hand over her heart. "And Zia, you bed Sylvia's daughter not two months after she turns eighteen. You couldn't wait to get your hands on her. A double whammy for my poor brother. Falling in love with the woman he chose to marry, and over twenty years later, fucking his daughter. It is a bit much, don't you think, Matthew, dear?" She rested her finger against her lips. "Maybe for some. But I . . . I find it deliciously naughty in the extreme."

"What will it take to keep your mouth shut, Chloe? My house? My half of Bridgewater? My savings? What will it take for you to walk out that door and never mention any of this ever again?"

She anchored her hands on his desk, leaned forward, and looked straight into his eyes. "I have money. I have my own house. I want what you said I could never have." She smiled. "I want you."

After they were finished shopping, Zia went home to an empty house to change. Her mother was meeting clients, and her father, as always, was at his office.

She arrived with a few minutes to spare, but Matthew's receptionist let her pass, saying as she rushed by her desk, "Your aunt is with him."

Ugh. She didn't want to see Aunt Chloe now. If any good came out of this, it would be she could finally tell her aunt to keep her creepy hands off Matthew. Everyone knew she followed him around like a puppy, hoping to make him husband number five. Thank God he was able to see through her façade and peg her as the woman she was—a self-absorbed, selfish bitch.

Zia rapped on the door and pushed it open, expecting to see Chloe slinking around Matthew's office reeking of that godawful perfume she liked, and Matthew, handsome in his suit, his face clean-shaven, wrinkling his nose in distaste.

What greeted her was anything than what she thought she'd find.

Chloe sat in Matthew's lap, and they were kissing, so absorbed in each other her entry hadn't made either of them look her way. Matthew's hand was up Chloe's skirt, and she rocked against him, moaning. He knew exactly how to use his fingers. Chloe's whimper was the real thing.

Tears filled her eyes, and she forgot to breathe.

This couldn't be happening.

This wasn't her Matthew. This wasn't her sweet darling Matthew who had taken her virginity, who'd given her the necklace that hung around her neck.

He wouldn't do this to her.

Yet, he was.

This wasn't a nightmare.

The scent of sex permeated the air, and just as she was about to turn and run, her aunt came against Matthew's hand, her whimpers turning into a sob of satisfaction.

Zia gasped.

Chloe tore her mouth away from Matthew's, and Matthew, looking abashed, withdrew his hand. His fingers were wet.

"Zia, darling, what are you doing here? You should knock first. I know your mother taught you better manners than that. Perhaps you were gleaning a few tips for yourself?" Chloe smiled, righted her skirt, and slid off Matthew's lap.

He pulled a tissue out of the box on his desk and began to dry is fingers.

The casualness of it made Zia shake with rage. Like he wasn't tearing her heart in two.

"What are you doing?" she whispered. "Matthew, what are you doing, when we—" She couldn't what they'd done in front of Chloe. "When you said—"

That wouldn't work either. Would he admit to saying he loved her with Chloe here? Doubtful when he'd just gotten her off.

"When we did what, Zia? When I said what?" His hateful stare pinned her to the carpet, and she died a little with the coldness of it all.

"But I thought we . . ."

"You thought what? We'd have a future? You and your little crush on me? You thought we'd turn that into a life? Grow up. You're eighteen. Go to school. Tease the boys with your sexy little ass, let them taste your juicy cunt. Paint your stupid pictures while the grownups make money so you can fuck around."

Her vision blurred. Not with tears, but something else. Some kind of hurt she'd never be able to describe even with all the words in the world.

She'd given herself to him, laid herself bare in his bed, spread her legs and offered herself out of love, and he turned that into something so ugly she could physically feel her light sputter out.

It was as if a power outage took out her entire body, and there was nothing in her mind, in her heart, in her soul, but a blackness she couldn't see through, couldn't feel through.

She feared she never would again.

What hurt worst of all wasn't the vile things he said about her body, but about her work. He knew how much painting meant to her. He knew she poured every fiber of her being into each piece. To turn her passion into a way to waste time and "fuck around" hurt more than anything he could say about her body.

"I'm . . . I'm sorry to have bothered you." She stepped back and felt behind her for the doorjamb, unable to take her eyes off Matthew, hoping that at the last second he'd tell her it was a joke, to stay, let's go to lunch, that everything would be all right.

He said nothing as he watched her grapple for the doorway while her aunt stood next to him and pretended to be sorry, the light of victory blazing in her cold eyes.

Finally, the doorjamb bit her back, and she snapped out of her trance. "Sorry," she said again, her voice meek. She couldn't feel anything, couldn't infuse any emotion into her voice.

"And Zia? Don't *ever* contact me again."

Violently, she nodded.

She whirled around and ran past Matthew's confused

secretary and down the hallway. She didn't wait for the elevator, instead pushing through a fire door to find the concrete stairway. Between the fourteenth and thirteenth floors she sagged against the wall, clutching at her chest, sure her shattered heart would fall onto the ground, little pieces everywhere.

Matthew swung his gaze to Chloe hurting so terribly he felt like he was having a heart attack. Pain ripped through him, the look on Zia's face etched permanently into his brain.

Oh, his Little Star.

What he'd done to her to save himself.

"Is that what you had in mind?"

Chloe's arousal and sickening perfume hung in the air, and the smell churned the bile in his stomach. He'd need to get used to feeling this way.

What Chloe had offered him to keep his secret was far more than he could pay.

She brushed her fingers through his hair. "You did well, my love. Much better than I expected. Now close the door. I need a good fuck after watching that. I trust you'll give me what I want, for as long as I want it."

He closed the door and loosened his tie.

Zia was better off without him.

He'd fucked up his life, and he'd be damned if he'd fuck up Zia's, too.

She spent over an hour in that stairwell, crying until she thought she'd throw up, but once her tears dried and her shaking hands steadied, she rode the elevator to the lobby.

A plan had come to her while she bawled her eyes out, but she needed to speak to her mother. She wouldn't wait three months. She'd leave now. Today. She'd use the time to get to know the area, the campus, before school started. It was smart. Rational.

It would get her out of Lake Kenosha and away from Matthew and Chloe.

She wouldn't come back. No Thanksgivings, where, as a couple, Matthew and Chloe would share a table with them. She wouldn't visit for any Christmas, didn't want to watch her mother take Matthew and Chloe's picture in front of the Christmas tree. It would break her mother's heart, but she'd cross that bridge when she came to it.

For now her plans were all about the quickest escape.

Her mother, though confused, reluctantly agreed, and later that evening, Zia packed, tears streaming down her face.

Aimee knocked on her bedroom door. "I wanted to see how your talk with Matthew . . . went . . ." Her voice faded. "I'm guessing it didn't go well."

Zia wiped her cheeks. "I went to see him. At his office. Aunt Chloe was there." Images of her aunt squirming in Matthew's lap made her gag. "I guess they're a couple now."

"You can't be serious," Aimee said, sitting on her bed. "He hates her."

"If his hand up her skirt getting her off is hate, I'd like to know what love looks like."

She thought she'd known. When Matthew had slid his cock inside her, his eyes smoky, full of love and need.

"You saw him doing that to her?" Stunned, Aimee covered her mouth with her hand.

"Stood there in stupid shock, too. Chloe accused me of watching for pointers. I'm leaving early. I can't stay here. He told me. . ." She took a deep breath to continue. "He told me to go fuck the college boys, to go play with my paints, and to leave being a grownup to the people who knew what they were doing. I thought he saw me as a woman, someone he could relate to on that level, but he was only fucking with me."

"I'm so sorry."

She sank onto the bed next to her friend, her suitcase bumping into her hip. "I am too. You warned me, but I didn't listen. My mom didn't understand, but I didn't mention Matthew at all. I told her it made sense to go early so I could get to know the area and to have more time to settle into an apartment." She rested her head on Aimee's shoulder, and Aimee put an arm around her. "I'll miss you. I was looking forward to hanging out with you this summer."

"I'll miss you, too. But you'll be in California, girl! I'll come visit you."

Aimee had been accepted into university as well, planning on an art history degree. It was the love of art that drew them together in the first place, and they had big, shiny plans. Aimee was going to open her own gallery, and Zia would show her work there. Her painting wasn't child's play.

She'd prove that to Matthew.

"You'll do great in school, Aim."

"So will you." She sighed. "You're leaving tomorrow, then?"

"Yeah. Mom's packing, too. She's been great about it, though she said it's putting some of her clients in a tough spot. I felt bad, but I can't stay here a second longer." Tears crept into her voice, and she wondered if she'd ever stop crying about what Matthew had done to her. "I thought he loved me."

"Some men will say anything to get into your pants, or up your skirt," Aimee said, rubbing her back in slow, steady strokes. "You just have to be careful next time."

"There isn't going to be a next time. He broke my heart."

"Broken things let the light shine in."

She lifted her head, snorting a laugh. "You sound like my Facebook timeline. Knock it off."

Aimee smiled. "That's what I was shooting for." Hugging her tightly, she said, "Don't forget about me."

"Never. Remember, you're going to be the famous gallery owner, and I'll be the famous *artiste*, showing my work there. We're gonna make it, Aim. We're gonna make it." She stuck her hand out, and Aimee clutched it, squeezing firmly.

"Deal."

That night, in her small studio in their backyard, Zia painted Matthew the way she remembered him, consuming her, love in his hazy blue eyes, his dark hair shining in the candlelight.

Soft paints, blurred, as if looking through tears, or petroleum jelly smeared on a camera's lens. Out of focus.

Him touching her, gently sucking her nipple, so careful not to hurt her.

That was love.

She'd choose to believe he'd loved her because it's what she wanted to believe. It's what would get her through these next few weeks, these next few months.

She didn't want her last memory of Matthew to be with Chloe in his lap, his hand between her legs.

That wasn't the Matthew she loved. Maybe that Matthew didn't exist. He was only a figment of her imagination. What she wanted him to be. Who she needed him to be.

Her flight left early in the morning and there wasn't adequate time to let it dry. She carried it to the apartment above their garage. Her parents hadn't rented it out in many years, and it was empty, only a cleaning lady giving it a light dusting once a month.

Zia hid the drying painting in the closet of the second bedroom. No one would think to look there.

She shut the door.

The latch clicked in the doorjamb, the only sound except for her pounding heart.

She walked away, leaving Matthew and her love for him behind in a small closet she vowed never to open again.

"We need to talk."

Matthew sat up in bed, his mind swimming with the three fingers of scotch he'd downed moments before. Chloe laid next to him, an eye mask over her eyes. A good fucking and a bottle of wine knocked her out cold, yet he still slid as carefully as he could out of bed, padded into the hallway, and lightly trotted his way down the stairs.

"Sylvia. What's wrong? Is it Zia?"

"No. Yes. She wanted to leave early, and we're flying out in the morning, but I need to talk to you. Can you meet me? At The Ragdoll?"

Matthew glanced at the ceiling. He'd need permission. That was his life now.

"I can. But . . . I'll need half an hour or so."

"Lady company?" Sylvia asked.

"I'll explain when I see you."

"Okay." Sylvia disconnected.

The meeting was an inconvenience, but needed.

He knelt by Chloe's side of the bed, slid the comforter down, and nudged her slim thighs apart.

Sex was Chloe's currency of choice, and he needed to pay the bill. Even in sleep she was wet, and his fingers slid inside her slick heat without resistance.

The woman was insatiable.

As long as he could get it up, he hoped Chloe wouldn't cause him too much trouble.

His thumb worked her clit and her hips rose to increase the pressure.

Matthew kissed her and slipped his tongue between her teeth.

Mewling, she widened her legs, and he pushed a third finger inside her, already knowing she liked a side dish of pain served with her sex. A bite to the nipple, his cock rough, a tug of her hair. She loved it all. At the same time.

He bit her bottom lip and she came, whimpering as she climaxed around his fingers. He swirled his thumb around her quivering clit until she jerked away. She pushed the mask off her face and regarded him in the hallway's light. "You do that so well, my love."

Kissing her cheek, he whispered against her skin, "A client's having trouble. He wants to meet for drinks."

"Let Raymond take care of it and come to bed," she said, wrapping her arms around his neck. Like a noose.

"I can't. This one's mine, and he expects five-star service."

"You know how to give it," she said, then growled. "When you get back, I expect more."

"Of course, darling," he agreed, wiping his fingers on the sheet. "Anything you want."

"I know."

He dressed in slacks and a light blue shirt, palmed his keys and wallet. He sucked in a breath of pure, cool, Minnesota spring air. Anything to get the smell of Chloe's perfume out of his nose. If he could convince her to wear something else, their arrangement could be . . .

No. Their arrangement would be nothing less than hell on earth.

A little jazz club downtown, The Ragdoll sat on a small

corner lot, and though it was past midnight, traffic clogged the narrow streets. He was later than the thirty minutes he'd told Sylvia he needed.

She waited at a table in the back, her spine stiff, her shoulders rigid. Whatever news she had to tell him wasn't good.

"Thanks for meeting me."

"It took some doing," he said. "Why here? I haven't been here since I came home from school."

"I wanted to meet somewhere quiet, where we wouldn't run into anyone we know."

"Are you all right?" He nodded at a waitress who approached their table and ordered a beer. He wanted something to sip on so he'd blend in. Sylvia had a drink in front of her, but it could have been a Coke for all he knew.

"I . . . I gave Chloe a couple of steamer trunks. She'd been admiring them for a while . . . but the movers took one of my personal ones. I was at a client's house, looking over . . . well, that doesn't matter . . . and I wasn't there to supervise." She rubbed her temples. "The love letters you wrote me were in it."

"I know."

Tears sparkled in her eyes, the vodka sign attached to the wall behind him turning them neon blue.

"She's already said something, hasn't she?"

He nodded, ignoring the waitress as she placed the bottle of beer on a napkin in front of him. "She's blackmailing me. She said she'd keep her mouth shut and not tell Raymond or Zia if she and I were a couple. That was this morning. I agreed and she already moved into my house."

Sylvia cried into a napkin.

Matthew waited her out.

She wiped her eyes, her hand shaking. "I'm so sorry. If we could find the letters, if we could destroy them, it would be her word against ours."

"Are you kidding me? Syl, she's not that stupid. Even if we could get our hands on the originals, you don't think she has copies somewhere? As it is, she probably has them locked in a safe deposit box, God knows where. She holds the cards."

"There has to be something we can do."

He sighed, choosing right then to come clean. "She's got more on me than just the letters." He took a long drink of his beer. He needed it after all.

Worrying the damp napkin in her hands, Sylvia asked, "What could you have possibly done? Embezzled from the company?"

"I slept with Zia, and Chloe knows."

"You did what?"

"The night of Zia's graduation party. She didn't go to Aimee's. She came to my place, and we made love. I swear to God, I would never hurt her. Ever. She wanted it, I wanted it. It was mutual," he babbled. "She said she loves me, and I love her too, if it means anything."

Sylvia stared across the bar. A tall, thin Black woman stood on a dais crooning Ella Fitzgerald into a microphone. Her green strapless dress sparkled in the spotlight.

"Is that why she wants to go to California early?" she finally asked.

He tried to read her face, but she gave nothing away.

"That's probably why, yes. We were supposed to have lunch today, and I asked her to meet me at my office. Chloe wanted me to fuck her, and I complied, knowing Zia would see us. I figured it would be easier all around if she hated me."

She sat quietly for so long he couldn't stop himself, and he asked, "Do you hate me, too?" She had every right.

"When I sent you to find her at the party, I wanted you to cheer her up. You two have always been close, but I had no idea you felt that way about each other."

Matthew beckoned to the waitress and asked her to bring Sylvia a stiff drink. He waited to speak until the waitress set it on their table and hurried away. He pushed the glass toward her. "Drink this."

She sipped at the lowball of scotch, her eyes closed, her skin pallid. Her dark red hair, darker than Zia's, and straight, hung in thick layers to her shoulders.

Chloe had been right about one thing. When Raymond had expressed interest, Matthew should have backed off. There was no excuse then, and he had no excuse now.

When it came to the Bishop family, all of them, he had truly fucked himself.

"This is my fault. Chloe never should have gotten her hands on those letters. I gave her the leverage, and you did what you had to do."

"That's not what I asked."

"You asked if I hate you, and I don't."

"That's not really what I asked."

She sighed. "I know. You want my blessing, but I can't give it to you. She's eighteen, Matthew. You're old enough to be her father. Could have been, if circumstances had turned out differently."

"That's not something I'd like to dwell on," he said, his mouth twisting.

"At least you showed her what . . . oh, God, never mind. I can't talk about this with you." She buried her face in her hands.

Matthew grabbed her wrists and pulled her hands away from her face. "None of that matters now. What matters is what we do next. Zia's leaving. That's good. She hates me, and that's good, too. She can't know about the letters. Okay? And Raymond can't know anything."

She shook her head. "No. That's too much for you. I won't let you. Chloe will take advantage of this forever if you let her. What else is she asking for? She's already living with you. Will she want you to marry her? You hate being around her. *I* hate being around her."

"Yes, but don't you see? Raymond will love it. Zia will be gone, and Chloe won't be his problem. After Zia moves out, tell him you're lonely without her in the house and ask to go on a vacation. Just the two of you. Fuck his brains out. I'll give Chloe what she wants and hope to God in time things smooth over."

"How long do you think we can keep Ray from finding out? About us? About you and Zia? It's a fool's errand. And trusting Chloe to keep her mouth shut . . ."

Matthew finished his beer but resisted ordering another. Chloe would want a good screw when he went back, and he had to be up for it.

"She can't say anything to anybody if my dick's in her mouth. I'll do it for as long as it takes. This is my fucking mess. I'll clean it up."

Sylvia picked up her purse and stood.

"Sylvia."

She looked at him. Misery, disappointment, and fear shadowed her beautiful face.

"I love Zia. As much as I loved you, back in the day."

"That didn't get you very far, did it?" She paused. "I'm sorry."

"Yeah, me too."

Zia leaned against the baby blue SUV her father had given her for her sixteenth birthday.

Crickets chirped, stars shone, and a light breeze blew against her skin. She shivered. The way Matthew treated her while they made love and what he said to her in his office tangled in her heart. How could he be so gentle one moment and so hateful the next?

She hadn't thought to take the necklace off. The disk felt smooth beneath her fingers, the letters catching on her skin.

She tugged at the delicate chain, tempted to yank it from her neck and fling it into the grass, but she couldn't bring herself to do so. She dropped her hand, rested her head against the window, and closed her eyes.

An engine's soft purr cut through the quiet, the blazing beams of headlights slicing through the darkness. Her mother's car turned into the driveway, and Zia frowned.

Instead of raising the garage door, Sylvia parked next to Zia's truck.

"What are you doing up?" Sylvia asked, adjusting her purse strap and smoothing her dress over her hips.

"I could be asking you the same thing." It wasn't like her mother to be out so late, unless she and her father were attending a function.

Sylvia rubbed her cheeks. The security lights mounted over the garage doors highlighted the fatigue and worry on her mother's face. She'd always thought her mother was aging well, maintaining her slender figure and keeping her hair color bright. But tonight lines dug into her mother's smooth skin and she appeared older than her forty-six years.

"Is everything okay?" Zia asked, her heart slamming in panic. Maybe something happened to Matthew. Maybe he was in trouble and that's why he'd treated her so terribly.

"I couldn't sleep. I needed some fresh air to clear my head. What about you, sweetie? Too excited to sleep?"

She flicked her gaze to the apartment above the garage. She couldn't tell her mother the truth.

"I guess so," she mumbled. "Maybe this isn't such a good idea."

"Come with me. Let's go into the backyard."

Sylvia dropped her purse on the porch and held Zia's hand.

She grasped her mother's fingers like a little girl, trusting her to show her the way.

Remnants of her party had been cleaned up days ago, but the fairy lights decorating the maze still twinkled.

Sylvia sat on a wicker loveseat and nodded at Zia to sit near her.

The stars and the city lights fought for attention, and the crickets' singing grew louder. Several blocks away, a neighbor's dog barked.

She should be happy, sitting with her mother, a quiet moment in which to share the worries of her heart and mind. Her relationship with her parents made her the envy of all her friends. She'd always been able to confide in her mother about anything.

Her mother wouldn't understand sleeping with a man twenty-eight years older than she was. Wouldn't understand the heartbreak that had come with it.

Sylvia ran her fingers through her hair. "What I'm going to tell you won't make you feel better. It won't take away the uncertainty of the future. You've just graduated high school, and you must feel so lost, but you have such talent, sweetie. People say I have talent. I can fill a room with pretty things and make it look nice. Not so hard to do, really. You, you can create something of value. Of worth. Nothing I do can match what you do with your painting."

"It's nice to hear you say that." She'd always known her mother supported her, but it helped to hear it. Especially after the ugly things Matthew told her. She thought he was proud of her, but maybe she was wrong about that. He'd been placating her, humoring her. His business partner's daughter.

"Things feel crazy now. Moving so far away. Starting school. You're going to be homesick, but you'll meet new people. Men who share your passion for the arts." Sylvia fingered her necklace. Zia scrambled for an explanation in case her mother asked, but she only continued. "You've grown up with Matthew watching over you. You've been the apple of his eye since you were born."

Zia trembled.

"You'll miss him. My sweet baby," Sylvia whispered, brushing Zia's unruly curls. "Matthew's going through a rough time. I don't want you going to California believing one thing when something else is true." Her mother stood and kissed the top of her head. "Just remember, things are never what they seem, okay? We need to be at the airport in a few hours. Get some sleep."

With her heart in her throat, Zia watched her mother walk away, her head down, her arms wrapped around herself.

Her mother knew something. Maybe not all of it, but she knew something. Maybe Zia's first thought had been correct after all. Maybe Matthew was in trouble.

Yet, she was only eighteen. She'd be no use to him, no matter what kind of trouble he found himself in.

Zia had tried to play a grownup's game.

She'd lost.

CHAPTER FOUR

"Zia, you need to come home."

An objection came fast to her lips, but her mother, used to her deflections, cut her off. "Your father's sick. I know you have a full calendar, but make time for him, for me. I miss you. I haven't seen you since Christmas."

For seven years Zia worked on her art. She'd graduated from the Art Studio. She met Reid, and over a bottle of white wine, hors d'oeuvres, and a shared dislike of phallic sculpture, they'd clicked. With this help, she'd grown into an accomplished young woman of twenty-five. Sleeping with him had nothing to do with it.

She hadn't been back to Lake Kenosha. At her insistence, her parents celebrated the holidays with her and Reid in California.

Sometimes she missed the snow.

Sometimes she missed Matthew, though she rarely gave herself permission to think about him.

Sometimes she wondered if he ever thought about her at all.

"But, Mom, I have a—"

"Zia." Her mother's voice was sharp, and she flinched. Her mother rarely spoke to her that way. "Your father's sick. He has cancer. I didn't want to tell you over the phone, but you leave me little choice. If you won't come, you won't be able to tell him goodbye."

"Goodbye?" Zia cried. "What do you mean?" Clutching her cell phone to her ear, she paced the living room.

Reid heard her outburst and rushed out of the bedroom where he'd been dressing for dinner.

Her heart did the heavy thumping it always did when she saw him. He wore his brown hair in a short, professional cut, and his warm brown eyes usually twinkled in amusement, loving a good joke, loving his life, but now concern shadowed them instead. Trim and fit, rich and sexy, he screamed sophistication. Connected in the art world, Reid Vaughn had taken one look at her paintings and had thrown all his strength at her career.

It had paid off.

Her last painting sold for twenty-five thousand dollars.

Reid wrapped his arms around her, and she leaned against him. He was everything she should have wanted.

"I haven't said anything because I'm tired of the excuses. You're painting. You have a showing, a benefit, a dinner."

Zia colored, heat flaming her cheeks. None of those things had been a lie. Reid kept her schedule full. As she paid him to. In and out of bed.

"You said cancer. People live—"

"His oncologist gives him a month, two at best. Pancreatic cancer is very aggressive, Zia, and I put this off longer than I should have. Months. For you. We don't know how long he'll be with us." Sylvia started to cry.

"Of course, Mom. I'll come home as fast as I can."

"Thank you." Sylvia sucked in a watery breath. "Let me know your flight number. I'll pick you up at the airport."

"Okay. Bye," she whispered, dazed.

"Fly safely. I love you."

She disconnected the call and dropped her cell phone onto the couch.

Reid rubbed her back through the sheer material of her robe. "What is it?"

"That was my mom. My dad has cancer and I need to go home."

"We'll have to reschedule the showing . . . the governor—"

"I know. I'm sorry."

Reid leaned away and gripped her arms with his strong hands.

Hands she'd painted many times.

Capable.

Steady.

Loving.

"It'll be okay. We'll call the airline on the way to dinner. We'll fly out in the morning."

"You don't have to—" Zia wanted him there, yet, she didn't. She wanted to face Matthew alone. Show him how tough and independent she'd become without him. But in the evening, after she looked into his eyes, maybe it would be nice to have someone hold her while she fell apart.

"I like your parents, and maybe I can help in some way? Don't worry, I can still do a lot from there. I want to support you, if you'll let me."

He repped other artists, and it seemed the best of both worlds if he was with her, yet occupied with other things. "Okay."

"Thank you." He kissed her, and she let him, his firm lips moving over her hers.

She liked sex with him. He didn't rock her world, but only one man had ever been able to do that. She didn't expect to find another who could do the same.

But Reid was a generous lover and let her take. High after a painting session or tipsy after a party. Elated, after a sale. She took, and he gave, with no complaint.

Even now, he brushed his lips over her neck, down her breasts, past her belly where he slipped off her panties and nudged her thighs apart. He gently pushed two fingers inside her.

Zia widened her legs, tipping her head back and lacing her fingers through his hair.

As Reid ate her out, the sensations brought her back to the first time Matthew Harcourt touched her.

His tongue brought her to climax, her clit quivering with every lick, and gasping, she curled her hand around the necklace hanging around her neck.

In all of seven years, she hadn't taken it off. Not once.

Her father's appearance made her crumple at his feet. Weak from chemotherapy that had been of little to no help, jaundiced and bone-thin, Raymond Bishop sat with an IV attached to his arm, a cannula hooked around his ears to keep it in place under his nose, and an oxygen tank secured to the back of his wheelchair.

When Zia walked into the library, she almost hadn't recognized her father, once a strong, vibrant man who could run Bridgewater Financial standing in the middle of a golf course and often did.

She sobbed in his lap, his trembling hand resting on her head.

"I'm so sorry, Daddy," she whispered.

"It's all right, Zia. I asked your mother to keep it a secret for as long as we could. You've done well for yourself. Look at you." Ray smiled, his lips barely moving.

His nurse hovered in the corner. He was never left alone, and as her mother explained on the drive from the airport, they were fortunate to afford twenty-four-hour care.

Raymond insisted Sylvia live as normal a life as possible, and she was often on site doing a consult or supervising the interior design of a house. In the years Zia had been away, Sylvia's business flourished and thrived, and she'd been forced to expand her staff to keep up with demand.

"I'm so proud of you. And Reid—" Ray coughed, his voice raspy and dry. "He's a good man. He loves you. I can see it. He'll take care of you."

"Daddy, we don't need to talk about that right now."

"Yes, Zia. I don't have much time left. My doctor's one of the best, but he isn't a miracle worker. I want to see everything settled before I move on to my next life."

"I'll do anything you want. Just tell me." Zia held her father's hand, his skin smooth and pale.

Raymond Bishop had turned fifty-three years old that year, but he looked eighty.

He coughed and weakly gestured at his nurse. "Stay with your mother. She's going to need you. I have to lie down. We'll talk more later."

She swallowed as the nurse wheeled her father out of the library.

How could she promise her father she'd stay in Minnesota after his death? Her life was in California.

But my heart is here.

She brushed the thought away. Matthew couldn't be a consideration in any of her plans. She needed to do what was best for her, and that meant staying as far away from him as possible.

Matthew knew the moment Zia's plane touched down, knew the minute she arrived home, knew the second she spoke to her father.

No one told him a word.

Seven years had come and gone, yet the moment she stepped onto Minnesota soil, those years had turned into seven seconds.

Everything had changed, but everything remained the same.

The morning after Zia and Reid's arrival, Matthew went for a run with Tucker.

He'd kept up the ritual, more to maintain his mental health than physical, though despite daily runs, both had suffered under Chloe's hand.

Matthew trusted Tucker more than anyone. Even Zia. He hadn't been entirely sure she'd keep their secret, but as the years dragged on, he relaxed, in that aspect, at least.

He'd told Tucker everything from his long-distance love affair with Sylvia in college, the letters sent through snail mail and Sylvia keeping them for Chloe to find, to admitting to Sylvia he'd fucked her eighteen-year-old daughter.

Not that she'd held that against him.

Bless her.

Things hadn't gone entirely back to the way they'd been between them—an easy-going friendship built on mutual respect and admiration—but he and Chloe were a couple and over the years they did things with Sylvia and Raymond that would have been impossible had she hated him.

Matthew pounded the pavement, fatigue weighing him down though they'd only just begun, Tucker silent beside him.

It had taken several weeks of running the trails before Tucker talked to him again. They'd meet, nod at each other, run. A handshake afterward, then Tucker would drive away. One morning, out of nowhere, Tucker asked him if he was okay.

Matthew had almost cried in relief.

The sun rose over the golf course, the sprinkler system keeping the grass a brilliant green despite the August heatwave.

Seven years and three months.

He hadn't seen Zia in person in all that time.

While she'd been gone, Chloe in his bed, he often wondered how much more pain he could stand.

It appeared he was going to find out.

"Chloe still wants to throw you that birthday party?"

Matthew grunted. "It's in poor taste, if you ask me, with as sick as Raymond is. But he insists, and she wants to, so what can I say? When she says jump, I ask how high."

"It might give people a chance to tell Raymond goodbye."

"That's what funerals are for," he muttered.

Chloe wanted to show off, play the part of loving partner as she'd done every year they'd been "together." The parties were more for her than they were for him, but he'd be gracious. Without the party, he may not have a reason to see Zia.

Tucker read his mind. "Zia will be there."

"Yes." He said the simple word calmly, though his heart pounded. It wasn't because they'd nearly finished a ten-mile run.

"Will you be able to keep your hands off her?"

Tucker sounded like he was joking, but he glanced at his friend to be sure. Zia remained a touchy subject between them.

"Chloe will make sure of it, Tuck. Zia and I are over. There are too many years between us."

They finished their run, stopping in the parking lot near their vehicles. Matthew leaned heavily against his truck. Not eating properly, lack of sleep, and living with someone he despised . . . after seven years, well, he wasn't the man he used to be.

Only pride and a valid reason to hide from Chloe for a couple of hours every day kept him from throwing in the towel and canceling the runs altogether.

The sun had dried the early morning dew, heat permeating the air. It would be another hot one.

"Can I ask you something?" Tucker wiped his face using the hem of his tank top.

He nodded and dropped to the ground, intending to stretch, needing the rest.

"Why'd you put up with it all these years? You could've retired, lived off your investments. Why put up with the Bishop bullshit?"

"And leave Sylvia to pick up the pieces after Chloe went to every gossip columnist in Lake Kenosha, my love letters clutched in her tight little fists? I know you think I'm a bastard, but I could never do that. Besides. I love her."

Tucker raised his eyebrows. "Sylvia?"

"No. Zia. I loved her then, my Little Star, and I love her now. But you're right," he said, the idea clicking perfectly into place, "after Raymond passes and I know Zia's safe with the man she brought home, I'll take off. Sylvia can have Bridgewater. She'll have Raymond's half and I'll sign over mine. Chloe can tell whoever will listen all my dirty secrets, but without Raymond around, no one will care."

"What if Zia still loves you?"

"What she had was a child's crush. I took advantage of that.

She's a woman now, who has a career, who's in a real relationship. After what I said to her the day she walked in on Chloe and me, I'd be lucky if she threw a thimble of water on my burning body." He hefted painfully to his feet. "Nope. When Raymond passes away, I can finally tell Chloe to fuck off, and I can, as you called it, put all this Bishop bullshit behind me."

Zia shifted on the hard, plastic chair of the waiting room. Fish swam in an aquarium against the far wall. A table sat in front of her, full of parenting and working woman magazines. A receptionist answered a constantly ringing telephone.

Reid had wanted to come with her and hold her hand during the exam, but she told him to make his phone calls and use the couple hours she'd be gone to answer email and touch base with his other clients. Now that she knew her time in Minnesota would turn into longer than a brief visit, she needed her yearly gynecological exam to refill her birth control pill prescription.

She hadn't told Reid what her father asked of her.

Not knowing what to make of it herself, she kept quiet. She didn't know if her mother would want her to stay after her father passed away.

That she'd leave before then was out of the question. She wanted to see her father as much as possible, and that meant making an appearance at Matthew's birthday party.

Just because she went didn't mean she had to talk to him. She'd stay close to her father, mingle with the other guests whom she hadn't seen in many years, and introduce Reid to her friends. She'd ask Aimee to attend, as well. She hadn't seen her friend since she came back, and catching up would be welcome.

A nurse called her name, led her down a short hallway, and gestured to an exam room. She took her temperature and blood pressure and said, "Please change into a gown, Dr. Jennings will be with you shortly."

She hated the gynecologist's office and reluctantly changed into the thin white gown, with what looked to be blue snowflakes stamped into the material. She sat on the exam table, the white paper crinkling under her butt, and frowned at the stirrups she'd be putting her feet into soon enough.

Someone knocked lightly on the door, and a curvy blonde woman who looked no older than she stepped into the room, smiling and holding a file folder. "Zia, I'm Dr. Jennings, so nice to meet you."

She shook the doctor's hand. "Thanks. It's nice to meet you, too, though circumstances could be better."

"Well, I have to admit, I'm thrilled to have you as a patient," Dr. Jennings said, sitting on a stool and opening the file. "My husband and I recently bought our first Zia Bishop and hung it over our fireplace. It's magnificent."

"Thank you. It's always nice to hear." It *was* lovely to hear compliments about her work, but this woman's fingers would be poking inside her and she didn't feel like making small talk.

"Will you be doing any showings in Lake Kenosha?"

Despite being uncomfortable, she tilted her head in consideration. She hadn't thought of it, but maybe Reid could arrange something. She didn't have any paintings here, though. "I'm not sure. I'm home visiting my parents and don't have a collection available at the moment. But it's something to think about, being I'll be in the area for a while."

"Please let me know if you do. My husband and I would love to attend. Do you have any concerns or questions before we begin?"

"No. I'm only here because I need to refill my birth control pills. My exams are always on time."

"Yes, I saw that. Your previous doctor sent us your records and I looked them over this morning. Everything seems to be in order, but I'll be doing a full workup, if you don't mind."

"No, it's no problem."

"Let me get my assistant, then we'll start." Dr. Jennings pressed a call button and a moment later a nurse stepped into the room. "This is Linda. She's going to help me."

Zia timidly smiled at the nurse who stood in the corner, her hands behind her back. This was so awkward and she just wanted to get her prescription and leave.

"If you could lie down, scoot your butt to the edge of the table, and put your heels in the stirrups . . . I'll start with an external exam to look for skin cancer and the like," Dr. Jennings said, tugging gloves onto hands.

Zia thought about other things while the doctor examined her labia and vulva and tried to tune her out when she indicated the internal exam would begin. Dr. Jennings slid the cold speculum inside her, and she flinched.

"You'll feel a pinch now. All of your tests have come back normal and I don't anticipate a problem this time around."

"Okay."

Dr. Jennings removed the speculum, dropped it into a trash can-like bin, and wiggled the gloves off her hands. "We'll let you know the results in about a week."

She sighed in relief her exam was over. "That's fine."

"You can move your feet out of the stirrups, but I'd like to do an ultrasound, if you don't mind. It's just a precaution to make sure I didn't miss anything. You can put your head on the pillow. I'm going to find an available machine."

Zia's heart skipped. She'd never had an ultrasound done before. "Is there something wrong?"

Dr. Jennings patted her shoulder. "Not that I could see, but because you'll be my patient for the next little while, I want to start your file with all the information. We'll also send the results to your primary care provider and they'll add them to your chart. Okay?"

Zia nodded. "Okay."

She and the nurse left leaving Zia alone lying on the exam table. She should have said she didn't want an ultrasound, made up another appointment she couldn't miss. The gynecologist she'd been seeing never mentioned an ultrasound, and she thought this was a waste of time.

The doctor returned pushing an ultrasound machine into the room. "You look irritated, and I'm sorry. We'll take a quick look, then you'll be free to go. Here, you can cover your legs," she said, draping a scratchy sheet over her thighs. "You're probably cold, but this won't help." She pushed the hem of Zia's gown up and exposed her belly. The gel Dr. Jennings squirted onto her skin was freezing, and it annoyed her even more.

Suppressing a scowl, she said, "You're right. It doesn't."

To her credit, Dr. Jennings laughed, unperturbed by her bad mood. "I apologize. This shouldn't hurt, but you may feel some pressure." She pressed a wand into her abdomen and stared at the small screen. "Hmm."

"What is it?" She didn't like the way the doctor studied the images, like she'd found something bad.

Dr. Jennings wiped the gel off her skin. "Why don't you change into your clothes? I have a couple of questions to ask before you leave."

"All right."

Worried and agitated, she changed into her sundress. She wanted to know what Dr. Jennings found but at the same time she didn't. She wasn't in pain, so she didn't think it could be that serious, but her father had cancer. Maybe she did too.

Ovarian cancer. Uterine cancer. She'd been on the pill since she was eighteen. Birth control could cause cancer, couldn't it? Maybe she had endometriosis. Maybe her pill failed and she was pregnant.

She sat in the chair near the desk and told herself to calm down. Her leg jiggled.

Someone knocked on the door and Dr. Jennings and poked her head into the room. She saw Zia was dressed and stepped inside, closing the door behind her. Sitting on the stool, she said, "Zia, I'm wondering what your family plans look like right now."

She wiped her sweaty palms on her skirt. "My father's sick and I don't think he'll be with us much longer," she said, her voice raw. "He asked me to stay with my mother, but I've been living in California—"

"I appreciate the information," Dr. Jennings cut in, "and if you feel you need a therapist to talk through what's happening, I can give you a referral, but I meant *your* family. You're twenty-five. Are you planning to have children?"

"Oh." She flushed. "No wonder I didn't understand what you meant. I've been so busy with my painting I haven't given babies much thought. My boyfriend, Reid, is only a few years older than me. We haven't talked about it."

"Okay. I'll send the film to my tech, but from my initial observation, you have scarring in your fallopian tubes. Have you had any abdominal surgery or an STD your records don't contain? Maybe as a teenager you were treated at a Planned Parenthood because you didn't want to tell your parents you were sexually active?"

She bit her lip. "Ummm, ten years ago my appendix burst. Does that count as abdominal surgery?"

Nodding, Dr. Jennings said, "Yes. I'm rather surprised your

gynecologist didn't catch this. Your tubes have substantial scarring."

"What does that mean?"

"It means," Dr. Jennings said and took a deep breath, "when you decide to have children, you're going to have issues." She picked up a plastic model of a uterus, fallopian tubes, and ovaries and pointed. "Do you see the thin tubes that connect your ovaries to your uterus?"

"Yeah." She'd taken health classes and knew all her reproductive parts.

"When there's scarring in the tubes, it can prevent a healthy pregnancy in two ways. One, it prevents sperm from being able to enter the tube to fertilize your egg. On the off chance a sperm can make it that far and fertilizes the egg, it may not be able to travel out of the tube to attach to your uterine wall, where the egg grows into a fetus. In most cases, this can result in an ectopic pregnancy."

"What can I do?" She hadn't thought about kids. Not with Reid. They'd been too busy having fun. The parties, the showings. When she wasn't with Reid, she was painting. She hadn't thought of babies. Children. A family. That kind of future had gone up in a puff of smoke the morning she found Matthew finger-fucking her aunt.

"There are a few options. We can try surgery, clean out that scarring. Or," Dr. Jennings said, eyeing her carefully, "you can try IVF treatments when you're ready to start a family. That's placing already fertilized eggs inside your uterus and hoping one attaches. It bypasses the need for healthy fallopian tube function."

Zia rubbed her belly. "What if I don't want IVF? What if I want to get pregnant as naturally as I can?"

Dr. Jennings set the model aside and sighed. "Your scarring

is really bad, Zia. I don't like saying something like that unless my tech can back me up, but I saw it on the screen myself. We can clean it out. There are other options, but I have to tell you, if you want kids naturally, whatever you choose to do, you should do it soon. You're twenty-five, and the sooner you decide to have children, the easier the procedures will be and your pregnancies will be healthier, too. When you approach thirty, thirty-five . . . we've come a long way, but some things, like having babies, well, it's still better to do it younger. Do you understand?"

"Yes. Thank you."

Scribbling on a yellow pad, Dr. Jennings said, "I'll refill your prescription. They'll prevent an ectopic pregnancy. If you feel any cramping, besides the discomfort that my exam may cause you later, if you feel something's off . . . you're sexually active now, I'm assuming, since you're here?"

Zia nodded.

"If you feel any pain or severe cramping, go to the ER. Chances are nothing will happen . . . but the body's a mystery. It's a miraculous mystery." She handed the slip of paper to Zia. "This is your copy. I'll send your script to your pharmacy."

"Thank you."

"I'm sorry about your father. If you need to speak to someone, my office can refer you to several therapists."

"Thanks."

Zia picked up her purse and shoved her hair out of her face, her hand shaking.

Infertile.

She couldn't have babies.

That wasn't what the doctor told her, but she could read between the lines.

Outside the clinic, she leaned against the brick wall and held back tears.

She hadn't thought about kids until . . . until the moment she was told she couldn't have any.

How unfair.

Zia crumpled up the yellow piece of paper and threw it in the garbage. She wouldn't refill her prescription. What good would pills do her?

She already couldn't get pregnant.

No point in trying to remember to take a pill every day. Her body was already doing the work for her.

In the apartment above the garage, Zia stood in front of a full-length mirror in the larger of the two bedrooms. She and Reid had opted to sleep there instead of staying in the house or renting a hotel room. Her mother had offered them a guest room or her childhood bedroom, but it felt wrong, somehow, to be under her parents' roof, sleeping with a man who wasn't her husband.

"Who's this guy again?" Reid asked, standing behind her, adjusting his tie.

"My father's business partner, Matthew Harcourt."

She jammed a pin into her hair, trying to wrestle the thick strands into a bun, but her hair wasn't cooperating, the wild curls easily escaping. Her mother and father had already left for the party, but she hadn't wanted to be one of the first to arrive. She still clung to the idea she wouldn't talk to Matthew if she didn't have to. Not to say hello. Not to tell him happy birthday. She planned to sip champagne, chat with old friends, and try to convince Reid to leave early.

Parties were his specialty. Networking. Glad-handing. Within half an hour he'd know the who's who of the art world in Lake Kenosha. It wouldn't be the same as a California party, but Reid would enjoy himself nonetheless.

"Argh," Zia growled. "This isn't working." She jabbed at her hair with another pin, suddenly near tears.

"Hey, hey. What's the matter?" He steadied her hands. "Stop. Why are you trying to put your hair up? You never have before."

"I . . ." She couldn't tell him the real reason. Didn't want to admit it to herself. She wanted to look good for Matthew. Sophisticated. Elegant. She wanted to show him all he'd missed sending her away.

Reid slid the pins out of her hair as tears trailed down her cheeks. "There now. There's the woman I love."

Her image blurred. Her hair, a wild mess, her eyes, glittering green against the gold silk dress. The rose gold necklace tarnished and worn from so many years rubbing against her skin. Gold sandals that had straps so thin she could barely see them.

Clearing his throat, he pulled a small black box out of his pocket. "Zia, I know this is a terrible time. You're upset about your dad, you haven't painted in a while and I know how you go through withdrawal, but I love you and I want to be there for you through all this. We make a good team. You fit into my life like you were made for me, and I hope you feel the same way. I've never been happier with another woman. Zia, honey, will you marry me?"

He stood in front of her with hope in his eyes, holding a gorgeous diamond in his shaking hand. Handsome, loving, kind. Rich, if she cared about that kind of thing. Reid would be her perfect match. They'd take California's art world by storm. They already had, in many ways.

Her father could die happy, knowing she'd be taken care of.

She thought a moment too long.

Reid lowered his hand and closed the lid on the box. It snapped shut. "Maybe I was too presumptuous."

"Reid, I . . . It's not that I don't . . . You're right. This is a tough time for me, and . . . I didn't tell you. The first time I saw my father, when we spoke . . . he asked me to stay here. To look after my mother."

He frowned. "You're going to stay in Lake Kenosha? I don't understand. Your life's in LA."

"I don't know. It's been hard on my mom to have me so far away. I don't know how she's going to feel after Daddy—" She covered her mouth with her hand. She couldn't talk about her father dying. It would happen soon and she was nowhere near accepting it.

She and Reid had been in Lake Kenosha for only a week, and every day her father deteriorated a little more. It wouldn't be long, and she couldn't talk about it.

"Come here," he said, dropping the box on the floor and wrapping his arms around her. "We'll work it out. I'm sorry. I should have known better. Let's not think about it now, okay? I'm sorry."

Resting her cheek against his chest, she said, "It's okay, but I don't want to hold you back. Minnesota isn't California."

Reid kissed the top of her head. "I wouldn't choose California over you, Zia, but we have to admit the art scene in Cali's a bit more lucrative than it is here, yeah?"

She sniffled a laugh at the understatement. "Yeah."

"Come on. We've waited long enough. We're later than fashionable now."

"All right. I'm sorry."

"Nothing to be sorry for. My timing was off. You're just so beautiful, any man who looks at you would be a fool not to want to keep you forever."

She rose to her tiptoes and kissed his cheek. "You don't have any competition."

"Sometimes I don't think that's true." He brushed his fingers over her necklace. "Let's go."

The minute they stepped into the ballroom of the elegant downtown hotel, Zia scanned the room for Matthew. She wanted to see him so badly her heart hurt, yet if she had the choice of not seeing one glimpse of him all night, she would have taken it.

"Zia, Reid, you're finally here." Sylvia swooped in giving them hugs and kisses, though she'd seen them not two hours before. "Let me introduce you around. Reid, you haven't met Chloe, my sister-in-law, Ray's sister. She's throwing the party for Matthew. They're in the corner, near the champagne fountain. It wasn't enough to have waiters walking around," Sylvia *tsked*.

"Mom," Zia said, tugging on her mother's hand. "We have plenty of time to see them."

"Come, now," her mother said firmly. "You haven't seen Matthew for years. The least you can do is tell him happy birthday."

Reid wrapped his arm around her. "I'd like to meet him, honey. He's your father's business partner. After all these years he must feel like he's part of the family."

Zia flashed to Matthew between her legs, pushing his cock inside her. Invading a space no other man had. Whispers. Kisses. Love. "Yeah, part of the family," she muttered.

His back was to her when they approached, but Sylvia said, "Matthew, Zia and Reid are here," and he slowly turned.

Her legs shook so badly she thought she'd collapse. She'd

dreamed of this for years, though the scenarios had always differed. In one, she threw a drink in his face. In another, she threw herself into his arms and begged him to love her.

In the middle of a party, with Reid by her side, she'd do neither. She steeled herself to be civil. Polite. Do her duty and then she and Reid would work the room and leave.

She wished she had a glass of champagne. She'd counted on being tipsy.

Matthew faced her and she staggered backward, her heart pounding.

"M-M-Matthew?" she stammered.

"Zia, it's nice to see you again," he said, holding out a hand.

He'd changed in the seven years since she left, and the years hadn't been kind. Deep grooves marred his face, and his complexion had taken on a sickly pallor she didn't understand.

His grip was still firm, his skin warm and dry against hers.

Chloe sidled up to them and wrapped her arms around his waist, anchoring him to her.

Matthew dropped her hand and shook Reid's briefly. "How's Raymond?" he asked Chloe.

"Good. He's chatting with some of his friends. Zia, darling, I'm so happy you're here. Your father and I have missed you so much. I can't believe how well-known you've become! Who knew your little paintings would fetch so much money!" Chloe smiled, her features brittle, and she wanted to slap her.

But not for what she said.

How could her aunt look at Matthew and not think something was amiss?

How could anyone look at Matthew and not wonder what the fuck was going on?

She forced herself to smile. "It's thanks to Reid, Aunt Chloe. I wouldn't have a career if it wasn't for him."

"Reid, tell me all about it while I introduce you around,"

Chloe said, latching onto him, too closely, if she had anything to say about it.

She let them go, Reid, amiable, a perfect gentleman. He didn't know there was bad blood between her and Chloe. He didn't know much about her life when she lived here. Didn't know that once upon a time she'd been in love with the man who stood in front of her, looking as if he was well on the way to his grave.

"I'm going to check on your father. I don't trust Chloe's opinion." Sylvia kissed her on the cheek and walked away, but she barely noticed.

Matthew stared at her, starving, like a man who hadn't eaten a meal in a week.

She felt the same, her eyes devouring his face, but she hoped it didn't show. She didn't want him to know how much his appearance affected her.

"You kept it." He delicately rubbed his finger over the tarnished necklace.

"I did, though it was an uneven trade."

"What do you mean?"

"You gave me a necklace, I gave you my heart. Which one of us came out ahead, do you think?"

He flinched. He'd tried to prepare for this. He'd tried to harden his heart, greet her like any other guest who would arrive, wish him a happy birthday, perhaps give him some small token gift.

But his Zia, his Little Star, didn't pull any punches.

She laid it all out there, and he tried to be grateful for it. Tried to appreciate it after Chloe's mind games and tantrums, but she could have at least softened the blow.

"You look good, Zia," he said, savoring her name on his

tongue. He hadn't spoken it aloud in seven years. He offered her a glass of champagne, hating his hand shook so badly.

She waved it away. "You don't. What's wrong with you? You look like shit."

"Life hasn't been all turpentine and canvas," he shot back, setting the untouched flute on a table instead of flinging it across the room like he wanted. "It would've been nice if you would have come home once in a while. Your mother's missed you. Your father's sick and I've been running Bridgewater alone. Maybe there's a reason I look like shit."

It felt good to have blood pumping through his veins again. Especially anger. God, he had so much to be angry about. He'd been living in resignation. Acceptance that this was his life.

Until Raymond got sick.

But that presented its own hell.

"Why do you think I've stayed away? I couldn't stand to be around you. You and Chloe . . . the thought of you fucking like rabbits," she spat.

Matthew gripped her arm and dragged her across the floor, ignoring the inquisitive glances thrown their way.

"Hey," she objected, but he didn't stop. They'd have this out because he'd be damned if he'd walk on eggshells around her the entire time she was here. Raymond's time was limited, yes, but no one could know for sure how long he would stay with them.

He'd tell no one he prayed for God to put Raymond out of his misery.

He yanked her to a carpeted stairwell that led up to the sleeping rooms. The fire door muted the guests' murmurs and the five-piece orchestra Chloe hired to play.

Yellow light lit the narrow staircase, and Zia's red hair blazed, her skin shimmered like gold.

He'd missed her, his Little Star. She'd turned into a woman, all curves and smooth lines. She'd grown out her hair, lost the baby fat in her face. Elegant, refined. Her art setting the world on fire.

They stared, the first time in seven years seeing each other.

Suddenly, everything Matthew wanted to say, everything he was going to spew at her in a rage of fury and hurt, dried up, and he simply stood there.

Her green eyes glittered, her breath coming out in angry gasps.

"You don't know what's been going on between Chloe and me," he finally said, but he couldn't say more. The dam of secrets would burst after Raymond's death, but not before. Not before.

"I don't want to know," she said, lifting her chin, but then her shoulders sagged. "You look ill. Is it only Bridgewater, or is it something else?" She reached to touch his cheek, but he leaned away and she dropped her hand.

"It isn't only Bridgewater," he said, but left it at that. Chloe's blackmail had taken its toll, but it wasn't Zia's business.

She swallowed. "Are you . . . sick?"

He slouched against the wall, wishing for a drink, something stronger than the champagne he'd been nursing all night. He wasn't prepared for this conversation. Not so soon.

What had Sylvia been thinking, shoving Zia in his face the moment she arrived? Why couldn't they have circled each other, like lions assessing prey, before going in for the kill?

"You'd like that, wouldn't you?" he asked bitterly. "For saying the things I did the day you found me with Chloe."

Zia stood on the second step, and they were close. So close. He could count the freckles that speckled her cheeks.

When she was little, he'd count them, his fingers tracing over her skin. She'd sit quietly, legs tucked under her, her face upward as if she were praying to the sun. He'd count, and then, without warning, she'd burst into a fit of giggles.

It'd been so innocent, until one night they'd played the game. He forgot how old she was. Fourteen, fifteen, maybe. He touched her cheek, and there was an electricity between them that hadn't been there before. After that night, he hadn't allowed them to be in the same room together alone.

She wasn't fifteen any longer and he smoothed his fingertip across her cheek.

Someone bumped against the door and he stood frozen until the footfalls faded.

So close. Only an inch between them.

She smelled of roses.

And sex.

Their proximity made Zia wet, and her scent made him hard.

"Are you engaged to him? Married?" He hoped she hadn't married without him knowing, but a master of secrets himself, he believed she could've taken Reid's name and not told anyone.

Zia covered the necklace he'd given her the night he took her virginity.

It humbled him she still wore it.

It gave him hope.

Not that they could have a future. There was no hope for that, but hope she didn't hate him for what he'd done.

"No," she whispered.

"Good."

He couldn't stop himself any longer.

He kissed her.

CHAPTER FIVE

Zia fisted her hands in his hair as he ravaged her mouth. She moaned under his lips, and that spurred him on, peppering love bites down her neck. She reveled in the tiny shocks of pain, and heat and wet flooded her panties.

It'd been so long since she felt like this.

She grappled at his belt and he yanked her dress's hem up.

"Please, Matthew, hurry," she gasped, lowering herself onto the stairs. Not wasting a second to undo the buckles, she pried off her sandals, the straps cutting into her skin. She didn't care.

Matthew undid his pants and pushed his briefs down, freeing his cock, and she wiggled out of the gold thong that matched her dress.

She laid back, propping onto her elbows and spreading her legs, wet dripping out of her. She'd missed him so much. "Please," she begged.

"Zia, I don't have anything with me," Matthew said, dropping to his knees.

"We don't need anything, hurry. Hurry."

He slipped his fingers inside her, and she moaned.

"My God," he mumbled.

"I need you, I want you," she whimpered, bearing down on his hand.

This was wrong. Reid was out there, somewhere, mingling with her family and friends. It had taken her all of half an hour to cheat on him.

Thank God she'd been able to tell Matthew the truth. She and Reid weren't engaged, but an hour before, they could have been.

"Are you sure?"

"Yes," she panted. If he didn't make love to her right now, she'd go crazy.

He teased her with the tip of his cock, a light nudge against her clit, and then thrust into her. The stair cut into her back, but she didn't care.

She cried in relief as he filled her.

She hadn't realized how hollow she'd been feeling all these years. She hadn't realized how much she'd missed him and what they could have had together until that moment her eyes fluttered open, and she met his, so tired, so sad, yet still so full of love for her, she could feel it, like ribbons floating around the stairwell as he braced himself over her.

Wrapping her arms around his shoulders, she clung to him, pressing her face into his neck.

"God, Zia," Matthew rasped, gliding back and forth, his skin slick against hers. He slid his hand between them and rubbed her clit.

She exploded, her muscles clenching at his cock.

He responded in kind, his semen hot as it spurted inside her, and he held her steady as they caught their breaths.

She shifted, her back hurting. The thin carpeting gave her little protection and the edge of the stair bit into her spine. She missed his nearness when he too, sat up due to discomfort, but he kissed her again, his tongue playing with hers.

"I'm sorry, Zia."

His words brought her back to earth, and she crashed, an angel with broken wings.

"Will you ever be able to make love to me and not apologize afterward?" she asked, snatching her thong off the floor and shoving her feet through the leg holes. Angrily, she secured her sandals to her feet.

She stood, and Matthew's cum trickled out of her, wetting the insides of her thighs. She'd need to visit the ladies' room before she found Reid. If she didn't, he'd need no time at all to know what she'd been doing.

"I'm not apologizing for making love to you. I'm apologizing for hurting you. I can't seem to stop doing either, I'm afraid."

He tucked his dress shirt into his pants and pulled the zipper up. Bucking his belt and adjusting his cufflinks, he didn't meet her eyes.

She leaned against the wall, tired and sad. "Will you look at me?"

Once again at eye level, he met her gaze, and she ran her hand along his cheek and across a jaw that used to be so strong, but now sagged in age and something else she couldn't quite describe.

He held her hand and kissed her palm, his lips, oh so familiar, and little zings of shock sizzled up and down her arm.

"We need to figure this out," she whispered, rubbing her thumb against his lips.

"There's nothing to figure out," he said, looking away. "You're with Reid. In the brief time I saw you together, I could see how much he loves you, worships you. I can't blame him. You look like a goddess tonight, all gold and bright."

"But—"

"And I have Chloe."

"I don't understand that. You never seemed interested before. Why did you sleep with me that night if you wanted my bitch of an aunt?"

"Chloe and I are a good match, and it makes your father happy."

"That doesn't tell me anything," she said.

"It's enough. We better go. I'm sure we've been missed."

"I want to see you." It was stupid to insist, but now that she knew he still felt something for her, she wouldn't let him put her off. He loved her, even if he wouldn't say it.

He sighed and pressed his lips to hers. They smelled of sex, and his cologne would linger on her skin. "We're playing with fire."

She held him, wanting to soothe, somehow. His ragged appearance shook her. "I don't care. It's been seven years. Seven years wasted because of what, I don't know, but Chloe, Reid, they don't matter, Matthew. It only matters that we love each other."

Wincing, she bit the inside of her lip. She sounded like her eighteen-year-old self, the naïve little girl still trying to play a grownup's game.

He cupped her face in his hands, tears sparkling in his eyes. "I'm fifty-three years old this week, Zia. Think about that. I'm fifty-three to your twenty-five. You belong with a man who can give you a future. A man who can nurture your career, like Reid. I'm old, broken. You can see that for yourself. Look at me. Look at me closely, Little Star, and tell me I'm who you'd want for the rest of your life."

He didn't want her to. He wanted her to renounce him for his age, for his haggard appearance. She wouldn't, but she wouldn't fight with him, either.

Right now, she needed to do damage control. Starting with

wiping off Matthew's semen slowly dripping down the insides of her legs.

She brushed her lips against his. "Remember what it feels like to move inside me. Remember what it feels like to have my arms around you. After seven years, how did that feel? Did it feel like love? Because it did to me."

She walked out of the stairwell and didn't look back.

She stopped at the first women's restroom she found. Luckily, she didn't see anyone who would ask her where she'd been.

Looking in the mirror, the answer would have been evident, anyway.

Her eyes smoked, hazy with lust, her lips red and swollen. Her skin glimmered under the lights, sweat and sin.

She used the toilet and cleaned herself the best she could. His cum, and hers, drenched her thong, and on impulse, she threw it into the trash. Going without would be better. It would give her a chance to dry out, such as it were.

Wishing she had a purse to perhaps reapply some gloss or a mist of body spray, she did the best she could using the scented hand soap and a wet paper towel. She'd opted out of carrying one tonight as Reid had driven and she had no use for cash with Chloe's open bar.

Using her fingers, she tried her best to detangle her hair. Matthew's fists had ruined her curls, and it turned into a good thing she hadn't been able to pin it up. An updo would have been destroyed in seconds.

"Zia! Where have you been?" Reid caught her as she stepped into the ballroom. "I've been looking for you. You should have warned me your aunt was a barracuda. I'm lucky I escaped with my life."

She laughed, but it sounded strained. "I'm sure you held your own just fine. I wasn't feeling well, and I stepped outside for a moment. I should have told you. I'm sorry."

"Did Matthew go with you?"

Her heart pounded. She'd never been a good liar. "Why do you ask?"

"Because he came in from your direction. Were you out there together?" He narrowed his eyes. "Is everything okay?"

Forcing herself to wrap her arms around him, she smiled. "Yes, everything's fine. Let's go say hello to my father. Mom said he can't stay long at these things and I want to see him before he has to leave."

"Okay. I need something stronger than champagne, and I'm hungry. Chloe said she made sure the buffet was the best."

On Matthew's dime, no doubt, but she didn't say anything. Reid didn't need a play by play of her family's problems, though the longer they stayed, the higher the possibility he'd be treated to a front-row seat.

She spoke with her father, sitting in a chair beside his wheelchair while Reid stopped at the open bar. Raymond narrowed his eyes, as Reid had, and her smile faltered. Discreetly, she sniffed her shoulder and silently moaned in dismay. Matthew's cologne still lingered on her skin. The raspberry-scented soap hadn't done as good a job as she'd hoped.

Standing across the floor, her aunt glared at her, but she ignored it.

She couldn't understand why Chloe and Matthew were together. Chloe had hung on Matthew's every word, but, unless Zia had missed something, he'd never reciprocated.

Reid approached her holding a lowball of something, and he handed it to her, letting her sip. She needed it to calm her nerves, and she sighed as the amber liquid burned its way down her throat.

Chloe stepped up the dais' short set of stairs and the orchestra quieted. Zia resisted rolling her eyes. Trust her aunt to steal the spotlight in any situation.

Tapping a butter knife against a flute of champagne, Chloe said, "Can I have your attention, everyone?"

The crowd quieted.

Sylvia stood behind her father's wheelchair and rested her hands on his shoulders.

"Attention, everyone," Chloe said again. "Matthew, can you come up here, please?"

He stepped up onto the dais, his complexion not as pale as when she first arrived. The sight made her happy. She, not her aunt, had been able to lift his spirits.

Whether she wanted to admit it or not, they were a nice couple. Matthew, wearing a sharply-cut suit, his hair more gray now than black, made an imposing figure. Her aunt, even after seven years, still beautiful. Her hair fell in perfect waves around her shoulders, her slim figure elegantly encased in a black cocktail dress.

"Thank you for coming to Matthew's fifty-third birthday party. I hope you all are having a good time?"

Matthew's guests answered her question with a round of enthusiastic applause.

"Good, I'm glad," her aunt continued.

Zia held out her hand, wanting another sip of Reid's drink, and he complied, lifting the corner of his mouth.

"In honor of Matthew's birthday, a donation to the United Way will be made in his name. We ask that in lieu of gifts, anyone who would like to donate to a worthy cause do the same."

More applause.

"We also have one more announcement we'd like to share. Matthew, honey? Did you want to tell them?"

Zia stood, a shiver suddenly snaking down her back, slippery, foreboding.

Without the aid of a microphone, Matthew's rich voice carried across the ballroom. "First, I'd like to thank everyone who carved time into their busy schedules to attend this wonderful party. I appreciate all of you very much. Secondly, Chloe and I do have some news to share. It's the best birthday gift a man could receive. I've asked her to marry me, and she said yes."

She dropped the crystal lowball onto the carpeted floor. The contents splattered over her feet, but she felt nothing.

"Zia, darling, are you all right?" Sylvia asked, alarmed.

Chloe flashed an enormous diamond to the crowd, and Matthew kissed her. The audience shouted well-wishes and congratulations.

Matthew's cock had been inside her not twenty minutes ago, and she'd been glad then she hadn't accepted Reid's proposal.

Apparently, Matthew had no such qualms fucking her while engaged to her aunt.

"Now, Zia, if we could get an announcement from you and Reid such as that, I would die a happy man," her father said.

She flinched.

He sagged in his wheelchair. "I'm ready to go. I've stayed for as long as I can."

A weight settled onto Zia's shoulders, and she looked at the dais where Chloe still accepted congratulations, holding out her hand, granting permission to those asking to see her ring.

She met Matthew's eyes.

His pallor had come back, his skin waxy with sweat.

Slowly, she took a step backward, then another, never breaking eye contact. Another step, and then, before she knew it, she was running, running, as far and as fast as her heels would carry her.

"Did we have to do that tonight?" Matthew asked, unknotting his tie and throwing it across the room. It brought him no satisfaction as the piece of silk did nothing but flutter to the floor.

The look in Zia's eyes as she backed away cut him to his knees. Back and forth, the horrified look on her face when she'd caught him fingering Chloe in his office so long ago, and her expression tonight, back and forth, flashed through his mind.

Her chin tilted in anger, her eyes flashing fury, Chloe stood in the middle of the bedroom. A bedroom she'd redecorated more times than he could count during the time she'd lived there.

Once he asked her why she didn't want to move into a newer, bigger house, and she said she took pleasure in sleeping in the bed where he'd taken Zia's virginity.

He told two hundred of his nearest and dearest he wanted to marry this lovely creature.

Goddammit.

"Yes, we did. And do you know why? Because I know where you were. Did you think I wouldn't smell Zia's pussy on you? This time I don't have proof, but I think a little birdie needs to visit Reid and tell him Zia has been a very naughty girl. What would he say?"

Matthew sank onto the bed. "You don't need to do that. I think I hurt her enough tonight she won't come near me, ever again."

"Good. That was my intention. Remember, I'll tell Raymond everything. From the letters you sent his precious Sylvia, to you fucking his eighteen-year-old daughter. After her disgusting display of emotion tonight, he'd believe me, without seeing the evidence I have. Unzip my dress."

"You don't love your niece at all, do you?" he asked, complying.

"That little bitch has everything she could want. She doesn't need the one thing I've been able to take for myself. Come to bed. I want you to give me what you gave her tonight. Is your cock still sticky with her cum?"

It wasn't too much longer, Matthew thought, mentally preparing himself to give Chloe what she wanted. A few more weeks at most until Raymond passed away, and then he could flick a match to this oil spill and watch as everything went up in flames.

For once, he'd be able to walk away without getting hurt.

Zia stepped into the apartment, exhausted.

Reid had been silent on the way back, but now that they were alone, he wasted no time picking at her wound.

"Zia, sweetheart, why won't you talk to me?"

"There's nothing to say."

Avoiding his eyes, she stepped into their bedroom and began undressing. She wanted to go to sleep and pretend this was all just a nasty nightmare.

"I think there is. I asked you to marry me. You said no, but I still think that gives me some rights. I love you, and you know I have since the moment we met."

"I didn't say no." She hadn't said anything.

"You didn't say yes."

She scoffed. "Then what does that mean? Maybe? Matthew was a childhood crush, that's all. Their announcement was a surprise." She sat on the bed and finally looked at him. Maybe she could smooth this over. She didn't want to fight.

Especially over Matthew, who had made his choice.

Again.

"You've spent time with her. Who in their right mind would marry that?"

"She's very beautiful," he allowed, undressing.

"Is that a man attitude? Women can behave how they like because they're beautiful?"

"No. I watched them together and it's obvious they love each other, but she seems . . . cold."

"She's a selfish bitch." She didn't believe for one minute Matthew loved her aunt. No matter how he acted in public. She dropped her dress onto the floor, and stood naked in front of the small closet, searching for a nightgown.

"I thought you wore a thong tonight?" Reid asked, his eyes roaming her body.

It used to turn her on when he looked at her that way.

When did it stop?

The minute her mother told her she needed to come home.

"It was uncomfortable so I took it off in the bathroom at the hotel."

"Right."

His one-word acceptance brought her back up, but she let it go. He had every right not to believe her because anything he thought would be true.

She gave up looking for a nightgown, pulled one of Reid's t-shirts over her head, and slipped on a pair of panties.

He finished undressing and changed into a fresh pair of boxer briefs and a t-shirt. He brushed his teeth and joined her in bed.

She turned out the light, praying he wouldn't ask for sex. She'd always been monogamous. After Matthew broke her heart, she'd gone to the Art Studio, licked her wounds and dated here and there. Slept with a man or two who caught her fancy to rinse the taste of Matthew out of her mouth, and it wasn't that long into her second year at school she met Reid.

Not one for browsing, she'd been happy with the choices she made.

Until tonight.

She wished it hadn't happened. She wished her heart wasn't so stupid soft. Matthew's ghastly appearance had appalled her, and all she'd wanted to do was kiss him and take away his pain.

She'd kissed him all right, but things had gone from bad to worse.

Reid cuddled her, his cock soft against her ass, and she relaxed in his embrace.

"I spoke to a couple of people tonight," he said.

She laughed. "Oh, you did? Good for you."

Reid tickled her and she squealed. "I mean, I talked to a couple of *art* people. There's a gallery downtown that seems rather prestigious for a city like Lake Kenosha. Post 15? Have you heard of it?"

She rolled onto her back and looked into his face. She didn't deserve this man, and she had to decide if she wanted him because it wasn't fair to either of them that she didn't know. "No. What's the address? Do you remember?"

"Jefferson Avenue?"

"Oh, I remember some kind of rundown gallery there, but if it's got something going on now, maybe it changed hands. Was the owner at Matthew's party?"

"No, but the director, Shirley Shapiro, was, and of course she's heard of you. Didn't know you were back in the area, but she'd love it if you did a showing. In fact, there's an event coming up that the downtown businesses participate in the first weekend of October? I forgot what she called it."

"*Fall and Foliage,* I think. That's what it used to be when I lived here."

He skimmed his fingertips down her cheek and over her jaw. "That's it. Shirley said it's a pretty big thing."

"It used to be. I don't know if it still is. Very high-society. A ball and everything."

"That's perfect then."

She sat up. "But that's not far away. I'd have to work like crazy to get anything ready. How much space is she giving me?"

"All of it."

Turning on the small lamp by the bed, she asked, "What do you mean 'all of it?'"

"The whole gallery. You'd be bumping someone, but Shirley didn't make it sound like a big deal. In fact, she sounded relieved you'd be available. I guess there aren't any good artists around here."

"I doubt that, but . . . okay. How many paintings? What's the square footage?"

"As many as you can get done. Earlier today, while you were at the house talking to your mom and dad, I found you some studio space, in case you wanted to paint, let off some steam. You can start on a collection tomorrow, if you want. I told Shirley I'd bring you by to meet her, and you can look at the gallery. It's close to two thousand square feet."

"That's a lot of wall space."

"It is. It's not California, but Post 15 is nothing we should turn down if we can ask a decent price for your work. She sounded very connected."

"My gynecologist told me she bought one of my paintings."

"How did your appointment go?"

She turned out the light. "I'm fine, as always," she said, lying down and adjusting the pillow under her head.

"Good. I'm sorry again about earlier, but a maybe sounds better than a no." He brushed a kiss over her lips.

"It's okay. You caught me off guard, that's all." She scrubbed the scruff covering his jaw. "Let me think about it, okay? I'm here for the time being, and . . . I haven't spoken to my mom at all about what she'll do once Dad's gone. You should go back to LA, Reid. You can only do so much from here."

He kissed her again, rubbing his hand up and down her leg, and she tamped back the guilt. She should have showered. "Maybe I have the *Fall* thing, now. We'll figure out your showing and go from there. Goodnight, Zia. I love you."

"Goodnight." *I love you too.* The words were there on her tongue, but she couldn't say them, couldn't mean them. Had she ever, or had she turned Reid's love into a substitute? A generic of the real thing she wanted?

She waited until he was sleeping soundly, slipped out of bed, and tiptoed down the stairs into the summer's night air.

Matthew's house was too far down the road to see if there were any lights on, if anyone was still awake. She leaned against her old truck and let her mind drift to his bed, the night he gave her the necklace. The night he made her a woman.

The night he made her feel like a queen.

"I took over as the director of Post 15 not long ago," Shirley Shapiro said, a tremor in her voice. "This would be a real coup for me, Miss Bishop, if you chose to show your work here during the *Fall and Foliage.* Your showing would be on a Saturday evening, and directly afterward, Lake Kenosha's mayor hosts an elegant masquerade ball. If any of your paintings are still available, they'll be transported to the hotel and displayed at the ball where everyone will have one last chance to purchase a Zia Bishop."

She walked around the gallery. Black walls gave paintings their own blank canvas. Flecks of silver sparkled in a black marble floor, and white pillars decorated the large area, the ceiling three floors above their heads.

She loved the space, the colors and feel of it, though it didn't quite give off the air of sophistication and money she'd come to expect from a gallery. "Reid, what do you think?"

"Is there something amiss, Miss Bishop?" Shirley asked, her forehead puckering into a frown. "I assure you, we can accommodate you by any means possible."

"I think what she's worried about, Miss Shapiro," Reid said smoothly, guiding Shirley away, a hand to her lower back, "is that she's afraid, and I am as well, that your clientele . . . how can I put this delicately? That your clientele won't be able to afford an original Zia Bishop . . ." His voice faded.

She blew out a breath. She hated talking about money, but she'd hate more not fetching a price she'd become accustomed to because of Reid's expertise.

"Zia!"

She twirled, her red curls flying.

Aimee Preston rushed across the floor, the heels of her plain black pumps clicking against the marble.

"Aimee! What are you doing here? And why weren't you at Matthew's birthday party? I was hoping to see you." Aimee could have talked her out of doing the stupid thing she did.

"I'm Miss Shapiro's assistant. It was a lucky break. Not many positions like this open up in Lake Kenosha. I had to miss because I was working a showing and couldn't get the night off. You know how it is."

Zia gripped the woman in a strong embrace. She hadn't seen her best friend since the night they said goodbye in her bedroom. They'd plan a visit, but then something would happen and plans would have to be postponed. After three years of failed attempts and Zia meeting Reid, they settled for FaceTime talks and long emails to catch up. "Yeah, I know," she said, leaning away. "It's so good to see you. I have so much news to tell you."

"It's good to see you too. I missed you. Are you going to do a showing here?"

"I think so. Reid's discussing the details with Shirley now. He's afraid no one will be able to afford me." She blushed. She sounded like such a snob.

Aimee only bumped her shoulder. "That's not a concern. There are more rich people than just your dad and Matthew who live here. Lake Kenosha's grown a lot since you've been gone." Her voice dropped. "I was sorry to hear about that, by the way, about your dad. How's he doing?"

"Not very well. Every second I'm not with him, I feel guilty."

"That's understandable." She paused. "Did you talk to Matthew?"

"Yeah, I did."

Across the large room, Shirley was showing Reid the gallery, pointing out every single feature, no matter how small, and he winked behind her back. He'd collaborated with directors who oversaw some of the most prestigious galleries on the West Coast. Post 15 didn't hold a candle to most of those galleries, but he wouldn't hurt her feelings. Zia wrinkled her nose, letting him know she knew exactly what he was thinking. They were always on the same page.

It'd be stupid to turn down his proposal, but ever since Matthew's party, ever since she looked into his eyes and saw the misery etched on his face, the resolve to want nothing to do with him crumbled like a sandcastle under an ocean's wave.

Aimee, her best friend for years, knew the truth. "You did more than talk."

She wanted to deny it, but she couldn't and looked away. A figure lurked in an alcove, spotlights creating shadows where the woman stood. "Who's that?"

"Don't try to change the subject," Aimee said, but she glanced in the direction Zia tilted her head. "That's Rebecca Gainsborough. She's a local artist. Oils, usually. She's shown here a couple of times so Shirley doesn't feel bad for bumping her off the *Fall and Foliage* program."

"Why is she hanging around? It's creepy."

Aimee laughed. "Zia, you're Zia Bishop."

"I don't know what you mean."

"I mean, she's probably too nervous to introduce herself. I would be too, if we hadn't grown up together, and if I didn't have stories like the time you licked a frozen light pole and stuck your tongue to the metal."

"She did what now?" Reid asked, draping an arm around her shoulders.

"Don't listen to her," she said and sniffed in mock disgust. "It was a long time ago."

Aimee laughed. "Not so long."

Her hands clasped in front of her, Shirley joined them. "Miss Bishop, I am so pleased you'll be showing your work at Post 15. Mr. Vaughn and I have come to a very satisfactory agreement. Will you be shipping your collection from California?"

The woman moved, and a willowy, platinum blonde stood in the spotlight, staring at their group.

"No . . ." Zia faded off, the woman's presence unnerving her.

Reid nudged her. "No. I've rented some space that will work as a makeshift studio. During the next few weeks she'll be creating an original collection for the showing. Being the event is called *Fall and Foliage,* we thought Zia would focus on the brilliant Minnesota fall. Autumn is a beautiful time of year, and we think it will give Zia adequate material to work with."

"Indeed," Shirley said, beaming. "Oh, Rebecca. Come meet Miss Bishop."

Everyone turned her way and the woman paled, but as she approached, she smiled and held out her hand. "I apologize for seeming odd, Miss Bishop. My heart's pounding! It's such an honor to meet you."

Zia shook her hand. "Pleased to meet you as well. I hope to see some of your work while I'm in the area."

Rebecca opened her mouth to respond, but Reid cut her off. "We best be going. We're pressed for time."

Hugging Aimee, Zia said, "We need to catch up soon." Tears scratched her throat. "I have so much to tell you."

"It's okay, sweetie, you'll be okay," Aimee whispered into her ear. In a normal tone, she continued, "Give me a call, and we'll have drinks."

"I will."

Reid held the gallery's door open, and Zia stepped onto the sidewalk, trying to keep her emotions in check. She didn't want him to think something was wrong.

She looked over her shoulder to wave at Aimee one last time, but Rebecca stood there, glaring.

Zia shivered.

Aimee assured them bumping the woman off the program wasn't a big deal, but it was apparent, to Zia anyway, that wasn't the case at all.

Matthew stepped out of the library where he'd been speaking with Raymond and slid the door closed behind him. The man tried his best to stay abreast of business dealings, but the details tired him, and Matthew had only been able to discuss half of what he wanted before Raymond grew too exhausted to continue.

As the months passed and cancer ate at Raymond, Matthew spoke to Sylvia more and more about business matters, and he went to find her now, searching the Bishop house. He had to keep her in the loop as she'd be able to share the information with Raymond later, and because it wouldn't be too far into the future Sylvia would inherit Raymond's fifty percent of Bridgewater Financial.

He rubbed his eyes and leaned against the wall cut away to reveal the kitchen.

He'd go to hell for looking forward to Raymond's death. He could wrap it in a pretty bow and say he wished Raymond was in a better place because that sure as hell was true. Though Raymond tried to hide it, pain ravaged him, and Matthew would be hard-pressed to believe Raymond cared about anything he had to say. It wasn't as selfless as that, and he knew it. Raymond's death meant freedom, and he could taste it, bittersweet, like Zia's kisses.

"Are you going to stand there all day, or do you want a cup of coffee?" Sylvia's voice carried through the white and blue kitchen, and Matthew scoffed in amusement.

"How did you know I was out there?" He set his briefcase on the floor and slid onto a stool behind the island. He'd spent many hours in this kitchen soaking up the ambience that made the Bishop family so special.

Sylvia didn't answer, only poured a mug of coffee and set it in front of him.

Shadows smudged under her dull green eyes, her skin pale. She'd lost weight, and her tragic beauty gave Chloe even more to hate.

"You made the right choice, you know, all those years ago."

Leaning against the counter, a mug cradled in her hands, she said, "I have few regrets. Ray's been good to me. Zia's the light of my life." She paused. "And yours."

He didn't want to talk about Zia. He hadn't seen her since his party, since he watched her back away, horrified, self-loathing in his heart for once again breaking hers. "I went over some things with Raymond, but he . . . he doesn't have the energy to care anymore."

"Don't change the subject. Zia hasn't been herself since, well, I was going to say your birthday party, but that's not true. Are you really going to marry Chloe? Hasn't this gone on long enough?"

"How long is too long?" He sipped his coffee.

"A minute's too long if Chloe's involved."

"We all do what we have to do."

"And what does that mean for you?"

"It means staying away from Zia. We never talked about what Zia and I—"

"It wasn't necessary. It's still not."

"You're right. She has Reid now. Which means she'll be happy and he'll take care of her."

"You would, too."

Annoyed, he pushed his mug away. "You can't want me with your daughter. You were kind not to hold my transgression against me and I value our friendship more than you can imagine, but I had no right to touch her. I still don't. I'm twice her age. She's going to want children someday."

"Why didn't you?" She touched his wrist, and he flipped his hand over, linking their fingers. An old love connected them, as did their friendship. As did their love for Zia. "Why didn't you marry and have children?"

He rested his back against the stool, the metal creaking. "I didn't have the want. Bridgewater has been my family. Raymond and I have nurtured that business for over twenty-five years. I didn't have time to find the right woman to spend the rest of my life with."

"Keep telling yourself that."

Laughing, he said, "I will. You ruined other women for me. No one could compete."

Sylvia arched an eyebrow. "Except my daughter."

"This is too close to becoming one of those gothic novels you liked to read in college." He tried to make light of the whole sordid mess, but she asked, "Do you love her? Do you still love her?" and his smile faded.

He stared into her eyes, and they were full of compassion and understanding. He could lay out all his hopes and dreams, tell her there wasn't anything he wanted more than to marry Zia and spend the rest of his life making her happy.

None of that mattered. After Raymond passed, he'd walk away, let Chloe do whatever damage she wanted, secure in the knowledge that Zia might hate him but would be all right without him.

Ignoring the question, he picked up his briefcase, set it on the counter, and snapped it open. "I have a few things to talk to you about."

"Matthew—"

"I love her, Sylvia. Is that what you want to hear?" he snapped. "I love her. The way a man loves a woman. But I'm not going to do anything about it. Do you understand all the fucking reasons why?"

Sylvia lowered her gaze to the countertop and nodded.

"Good. Now I need to go over this with you, then I have to get back to the office. Chloe monitors every second of my goddamned day and I've been here too long."

It pained him to hurt Sylvia that way, but she had to see the hopelessness of it all.

Between him and Reid, Reid was a better choice for Zia, and he'd make sure she made the right one.

Even though she shouldn't, she missed Matthew. Worried about him.

She helped the delivery driver unload the canvases, paints, and other supplies she'd need to create a new collection for *Fall and Foliage.* She only had six weeks to complete as many paintings as she could. The more she could finish, the more money she'd make, obviously, but like any artist, the need to create quality work warred with the need to supply the demand. She'd sell the best paintings. If they all met her standards, so much the better.

She signed the electronic pad the driver handed her, and tipping his baseball cap, he hopped into his truck and drove down the street.

Carrying a box of paint, Zia rode the service elevator to the top floor.

Blank canvases leaned against the wall of windows, waiting for her to bleed emotion onto the white.

She welcomed the chance to channel her misery into her art.

Reid had chosen a good space—a high rise under construction. This floor would become a law firm's office suite, but for now it'd be her temporary studio. The debris on the floor didn't bother her: saw horses, wooden planks, toolboxes, and ladders. The glorious floor-to-ceiling windows would let in the precious light she needed and made jumping over extension cords worth it.

A lovely late-summer evening, the sun turned a soft, buttery yellow against a brilliant, cloudless blue sky. Colors so splendid she could mix paint for the rest of her life and not match the beauty of what Mother Nature could do.

She sank to the floor, heartsick and exhausted.

Reid was very understanding, blaming her moods on her father's health, but being in the same city as Matthew, only blocks away while another man slept in her bed, shredded her heart.

She couldn't admit it to anyone.

Leaning her head against the window, she wiped her eyes. She hadn't tried to see Matthew since his party, and it hurt more than she wanted to admit he hadn't sought her out.

Hadn't wanted to see her, kiss her, hold her.

Explain this craziness.

She checked her phone. She had a couple hours before meeting her family to eat a late dinner.

She'd start painting tonight.

Why not? Pining over Matthew wouldn't pay her bills.

As she mixed paint, she remembered an afternoon when Matthew had taught her how to ride her bike, the training wheels taken off only moments before.

It had been fall, then, the leaves drifting from the trees, the scent of woodsmoke in the air.

A hint of winter already nipping at her nose.

Matthew ran alongside her pink bike as she wobbled, a

shiny silver bell she rang gleefully, a stuffed dog sitting in the wicker basket attached to the handlebars.

She was so proud of her new bike.

Losing her balance, she'd tipped over, scraping her palms and tearing a hole in the knee of her jeans.

She'd been but a second on the road, and Matthew had scooped her up and cradled her against his chest, murmuring promises into her ear that she'd be okay. She'd laid her six-year-old head on his shoulder knowing that as long as he was there to protect her, she *would* be okay.

In paint, she captured the feeling of his strong arms wrapped around her little body, his breath against her cheek, warm, as she cried.

She'd never felt a love as strong as when she looked into his eyes that autumn day.

Until Matthew told her he loved her and wanted to spend the rest of his life with her, she'd never feel that kind of love again.

Darkness had blanketed the city by the time her memories released her, and in the service elevator, she leaned tiredly against the wall. She walked through the high rise's lobby and stepped into the cool evening, tightening her sweater around her. Though the summer's heat still blazed during the day, the nights were beginning to cool and a breeze chilled her skin.

The sidewalk was empty, and she headed toward the parking ramp where she parked her truck. During the day, available parking was scarce, and the nearest parking ramp was located several blocks away.

She didn't mind. She loved Lake Kenosha, loved the people and the liveliness of the city, the energy of the lake that brushed the shores. She stopped in front of a few display windows, stores that hadn't existed when she'd lived there before.

She paused to admire a mannequin wearing a gauzy peach dress, fantasying briefly of Matthew bringing her on a romantic date. A flicker of movement caught her eye, and suddenly, her heart started thumping in apprehension. She clutched her purse strap and kept moving, this time at a faster pace.

She'd never felt threatened, walking alone in the city, never felt scared to be by herself, but times were changing and she didn't have any self-defense skills.

Turning the corner, the parking garage came into view, and she blew out a breath in relief.

Someone grabbed her shoulder, and she bit back a scream. She whipped around, preparing to fight.

"Matthew," she said, leaning against the building and closing her eyes. She ordered herself to breathe. Breathe. He wouldn't hurt her. Not like that.

"Zia, are you all right?"

"Yes, I . . . I thought someone was following me."

His lips quirked. "There was. Me. I've been tailing you since you stopped at that clothing store. You didn't hear me call out?"

She hadn't, but he wouldn't lie. Even after everything that happened, she still trusted him. Only time would tell if that proved to be her downfall. "I must have been wrapped up in my thoughts."

"You've been out all night and haven't been checking your phone. You missed dinner and your mother sent me out to look for you. She's worried."

"I'm sorry. I didn't think I'd start painting tonight, but I got caught up." Disappointed, she tugged at her sweater. Of course he wouldn't have come for her on his own.

"Let me walk you to your car. I parked at Bridgewater."

Nervously, she licked her lips. She couldn't let the chance pass her by. "Do you think we could go somewhere and talk?"

He stopped and studied her, his eyes narrowing.

Would he still like what he saw? She hadn't dressed well this morning, only in one of her poufy skirts, a peasant top, and a sweater her mother had given her years ago that had belonged to her grandma. She wore the necklace he'd given her, always, and gold hoops at her ears, her hair a wild mess.

Finally, he nodded. "Text your mother and let her know you're okay."

She did as she was told but shut her phone off afterward, not waiting for a response. She didn't want to lose these precious minutes with him. They walked down the empty side-walk toward a twenty-four hour coffeehouse, his hand resting on the back of her neck.

He opened the door, nudging her inside ahead of him, and she breathed in the sweet and earthy scents, craving a coffee and a pastry to raise her blood sugar after painting for hours without a break. She hadn't realized how shaky she was, or maybe that was just Matthew, finally having a moment to talk to him.

At the counter, he ordered for her. He knew what she liked best and she didn't object, but she carried her own coffee while he carried his and their pastries that shared a bright blue plate.

He chose a loveseat in the corner of the room, and they sat, hidden behind a bookshelf.

She hoped it was because he didn't want anyone to inter-rupt them, not because he wanted to hide.

She twisted sideways on the couch, holding her disposable coffee cup to her chest. He didn't look any better than the last time she'd seen him, standing on the dais at his birthday party, having just announced to everyone he loved her aunt enough to marry her.

"How are you doing?" she asked, the silence too much.

He sagged into the leather loveseat and closed his eyes. "Shh. Let me sit," he said, tangling their fingers.

She set her cup on a coffee table that was covered in magazines and tucked herself into his side where she'd wanted to be all her life.

He stiffened, then relaxed, sighing and wrapping his arm around her.

She rested her head on his chest and listened to his steady breathing. The bustle of the baristas and other customers faded, and she hugged him, her tears wetting his shirt.

He kissed the top of her head and then nudged her away. Wiping her cheeks, he said, "Things have been rough, Little Star, but nothing I can't deal with. Your mother has good business sense and she'll fit in well when . . ."

His voice faded, his thumb lingering on her cheek, and she fought the urge to turn her face into his palm. She hungered for any little touch he was willing to give her, but if she appeared too desperate, he'd push her away.

"He doesn't have much longer," she said, picking up her cup.

"No. I'm sorry."

"Thank you." She didn't know what else to say, didn't know what to think or feel about her father dying.

"I'll miss him. He's been a good friend. We never would have been able to accomplish what we have if he would've been anyone else. He's been a good husband and loves your mother very much. He's been a good father, even at times when it seemed he was too busy to be one. Zia, if there's anything you need after . . . let me know. I'll do what I can."

"I shouldn't need much," she said, because what she needed he wouldn't give her. "I'll stay long enough to see Mom settled. Dad asked me to move back home, but I don't know what he was thinking. Reid . . . his job . . ."

It seemed a betrayal to say Reid's name while she sat so close to Matthew, and she stumbled.

"Ray's in too much pain to think clearly, Little Star. I don't expect you to move back, and neither does your mother. She's told me quite a bit about your life in LA, and she understands you and Reid need to live there. She's very proud of you, and so am I. You've done well for yourself."

"With Reid's help." She met his eyes. "He asked me to marry him."

He held her hand, his fingers grazing over her naked ring finger. "You didn't say yes?"

She didn't want to wear Reid's ring. "I was hoping—"

"I know what you're hoping for, but I don't want your feelings for me to stand in your way. You may not love Reid, but if you think you're a good match, and by the way he looks at you, I think he is, then accept his proposal. Say your goodbyes to your father and after all that's done, leave Lake Kenosha because there won't be anything left for you here."

She jerked her hand away, immediately missing the warmth of his touch. "You can't mean that."

"You want me to be there for you, and I can't."

"But you'll be there for Chloe," she said bitterly, looking at the floor, unable to meet his eyes.

Gripping her chin in his hand, he made her. "I love you. Is that what you want to hear? I love you, and deep down, you know I do. That will never change. But sometimes love isn't enough."

Hope flared in her heart. "Yes, it is. I love you too, and I'm not going to let you walk away from me. You pushed me out of your life seven years ago, but I'm here, right in front of you, and you just told me you love me. That has to matter. That has to count for something."

He framed her face in his hands and she turned her cheek into his palm, relishing his caress. "Zia, my Little Star, you have no idea the hell I've lived with these past seven years, replaying the look on your face when you found Chloe and me in my office. I will never escape the shame that I hurt you so terribly. I choose Chloe because we're a good match, like you and Reid. She understands the kind of life we live. You removed yourself from that life, and the life you live now, in the art world, that world belongs to you. You don't belong here. We don't belong together."

"You're saying you don't want me."

The truth finally settled over her, seeping into her heart like poison.

He'd forced her to go to school in the most hurtful way possible, and that's why he hadn't sought her out since she'd been in the city. It was why he was telling her to go once her father finally succumbed.

Matthew loved her, but he didn't want her.

"I'm saying that if you ever find out the truth, you won't want to be here, and I'm giving you permission to leave. It won't hurt me when you never come back. It won't hurt me any more than I've already been hurt."

"I don't understand."

His pallor grew grayer, and once again he looked as he did at the party, sick and tired. Ready to be done with everything. "One day you will, and you'll hate me. More than when you found me with Chloe, more than when you watched her flash that ring at the party, laying her claim on me. What I'm saying is that when you find out the whole truth, you'll hate me, and I don't want to be around when you do."

Tenderly, he kissed her, his warm lips nudging hers, but she was too stunned to respond.

Her fingers skimmed the necklace. She could never hate him. "Matthew—"

"Excuse me. I need to go. Drive safely."

She threw their uneaten pastries into the trash. Their conversation left her without an appetite.

She found her truck without incident, and she didn't feel like anyone was following her, thank goodness. Maybe it *had* only been Matthew, trying to catch up with her, but still, she'd need to be more careful if she ever painted after dark again.

When she turned into the driveway, the lights were still on in their small apartment. Reid had waited up for her. She sighed and rested her head against the steering wheel, reluctant to go inside.

She was going to have to figure things out there too, because it wasn't right to keep him hanging on, waiting.

If she did what Matthew told her to do, she'd accept Reid's proposal, tell her father she'd be getting married, let him pass in peace, and then leave for good.

But something about that felt wrong. Something about that made her feel like she'd be abandoning both Matthew and her mother. She couldn't do it.

Matthew was keeping her in the dark.

There were secrets, skeletons, he knew she'd find.

Oh, she would find them all right.

Then she would make her own choices.

On the day Zia's mother summoned her to say her final goodbyes to her father, the weather had turned gloomy and cold. With an orange paint smear on her cheek, she rushed into her childhood house and into the library where everyone was waiting to say their last goodbyes to the man who had meant so much to them.

They all looked at her when she pushed her way into the room in a cloud of paint, grief, and rain. Reid stood from a chair in the corner, but Zia didn't have the chance to say anything. Her mother embraced her immediately and began to cry.

She met Matthew's eyes over her mother's shoulder. He wore a charcoal suit and sat next to Chloe, a lowball of something in his hand, almost empty. Chloe sniffed delicately into a tissue. He nodded at her once then wrapped his arm around Chloe who began to sob into his chest. Putting on a show, Zia thought with distaste.

"Your father's been waiting for you," Sylvia said, brushing a hand over her rain-soaked hair. "You're the last to say goodbye."

She tore her gaze away and let her mother lead her to the small room where Raymond laid in a hospital bed.

A nurse stood nodded toward the IV stand. "Your father's on a lot of pain medication, but he's still lucid. He's responsive if you'd like to speak with him."

"Thank you."

Sylvia backed out of the room and the nurse stepped into the hallway and shut the door to give them privacy.

"I'm so sorry, Daddy," Zia said, trying not to cry.

"I'm . . . so . . . proud of you," her father rasped.

"I'm glad. I wanted to make you proud of me."

"You and Reid . . . will be happy," he said. "Hold my hand."

Her heart sinking, Zia gripped her father's thin hand.

He'd lost too much weight and his skin stretched across his bones. His gray hair had thinned, almost non-existent. Deep grooves lined his face, and he squinted his eyes in pain and exhaustion.

She couldn't help but compare her father to Matthew.

Matthew, while not sick physically, had taken on a similar sallow complexion. How horrible his life had been these past seven years. What a beating his mental health had taken dealing with everything alone.

"Daddy, I have to tell you something," she said urgently. She couldn't let her father pass away without telling him the truth. "Matthew." She whispered the next, her heart's wish to her dying father. "I love him. I love him so much." Saying the words aloud broke a dam in her heart, and she sobbed into her father's side, relieved she'd finally told him her deepest secret.

Keeping it had torn her heart to shreds, and only now could she feel her soul begin to mend.

She lifted her head and pushed the tears down into her chest so she could speak. "I want your blessing, Daddy, to be with him."

"My little girl . . . things . . . will work . . . out. Let me . . . speak to Chloe."

Zia stood and kissed her father's papery cheek. "I love you, Daddy."

He patted her hand, his eyes dimming. "Chloe."

"Of course. I'll send her in."

Zia stepped into the library and everyone lifted their eyes to her, waiting to hear that Raymond had finally surrendered to the disease that ate his body from the inside out. She shook her head. "He wants to speak with Aunt Chloe."

Sylvia took a step forward, an objection on her lips.

Crowing with victory, Chloe leapt off the loveseat, tearing her hand out of Matthew's. She strode confidently out of the room.

Reid came up behind her and wrapped his arms around her. She turned and hid her face in his sweater. They stood in complete silence until Chloe stepped into the library.

"He's gone," she said, a smirk on her lips.

Sylvia cried out in dismay.

"Why didn't your dad want your mom with him?" Reid murmured into her ear.

"I . . . don't know," she said, confused, pulling away to comfort her mother.

Sylvia sank onto a leather couch and buried her face in her hands, keening in grief.

"I don't know. I don't know," she mumbled, stumbling toward her mother.

She sat on the couch and wrapped her arms around her.

She looked around the room. At Reid, who stood where she left him, helpless, not knowing what to do; at Matthew, who sat on the loveseat, his head cradled in his hands staring at the floor; at Chloe, who'd poured a glass of champagne and was now lifting it to Zia in toast.

"It will all work out." That's what her father told her. That's what someone said when they hoped things would go the way they wanted them to go.

Maybe he hadn't given her his blessing.

Maybe her way wasn't her father's way.

Zia smoothed her mother's hair.

Maybe she'd just made a terrible mistake.

The high rise towered over him, blocking out the September sunlight. Matthew sat in his car, parked in front of the building where Zia's makeshift studio was located.

He shouldn't be here, but he couldn't stand Chloe's smug expression a second longer. She wouldn't say what Raymond told her in the few minutes before he passed away, and he didn't press because it was of little to no consequence. Let her keep her secrets. It put her in a better mood, but he could still hardly tolerate her. The only thing that made him crawl out of bed that morning was the thought that this would all be over soon.

They'd closed the office until after Raymond's funeral. He had the day free as Sylvia said she didn't need help . . . with anything. Raymond left specific instructions in his will. He hadn't assigned a member of the family to be the executor of his estate, preferring his attorney handle everything. It had been another knife stuck into Sylvia's back, but no one could question the wishes of a dying man.

A reading of the will was scheduled after the funeral, and he didn't look forward to it. He'd have to deal with Chloe when she didn't inherit what she felt was her due share, and he was out of patience.

Just a little longer.

He pushed out of his car, cleared security, and rode the elevator to the highest floor. Support beams were interspersed throughout the huge space, and extension cords, tools, plywood, and everything in between were scattered haphazardly on the floor. Sawdust and the chalky scent of Sheetrock floated through the air.

He didn't blame Reid for accepting the real estate agent's offer, but it worried him that Zia was painting in a construction zone.

His concerns were laid to rest when he found her painting in the northeast corner of the building. The floor had been swept clean and the area was large enough to hold several easels. The windows let in so much light he wondered if she ever needed to paint wearing sunglasses.

Enchanted, he watched her. Focused on her work, she hadn't heard the elevator.

She painted a fall scene, browns and oranges, golds, dark forest green. The picture came to life under her brush, and the colors and strokes brought him back to the day he'd been with her.

He'd taken her to the state park. She'd been assigned a project in science class and she'd needed someone to drive her to the prairie. Raymond had been on the golf course, a meeting with someone or other, and Sylvia had committed to a consultation with a new client she couldn't reschedule.

Spending time with Zia had never been a hardship, and he'd volunteered, not the slightest bit sorry to be missing a day at home alone. At his insistence, they'd made a day out of it. How old had she been? Nine? Ten? They'd spent the day exploring, jumping onto rocks, wading in the shallow creek. Taken lots of pictures and collected the stones and plants she needed to complete her homework.

They'd packed a picnic and eaten under a tree, the leaves floating lazily onto their blanket.

He'd never realized how much that day meant to her until now. Or how much it had meant to him, until she captured it in paint.

"That was a good day."

Startled, she locked her eyes with his, tears dampening her cheeks.

"Zia."

She laughed and wiped her face using a handkerchief she kept shoved into the back pocket of her jeans. "Don't worry about it. I cry a lot when I paint." She studied the painting. "It *was* a good day. We had a lot of good days."

"They aren't over." He stepped closer to her.

"You said they are." She added flecks of gold to the sun sparkling in the creek.

"I meant, we'll have good days . . . with other people."

She shrugged. "Maybe I don't want good days with anyone else."

"You and Reid haven't been happy?" Part of him wanted her to say, yes, she'd been happy, was happy. Why stay with a man who didn't make her happy? But part of him wanted her to say no, she'd been miserable, all this time, without him.

"Reid's a good agent. He made my career what it is."

"That's not happiness."

"No, it's not, but I never said it was, did I?"

"No."

He hated they sounded like strangers. Polite. Distant.

He'd done that.

"I'm sorry about your father. How's your mother holding up?" He leaned against a window, his ass perched on a wide ledge where a secretary would set a plant or a desk calendar. A picture of her son or daughter.

"She can't figure out why Dad didn't want to be with her when he passed away, and she's sad and really mixed up. Wanders the house like she's lost. I understand now why he wanted me to stay here."

"Raymond may have been confused or he wanted to tell Chloe something about their parents, about their family. I doubt it has anything to do with Sylvia and she'll be okay." He paused. "How are you?"

Zia set her paint-smeared pallet on a makeshift table made of particle board and sawhorses and dropped her brush into a can of something. Water, maybe. She faced him, her hands at her sides.

She looked so grown up. He hadn't taken the time to look at her, really look at her, since she'd come home, and he did so now, his eyes memorizing her every feature. Her hair hadn't changed except that it was longer, still the fiery red he'd always adored. Freckles dotted the bridge of her nose and her cheekbones had emerged. Coral gloss shimmered on her lush lips.

Her collarbones popped whenever she moved, though her

breasts had gotten larger and her hips still flared. He could still feel her slim thighs wrapped around his waist while they made love. She'd grown an inch, maybe two.

She'd turned into a woman.

That woman stepped between his knees and wrapped her arms around his neck. She stood there, holding him, and he breathed her in, paint and perfume.

"I'm okay," she murmured, her head resting on his shoulder. "Tired. I'll need to find the energy to finish enough paintings to present a proper collection at the *Fall and Foliage.* After the ball, I guess I'll need to ask Mom what she wants me to do."

"Would you really stay? What about Reid?"

"He'd have to go back. He manages too many artists to move here, but I can paint anywhere."

"Could you be around me, Little Star, knowing we didn't have a future?"

She lifted her head. "I think the real question is, could you be around *me,* Matthew, and stay away?"

Raking her fingers thought his hair, she kissed him, and he didn't resist, diving into her passion, wishing he could drown.

"Spill it."

"Can't I order a drink first?" Zia dropped into the booth, pushing her purse against the wall.

Finally, she and Aimee had managed to settle on a time and make it work, and she felt like she could melt into a puddle, relieved to be with her friend, relieved she didn't have to keep up pretenses.

She needed to be steady for her mother. She needed to keep her real feelings about Matthew from Reid. Hell, she needed to keep her real feelings from Matthew, too, or she'd drop to her knees and beg him to take her, take her anywhere, so they could be together.

She was so proud of herself for the way she'd handled him in her studio. So proud that he'd stood there, all sexy scruff and long hair, and she hadn't done a damn thing but kiss him. So proud that she hadn't torn his clothes off and demanded he make love to her when he returned her kiss.

"Yes, but then I want to hear all about it."

"All about what?"

Aimee laughed. "Everything. From the minute I walked out of your bedroom the night before you left for LA, to now, when you walked into this bar." She sobered. "I told Shirley I was going to your father's funeral. That it was non-negotiable. Being we're best friends and you're doing her a favor showing in her gallery, she didn't argue. I'm so sorry about your dad, Zia. He was such a nice person and he always treated me with respect even though I was just a kid." She nudged her black-framed glasses up her nose.

"Thanks. He said many times he liked you too."

A waitress approached their table and asked to see their IDs. She glanced quickly at their driver's licenses and took their orders.

"I want a Cosmopolitan, and keep them coming," Zia said, shoving her ID into her wallet.

"A mojito, thanks," Aimee said, then to Zia, "Are you celebrating or drowning your sorrows?"

"Neither. It's nice to be with you, take a break. Things have been so crazy and I feel bad for Reid. He says he doesn't mind, but I think after the funeral . . . Well, he wants to go back to LA, but now he has to stay for the *Fall and Foliage.* I feel like I'm being pulled in a million directions but what I really want to do—"

"Is spend time with Matthew."

"You know me too well."

"Is he still engaged to Chloe?"

"Yeah, he is. I don't get it. You've been here, Aim, do you know what's going on?"

Aimee shook her head. "No. With school, trying to stay relevant in the art world, and paying my bills, I've been scrambling. Every now and then I would catch a write-up of them in the paper, or I'd help set up a showing at a fundraiser and they'd be there. He never looked good, and she always looked like a vulture circling around a fresh kill. You know how people look after spending a lifetime doing a job they hate? That's how Matthew looks to me. But I never heard why he's with her when it was obvious he doesn't want to be."

The waitress brought their drinks, and she sipped, almost draining the tart martini, the rush of alcohol buzzing in her blood the second she swallowed. It felt fabulous, and after the horrid past couple of weeks, she needed the fizz.

"Maybe he was doing it to make my father happy." He'd said as much, though it still didn't sound right.

Aimee frowned and played with the swizzle stick poking out of her glass. "Why, though?"

"I know Dad was tired of her living off the bank. Maybe he asked Matthew to take care of her, and Matthew felt obligated because they were best friends. That seems like a lot to ask though, and not like my father at all."

"Maybe Chloe has something on Matthew, and she's blackmailing him."

Zia giggled, the alcohol relaxing her. "Matthew's squeaky clean. The only thing he ever did was sleep with me, and how would Aunt Chloe know that? You didn't say anything to anybody, did you?"

Dragging her finger in an X across her heart, Aimee said, "Not a word."

"Then that can't be it. Maybe he really loves her and something else is dragging him down," she said, scrambling. There had to be a reason he threw seven years away on Chloe. There had to be a reason he spoke to her so harshly in his office. What had he and Chloe talked about before she walked in on them?

"No way. You've already had too much to drink. There's no way Matthew loves her, and you know it."

She drained her glass and caught the waitress's eye. She gestured, asking the waitress to bring her another. "Do you remember a long time ago you said I had to be careful because I was playing a grownup's game?"

"Yeah. I was so profound." Aimee laughed and sipped her drink.

"No, you were right. I still feel like that. Like people are keeping secrets to protect me. My dad saw Chloe last."

The waitress placed another Cosmopolitan in front of her, and she seized the dark pink drink.

It'd been a long time since she could be so unguarded.

Aimee froze. "What do you mean?"

"My dad, right before he passed away, he spoke to Chloe and not my mom. She was devastated. Still is."

"I'm sorry. I don't know what to say."

She leaned closer, truths and lies and vodka swimming in her head. "I told my Dad I was in love with Matthew. I think that's why he wanted to talk to Chloe. He told her what I said. It's my fault he didn't have enough energy to tell my mom goodbye." She blinked back tears.

"Oh, I don't think that's it," Aimee said, holding her hand. "He could have wanted to tell her anything."

Sniffling, she said, "That's what Matthew said."

"Did you tell Matthew what you told your dad?"

Zia freed her hand and sipped her drink. "Of course not. He would've been pissed. He'll find out, though, if Dad really did tell Chloe. It's such a mess. Dad's gone, so it shouldn't matter, but why do I feel like I made a really big mistake?"

"We all have regrets when someone passes away. It may not seem like it, but Matthew's on your side. So is your mom, and you have Reid," Aimee said, shredding a cocktail napkin. "Let's talk about something else. I helped Shirley hang paintings at the ball last year, and you'll have such a great time. Probably nothing as cool as what you get to do in LA, but for Lake Kenosha, it's pretty exciting. Do you have something to wear?"

"No. I suppose it's black tie."

"Yeah, and a masquerade. We'll have to go shopping, I've already worn all my good dresses. How are your paintings coming along?"

"Oh, fine," she said, carelessly flicking her fingers. "I'm at the top of a building downtown. Great light. I get so caught up in thinking about Matthew while I paint."

"What are you going to do about him?"

The waitress set fresh drinks in front of them. Snapping her gum, she said, "I started you a tab. Go up to the bar to pay when you're ready."

"Thank you so much." She drained her glass and handed it to the waitress. She sipped her third drink, reveling in the lightness of her body. Matthew was always a weight around her heart she couldn't shake off. "I've talked to him a couple of times. He wants me to go back to LA after the *Fall and Foliage*. I probably will. I can't make him want me."

"You have Reid."

Zia smiled, or she thought she did. She tried again, forming her lips into a moue. "Reid's lovely," she said, sighing. "Lovely . . ."

Aimee covered her mouth, hiding a laugh. "You're drunk. Did you drive here or did Reid drop you off?"

"I drove myself, but don't worry about it. I'll be fiiiiiine."

She sipped her drink. It was almost gone already. She wanted another, but Reid wouldn't be happy if she went back to the apartment falling-down drunk. Drunk-drunk was okay, but he'd probably want sex. They'd never gone this long without being intimate. Because of the circumstances, he'd been understanding, but there was a thin layer of annoyance that was beginning to come through whenever she turned him down.

"No, you won't. Give me your phone."

She handed Aimee her phone and said, "You can order an Uber, but don't you want to talk more? We only talked about me, and Matthew, and me, and Matthew. What about you? What have you been doing?"

"We talked about your dad in there, too," Aimee said, her thumbs flying across Zia's iPhone. "I'll see you at the funeral, and your mom's having people over to the house after that, right? I'll be there."

"Yeah. Thank you. I'm sorry we haven't been closer these past few years."

Aimee slid her phone across the table. "It's okay. We've both been busy. You're a famous artist now, and it would be really shitty if I resented you for that. I'm proud of you. We kept in touch in a way that worked for us. It's okay. You don't have to cry about it."

Blinking back tears, she said, "I'm not. You've been a good friend."

"You've been a good friend to me, too. When you're feeling up to it, we'll go shopping, okay? Have a girls' day. Maybe your mom will come. She's going to the ball, isn't she? It'd be good for her to get out of the house. Has she gone back to work yet?"

"I think so, but I'm not sure. I've been trying to paint and keep Reid happy, but I miss Matthew, and then I try to paint, and then I miss Matthew more . . ." She sighed and drained the rest of her drink.

"You can stop missing him."

"What do you mean?" She licked her lips and thought about ordering another. No harm in getting shiftfaced. No, that didn't sound right. Shitfaced. Right. Maybe she shouldn't drink anymore if she couldn't think straight.

"He's at the bar, probably paying our tab, like the gentleman he is."

"Whaaaat's he doing here?"

"I texted him to pick you up. I wanted to make sure you got home safely, and I wasn't going to send you off with a stranger in an Uber."

Matthew strode to them, but he didn't look mad. Whew!

"You could have given me a ride home."

Aimee blinked. "Yeah, I could have, but isn't this better?"

"Ladies," Matthew greeted them, stopping at their table. "You've been having a fun?"

She gobbled him up. His blue eyes, his whiskers. Aimee was right. This was better.

"We certainly have, Mr. Harcourt," Aimee said, sliding out of the booth.

"I think you can call me Matthew, Aimee. We're all adults, aren't we?"

"Yes, I'm sorry."

"Nothing to be sorry for. Thank you for asking me to pick Zia up. Are you okay to drive?"

"Oh, for sure. She was ahead of me all night."

Matthew chuckled. "Okay. Let Zia know when you get home, if you don't mind. I'll check her phone."

"Sure. Goodnight, Zia."

"Bye . . ." she sang. Grabbing her purse, she slid out of the booth and stumbled into Matthew. "Aimee's soooooo nice." She buried her face in the crook of his neck and he wrapped his arm around her to steady her. "You smell soooooo good."

"Thanks," he said, amused. "That's always a plus. Come on, let's get you home."

The bar swirled around her in a warm haze of neon colors. They reflected in his eyes, an electric blue, filled with kindness, and oh, yeah. Love.

She sighed. He loved her. She could see it on his face.

"Where's home, Matthew?"

"Sometimes, Little Star, I have no idea."

CHAPTER SEVEN

He wasn't going to bring her home drunk. He wasn't going to make sure she made it up the steps to the apartment she and Reid shared. He wasn't going to make sure she went inside without incident. Because in doing so, he was damn well making sure she fell into bed with her fiancé where he'd make love to her all night.

Nope.

Not going to happen.

If Zia made love to anyone tonight, it would be to him, and he wasn't sorry about it.

The sky was a deep purple and the first stars were beginning to twinkle. The days were slowly starting to shorten, and golds and browns and oranges would gradually turn leaves from their radiant summer green.

Matthew drove them out of the city, toward Lake Kenosha. In the late hour, a light breeze blew, and the fresh air would clear Zia's head.

She sat in the passenger seat of his SUV, her cheek pressed

against the back, humming, her eyes closed, a slight smile on her lips.

He kissed the back of her hand.

The minute Raymond passed away, Matthew had stopped telling Chloe where he was going, what he was doing. She knew things had changed and that she no longer had the power over him she'd enjoyed for the past seven years. She still kept the love letters he'd written Sylvia and she still had the pictures of him kissing Zia outside his house, but now that Raymond was gone, she no longer had anyone to show them to.

She could tell Zia about the letters, and without a doubt, Matthew knew she would. She hated her niece as much as she hated him, and that was the last play she had to hurt both of them.

It would work.

"Where are we going?" Zia murmured, opening her eyes.

"Just for a drive, to sober you up. How are you feeling?"

"Dreamy." She sighed, tightening her hold on his hand. "It's nice to be with you."

"Yes. I've missed you."

"Seven years is a long time."

"It is."

She went back to humming, a song he didn't recognize. He concentrated on the road. It'd been some time since he was out this way, but a walk along the water would perk her up. He'd brought a blanket and they could sit on the beach. If anyone accused him of pre-planning this seduction, he wouldn't, couldn't, deny it.

He was tired of staying away from her, and now that Raymond was gone, the only things standing in their way were the love letters and Reid.

They were enough.

That was fine. He'd take what he could get, and then after

the *Fall and Foliage,* she'd go back to LA with Reid where she belonged. He'd appoint a director at Bridgewater, leave all that mess in Sylvia's capable hands, and find a quiet place to live out the rest of his days.

It wasn't what he wanted, but anything would be better than the seven years he'd let Chloe torture him.

Things were finally about to come to a head, and he thanked God.

He parked in the empty lot. Water crashed against the rocky shore, and clouds crept across the sky, hiding the moon. They'd only have an hour, maybe a little more, before it rained.

"Let's go for a walk."

She cracked her eyes open. "Where are we?"

"The beach."

"Okay."

He grabbed the blanket out of the backseat, and she climbed out of the truck without her heels. The soft sand wasn't far, but he lifted her in his arms. "I don't want you to hurt yourself."

"No, you've managed to do that quite nicely."

"Those martinis loosened your tongue, huh?" he asked. "But you're no less correct. I've hurt you, and I'll never be able to tell you how sorry I am."

He let her down onto the sand.

She wrapped her sweater around herself and walked to the water's edge. The wind whipped her hair into a blazing tangle as she looked across the lake, a large tanker floating in the horizon.

There was barely enough light to take her picture with his phone. If he commissioned it, maybe she'd turn it into a painting.

If he couldn't have her, he'd like to keep one thing.

To remember what the rest of his life could have been like.

Had things turned out differently.

Had he made better choices.

Had he been a man who fought, who defended himself. Defended the women he loved.

All those chances had come and gone, and he didn't expect any sympathy.

"Zia," he called, "come here, we need to talk."

He tried to spread the blanket out, the wind catching the ends. She held onto the other side, and together they laid the blanket on the ground.

He sat and took his shoes and socks off and buried his feet in the smooth sand. Resting his forearms on his bent knees, he clasped his hands.

He owed Zia some truth. Not all of it, as he was too big of a coward to tell her everything. He wanted to wait. He wasn't proud of himself, but the longer it could be put off, the better.

"What is it?" she asked, letting a handful of sand trickle through her fingers.

"Tomorrow, after the funeral and the gathering at your house, an attorney will read your father's will, though what's inside won't be a surprise. Sylvia will inherit his half of Bridgewater, you'll receive some money, and so will Chloe. Enough to keep her, maybe not in the lifestyle she'd like, but enough so she'll never have to work if she's careful."

"Okay. Why are you telling me this?"

"Because I want you to be prepared for what comes next. I'm tired, Zia, and I don't want to run Bridgewater anymore, especially not without Raymond's help. I'm going to retire and try to heal from what the past few years have done to me."

She met his eyes, pushing her hair out of her face. "Where are you going to go?"

He shrugged. "I'm not sure. Lake Kenosha's filled with too many memories and I don't want to stay here."

"You're going to leave my mom? You're going to leave me?"

"Sylvia will be fine. She's a strong woman who's been running her own business for many years. She'll have no trouble taking over Bridgewater. You have Reid and your career. You don't need me. Neither of you do." Though it made him proud Sylvia and Zia would be okay without him, it saddened him to say it. He'd devoted so much of his life to Sylvia and his Little Star.

"That's bullshit. Why have you been with Chloe?" she demanded. "If you're leaving, you're not going to marry her. Why did you propose?"

He turned sideways and wrapped his arms around her shaking body. From cold? Emotion? It was difficult to guess. Probably both because God knew the temperature dropped twenty degrees in the last five minutes and this conversation was less than pleasant.

"All I can say is the past has a way of catching up with you. What I'll gain when I leave won't compare to what I'll lose. Do you understand what I'm saying?"

"No," she cried, burying her face in his shirt. "You love me, you said you do. I love you, too. If you don't want Chloe, why can't we be together?"

"I've never wanted her, and I hope you believe that. I've always protected you, and that's why we can't be together. I'm too old for you, Zia."

It was a stale, repetitive argument, but true, nonetheless.

"That's only an excuse," she said bitterly, pushing him away. "You're afraid."

"Yeah, I am."

She rose on her knees and framed his face in her hands. "You don't have to be. I'm right here. I'm right here, Matthew, offering you my heart, offering you my soul. You said you don't want to hurt me anymore, and you'll crush me if you don't take them."

"I can take whatever you'll give me, but I can't keep it. Not forever. You deserve more than what little I can give you."

"Then tonight, just for tonight. Please, Matthew."

He kissed her, softly teasing her lips until she opened her mouth. He slipped his tongue between her teeth and tasted her and the Cosmopolitans she'd been drinking. Without breaking their kiss, he laid her on the blanket and brushed his fingers over her thigh and under the hem of her sundress. He moved her panties aside, and she widened her legs, giving him permission to touch her.

She was hot and wet, and he pushed his fingers inside her, as far as they could go, wanting to touch her as deeply as he could.

She moaned.

He nudged her clit with his thumb, but she tore her mouth away. "No, don't touch me yet. I want to come while you're inside me."

"I don't have a condom," he said, gently sliding his fingers out of her.

"I said you didn't need one. We had this conversation at your party." She unbuckled his belt and unbuttoned his pants. Tugging at his zipper, she mumbled against his lips, "I want to sit in your lap."

He pushed the waistband of his boxer briefs down, grateful no one was around to interrupt them. Everyone sought shelter from the upcoming storm. Lightning flashed and crackled and the electricity sizzled in his blood.

He breathed in the damp air and guessed they had less than half an hour before the sky opened. The way he felt, he only needed five minutes, but he told himself to calm down. He wanted Zia to enjoy this. "One day, Little Star, I need to get you into a bed. This is fun, but I'm too old to do this on a regular basis."

She kissed along his jaw, pausing only long enough to wiggle out of her panties. She went right back to kissing him as she settled onto his lap. It was a tortured bliss she wanted him, and he greedily consumed it. "You're not old. Stop saying that."

He gripped her hips. "Yes, I am. Go slow now, or I'll be done before we start."

Huffing a laugh, she said, "We can't have that."

He positioned the tip of his cock at her opening, and she sank onto him, taking all of him as she always had, all his faults and flaws.

"Easy. Wait a minute." He kissed her, holding her heavy breasts in his hands, her nipples tightening under his thumbs. "I love you, Zia. No matter what other words come out of my mouth, they're all lies. I love you. That's the only truth."

She rocked, her head tipped back. "Yes. You're so deep. I need you so much. You're my whole life. You've always been my whole life."

"Little Star." He squeezed her nipples, loving that in response to the slight bit of pain her pussy clenched his cock. He spurted, close to losing control. "I'm there. Come with me."

"Touch me," she whispered, nipping at his neck.

He rubbed her quivering nub, and she convulsed around him. She cried out, the sound carried away on the wind.

Gripping her hips, he jerked upward, thrusting into her, and he came, hugging her to him as he emptied inside her.

They sat joined together, hearts and bodies, until big, fat drops of rain began to fall.

"I love you, Matthew."

There was no mistaking the hope and misery in her voice and he didn't need to see her face to know what she was thinking. Dark and cold, bleak. It was all around them.

"I've hurt you too much to deserve you," he said, brushing her hair away from her cheeks. "You're only twenty-five. A famous artist. You have so much ahead of you, my little girl. Don't let me hold you back."

Shaking her head in frustration, she asked, "Why won't you let me decide what I want?"

"I will, but I already know what you'll choose. We should go. We're going to get drenched in about two minutes."

She moved off his lap, his cock slipping out of her in a warm gush, and he sighed. Nothing would make him feel lonelier, or more alone, than the distance between him and Zia. Even if he was the one causing it.

He tucked his sticky cock into his briefs and zipped his pants. She put her panties on and adjusted her dress.

The rain began to fall in sheets, the wind whipping the chilly drops into their faces.

She shrieked, snagged the edge of the blanket, and ran toward the truck. Matthew followed, but cursing, he turned back to retrieve his shoes and socks.

Barefoot, she picked her way over the rocky parking lot. A flash of lightning lit up her figure and set her hair on liquid fire.

He opened her door, and she scrambled into the truck. Shivering and laughing, she met his eyes.

Kissing her, he didn't care the rain drenched his back, he didn't care he was freezing. All he cared about was his lips on hers, that she held him so tightly in her arms, her heart pressed against his.

"I love you, Zia," he mumbled.

"I love you, too."

Reluctantly, he broke away and shut her door, settled behind the wheel, and drove out of the parking lot.

After making love to her, he'd bring her back to her apartment where she'd spend the night in another man's bed.

It wasn't what he wanted, but it was the way it had to be.

The late night storm followed them into the next day, and rain beat against the windows of the Bishop house.

Every room was full of people and Matthew didn't have any luck finding a quiet place to hide. It seemed everyone wanted a piece of him. Word on what would become of Bridgewater or offering insincere condolences.

He sat in the corner he'd occupied when he attended Zia's graduation party. Sylvia had redecorated several times in the past seven years, and the chair he sat on wasn't the same.

But his feelings were. Watching Zia walk from group to group, her demure black dress contrasting with the wildness of her hair, the vividness of her green eyes.

Only now, Reid was with her, offering an arm, lending support.

"Trouble in paradise?" Tucker asked, handing him a heavy, plain white coffee mug.

Matthew should be grateful she had someone, but bitter it wasn't him, he looked away and addressed Tucker, accepting the mug in relief. "I hope you spiked this."

"You can't get through a day like this without a little help."

"Amen."

"How are you holding up?" Tucker asked, sitting in a seat adjacent to his.

"I'll be fine," he said, grateful he and Tucker had remained close enough friends he'd wanted to attend Raymond's funeral, to be there when the will was read. "Sylvia's a bit shell-shocked, but she'll come around."

"Zia grew into a lovely woman."

"Ah-huh."

"How are things going there?"

"I brought her to the beach last night and told her I was leaving after Sylvia settled in at Bridgewater. She didn't take it well, but hell, the past seven years haven't been fun for anyone."

"Is that all you did? Talk?" Tucker raised an eyebrow.

"I don't think Zia and I can be alone and just talk, but me being with her that way isn't right, especially with Reid here. Anyway, this is rehashing old news. My feelings for Zia are old news."

"You're looking better."

He quirked his lips. "Zia asked me if I was sick. Couldn't tell her I was sick of being blackmailed. Sick of Chloe. Sick of life."

"You could have. You should have. You can't know how she'd react."

"I know how Raymond would have reacted. I was protecting Sylvia as well as Zia, and I'd do it all over again. But yeah, I'm feeling better. Being around Zia does that to me. I missed her more than I ever thought possible. It's funny, you don't realize how much you've missed someone until they're right there in front of you."

"She's been a part of your life for a long time."

He nodded. "She has, but after today, I'm going to have to learn how to live without her. And so will she."

Panic squeezed Zia's lungs until she couldn't breathe, and she whispered to Reid, "I need a moment." She slipped out of the living room and ran up the stairs, leaving the murmur of voices behind her.

She had to get away.

The secrets and lies, Chloe's venomous looks, Matthew's sullen expression, and Reid not giving her any space, made it all too much to bear and she hid in her mother's bedroom. She toed off her black pumps and crawled into the bed, the blinds and the storm outside darkening the room.

She huddled under the covers, tears dripping down her cheeks.

Rumors started to spread, and as she moved from group to group to accept condolences, she overheard threads of conversation and gossip.

Aimee told her more of what people were saying. That Chloe and Matthew were going to elope. That Matthew was leaving Lake Kenosha because he'd secretly been in love with Sylvia, but she rebuffed him, still in love with her dead husband. The rumors ranged from scoff-worthy to downright ludicrous, but what hurt her most was that no one mentioned her. At least, not in conjunction with Matthew. Like there was no way they could be together. Like no one would have given it a single thought.

Reid had a lot to do with it. People couldn't stop talking about their engagement, some even congratulating them, not realizing she hadn't accepted. There wasn't any reason for anyone not to believe she and Reid weren't planning a big, beautiful wedding, though she wasn't sure how anyone knew he asked.

They were caught up in the romance of it. Leaving home at a young age, making her fortune, coming home to her dying father, a handsome, established man on her arm. If they knew she'd left brokenhearted and rejected, it would have added to the glamour of the story. Success in the shadow of defeat.

But success couldn't mend a broken heart.

She did revel in the fact that the more the rumors spread, the darker and bleaker the look became on Matthew's face.

"Zia? Are you in here?"

She peeked over the edge of the bedspread. "Yeah. I needed a minute. Are you okay?"

Sylvia stepped into the room, shutting the door behind her.

Silence blanketed them, and her mother slid into bed with her.

Zia snuggled in her arms, breathing in the scents of perfume and coffee.

"I'm fine, but I miss your father and the crowd was starting to become too much."

"I know how you feel," she said. "I couldn't stand listening to the gossip any longer, but I'm being rude." She moved to climb out of bed, but Sylvia tightened her hold around her.

"No, take all the time you need. I wanted to spend a few minutes alone with you, anyway. I asked Matthew to circulate and tell anyone who asks that I needed a minute to pull myself together."

"He's a good man," she said, resting her head on her mother's pillow.

"Yes, he is. He's been there for us for as long as I can remember."

"I heard an old woman say that you and Matthew used to be in love, and now that Dad was gone, you'd pick up where you left off."

Her mother's hand stilled on her back then resumed the soothing circular motion over her lace dress.

"We've been good friends since high school. Maybe someone would mistake that for love. It's unusual for men and women to be only friends. Some people say it can't be done, that one person will eventually fall in love and ruin the friendship."

She hadn't heard many stories of her mother's time in high

school or college. "Were you and Matthew ever more than friends?"

Sylvia paused. "No, sweetheart. There's only ever been your father, but . . . I can understand how a woman could fall in love with Matthew. He's so kind and handsome."

"Yeah, he is."

"Zia, he told me . . . he told me . . . he . . ." She sighed.

"What did he tell you?" Zia sat up, and through the darkness, she searched her mother's face.

Sylvia sat up, too. "I know he loves you. I know you two have been dancing around each other since you came back. You love him, too, don't you?"

"Yes," she whispered, so thankful she could finally say it aloud to someone other than Aimee. "Yes. But, Mom, I think I made a terrible mistake."

"Falling in love isn't a mistake—"

"No, not that," she said, hiding her face in her hands.

"Then what is it? I've tried telling him your ages—"

She dropped her hands and said, "When I spoke to Dad before he died, I told him I was in love with Matthew. I wanted his blessing. I thought if I had Dad's blessing, Matthew wouldn't be so reluctant to be with me, but I think that's why —" She stopped and tried to swallow back the sobs clogging her throat. She had to confess in case this all blew up in their faces.

"You think that's why what, sweetheart?" her mother asked gently.

"I think that's why Dad spoke to Chloe last. I think he told her. I'm sorry, Mom. I'm so sorry. I ruined your chance to say goodbye."

Relieved to have gotten that off her mind and heart, she broke down in her mother's lap and cried out all her sorrow of her father's death, loving and losing Matthew, her confusion about Reid, knowing she should tell him she didn't want to marry him but not quite being able to make herself do so.

She quieted and her mother handed her a tissue. "It's okay, sweetheart. You didn't do anything wrong. I don't know what your father would have thought about you and Matthew. I know he was hoping Matthew and your aunt would make a match, and when Chloe moved into Matthew's house, he was relieved she'd be taken care of. But what he would've thought about you and Matthew, it doesn't matter now, does it? He can't do anything from the grave. If he would have disapproved . . . Zia, I don't disapprove, but Matthew's a complicated man and I don't . . . I think that you shouldn't . . ."

"I know. He doesn't want me." Not forever.

"I'm sorry, baby," Sylvia whispered.

"No, I am. You don't hate me?"

Sylvia held out her arms and Zia fell into them. "Of course not. Little girls want to please their fathers. What did he say? When you told him?"

"That everything would work out."

Sylvia kissed her cheek. "See there? Your father was wise until the very end. Everything *will* work out. Maybe not in the ways we hope, but things happen for a reason. Sometimes, as much as it pains us, we never know what those reasons are. We need to keep faith." She blew out a breath. "We should go downstairs. We've been missing for a while, and poor Matthew, he's not patient enough to deal with the hordes."

She followed her mother down the stairs, and she met Matthew's eyes across the crowded floor.

Things would work out.

They had to because her life wouldn't be worth living if she had to spend the rest of hers without him.

"Spencer's ready to see us," Matthew said, meeting Zia and Sylvia at the foot of the stairs. "He's waiting for us in Raymond's office."

He'd been letting a grieving teller cry on his shoulder when Tucker pulled him away, saying the attorney had arrived to read Raymond's will. Ashamed, he'd been grateful he could untangle himself from the woman's teary embrace.

Silently, he'd led Spencer to Raymond's office, a smaller room off the library. Circling the house, searching for Zia and Sylvia, he accepted more condolences and reassured people Bridgewater would operate as normal without Raymond. He was relieved to find them trudging down the stairs like rejoining the repast was akin to facing a firing squad.

Zia's red eyes and wet cheeks hurt his heart, and he wondered what mother and daughter had been speaking of but thought it better if he didn't know.

"Let's get this over with," Sylvia said, smoothing a hand over her hair and adjusting her black dress.

He reached out to hold Zia's hand, but Reid pushed him aside and wrapped his arms around her. He nodded, thanking him, albeit reluctantly, for supporting Zia.

Reid nodded in return but narrowed his eyes.

That wasn't good. Apparently, he wasn't keeping his emotions to himself as well as he thought he was. He'd need to be careful and stop following Zia around with his eyes.

The four of them stepped into Raymond's office, and Chloe was already there. She held a white handkerchief in her hand and blotted her cheeks. She sat directly in front of Raymond's desk.

A dog doing tricks begging for a treat.

It'd be a pleasure to see her face when she inherited only a sliver of what she expected.

Zia and Reid sat on a loveseat under a picture window, and Matthew stood by the door near Tucker, too ramped up to sit without fidgeting.

Sylvia sat in the other seat in front of Raymond's desk.

"Thank you for coming," Spencer said, sitting at Raymond's desk, a sheaf of papers laying on the blotter in front of him. "I apologize I was the one who had to put the funeral together, Sylvia. I can only do what my clients direct."

"I understand," she murmured.

The attorney adjusted his glasses and cleared his throat. "Thank you. Raymond was very forthright in how he wanted his estate broken up. To be clear, there were several witnesses who will testify he was of sound mind, if, or when, anyone wants to dispute this will after the reading. There are no loopholes. Raymond was too smart for that. Does anyone have any questions about what I've just said?"

He stood near Tucker and watched without responding to Spencer's question. He didn't expect to be named in Raymond's will. Chloe lifted her chin, confident. Sylvia sadly shook her head. Zia stared at her lap.

"Good. Then let's begin. There are the normal bequests to charities that Raymond championed during his life: the National Humane Society, the Special Olympics. Grace Lutheran Church, the church he attended as a child, and the Lake Kenosha Public Library. Raymond granted those organizations small sums and that information will be available to you upon request, as I won't waste time with that here. Shall I continue?"

Impatiently, Matthew shifted on his feet. Spencer was taking too long in telling everyone what they already knew.

The room remained silent and Spencer said, "Good." He

began reading: "I, Raymond Carver Bishop, a resident of the state of Minnesota and county of Itasca, and being of sound mind and memory, do hereby make, publish, and declare, this to be my last will and testament, therefore revoking and making null and void any and all last will and testaments and/or codicils to last will and testaments heretofore made by me. All references herein to 'this will' refer only to this last will and testament." He paused and sipped something clear.

If it were Matthew, it would have been vodka.

"Having said that, I'll be going over specifics with Sylvia, but the most urgent thing here is the inheritances. I'm sure you all are wanting to know to whom Raymond left what." He shuffled the sheaf of papers and began reading once again. "I give to the person's name below, my Primary Beneficiaries all of the residue and remainder of my gross estate, real and personal, wherever situated, after payment of all my just debts, expenses, taxes, and specific bequests, if any, in the percentages and rations set forth below. Unless otherwise indicated in my Will, these shares shall be distributed outright and free of trust. Sylvia Elaine Bishop: the house located on 2613 Hemingway Court, Lake Kenosha, Minnesota. The vacation house located on 10 Pebble Beach Drive, Miami, Florida. My vehicles, clothing, jewelry, and collections. To my sister, Chloe Grace Bishop—"

"Wait," Matthew burst out. "You're not done reading what Raymond left Sylvia. It was understood he'd leave all that to her. Her name should already be on the house and the vehicles and—"

"Matthew." Sylvia shook her head.

"Let me continue, Mr. Harcourt," Spencer said, straightening. "There will be time for questions after the reading is completed. To my sister, Chloe Grace Bishop, fifty percent of Bridgewater Financial."

"What?" he rasped under Chloe's delighted squeal.

"Matthew, be quiet," Tucker warned, a hand to his shoulder.

Spencer glared at Chloe, disapproving of her unladylike outburst. "Including, but not limited to, all past, present, and future income, as well as any and all decision-making responsibilities pertaining to the shared CEO position."

Chloe beamed.

Sylvia sagged in her chair.

"Past income?" Matthew asked faintly but knowing the answer. Raymond didn't leave his wife any money.

"Raymond had set aside in savings a large percentage of his income. Stocks, bonds, CDs, which are now Chloe's. She will begin collecting income from Bridgewater immediately." Spencer paused. "I'm sorry, Sylvia. I tried . . ."

"It's okay, Spencer. Was there anything else? Anything for Zia?"

Spencer nodded. "Yes. To my daughter, Zia Raine Bishop, a sum of five million dollars which will be held in trust until her firstborn child reaches age twenty-one. Zia, there's an addendum that states you are to receive a payout of the interest each month to help care for your child or children."

Zia lurched to her feet, panting, her cheeks stained pink.

Sylvia buried her face in her hands, her shoulders shaking.

"Why? Why would he do this?" he demanded, zeroing in on Chloe. "Why would Raymond leave everything to you?"

"I'm his family. Maybe he trusts me more than he trusts any of you."

He swore. "This has to be a sick joke."

"Then the joke's on him," Zia spat, clawing at her throat. "Then the joke's on him because I can't have children."

Sylvia jerked, blood draining from her face. "Zia, what do you mean? Who told you such a thing?"

Reid staggered off the loveseat. "Honey, why didn't you tell me?"

He resisted the impulse to hold a distraught Zia in his arms and instead slipped out the door, leaving the Bishop family alone to deal with the ramifications of the will. He sank onto a decorative bench outside the library, escaping the chaos.

"Did you know?" Tucker had followed him out of the library.

"No. Not any of it. Raymond didn't tell me a damned thing."

"Matthew." Spencer carried his briefcase and a white business-sized envelope. "I'm sorry for how all that went down. I tried to reason with him, but he had his own ideas, and in the end, all I can do is what my client wants."

"Just tell me one thing, Spence."

"If I can."

"Why did Raymond leave Sylvia their house, their vacation house, the vehicles? Didn't she already own half of those things?"

Spencer shook his head, an unhappy frown pulling at his mouth. "You'd think so, but no. Sylvia's name isn't on anything but her business and the vehicles she owns in conjunction to that business. If Raymond wouldn't have left her their property, she'd be out on the street. Not literally, of course. Sylvia's design business does quite well, which is why Ray felt he could do what he did. Sylvia's more than capable of taking care of herself."

"And there was nothing else? No reason, no explanation, why Sylvia didn't receive his half of Bridgewater?"

"The only thing I can deduce is that it has to do with this." Spencer gave him the envelope, and he took it, his hand trembling. "He told me to give this to you at the reading. I don't know what's in it, but I'm assuming it explains some of the decisions he made."

"Thanks." He wanted to rip it open devour what was inside, but he didn't because he already knew.

"I'm sorry for your loss. Raymond was a good man. Listen, Zia's going to have some questions. Raymond didn't consider she couldn't have children . . . but there are things she can do and still inherit. Tell her to contact me, after the shock passes, and I'll go over some things with her."

"Thank you. She'll appreciate that," he murmured, fingering the envelope. He didn't watch Spencer walk away.

"I'll leave you alone," Tucker said, "but I'll hang around in case you need to talk."

"Thanks."

The commotion in the library hadn't lessened. Someone was crying, the sobs sounding like Sylvia. He should be in there, but he couldn't face Chloe's gloating. Not now.

They owned Bridgewater together, and that was something he was going to need a lot of liquor to come to terms with because he knew, without a shadow of a doubt, that it was Raymond's payback.

His heart pounding, he opened the envelope, confirming his worst fears.

On the company letterhead, there were only two words written in wobbly script:

I know.

CHAPTER EIGHT

In her makeshift studio, Zia set up an empty canvas. Reid's angry words still echoed in her ears. "Why didn't you tell me you can't get pregnant? We've been together for five years, and not once did you allude to anything of the sort. I asked you to marry me and you didn't say one damned thing."

She hadn't wanted to argue, wasn't going to defend herself. She didn't care what Reid thought. She'd only wanted to know what Matthew thought of her, if he saw her as less than a woman because she couldn't have children, but by the time she'd freed herself to look his way, he'd gone, and all she could think of was freedom.

It hadn't been very mature of her, to leave all the damage control to her mother. Especially since Sylvia took her announcement the hardest. Being she was an only child, Sylvia hadn't taken the news of never having the privilege of grandchildren lightly.

It wasn't easy to digest what her father's will had decreed, either. She did all right with her paintings so the need for money wasn't there, but to be cut out like that, to not inherit unless she had children . . . it was crazy five million dollars would just rot in a bank, a Bridgewater bank, but a bank nonetheless, because she'd never be able to claim it.

Needing to remember happier times, Zia began to paint. Because of her father's illness and subsequent death and funeral, she'd had little time to work on her collection, and she had just as little to show for it. The gallery showing and ball were four weeks away. She'd need to paint at least three paintings a week until then to have a satisfactory collection to show.

It was easy to get caught up in the reminiscences, and hers and Matthew's intimate time on the beach the night before brought back memories of him taking her to the same beach years and years before.

The leaves in the trees turning their burnt oranges, rugged browns, and crisp reds crowded the shoreline, and the wind blowing over the lake misted their faces. Deeper into fall then, she'd needed a jacket. She'd been young, maybe around the time she'd fallen off her bike.

Her parents had been fighting. She remembered that clearly, something about meetings or work, something about being too busy to take care of her. Something that had put a pit in her little stomach.

Her parents fighting over her.

They hadn't done it often, which made when they did that much more terrible to her tiny heart.

Matthew, in his way, had swooped in, claiming he needed help finishing a project, and only Zia Bishop's help, no less, as he tickled her belly.

She captured them, a man and child, walking one of Lake Kenosha's beaches, her small hand in his.

He would have been thirty-four, give or take, she mused as she painted.

Thirty-four to her six.

He always called himself old, but she never thought of him that way. When she thought of their ages, she only considered herself finally caught up with him.

When he looked at her, he probably still saw that little girl who needed him to rescue her.

She still did. Needed him to rescue her, that was.

But whenever they were together, there was a spark in his eyes, a healthy pink to his cheeks.

He could deny it all he wanted, but she was good for him, too.

She hummed, letting the simple joy of her six-year-old self spending time with her hero fill her. The way she felt about him now wasn't so different than the way she'd felt about him then. More mature, but the love was the same. Honest. Pure.

Unconditional.

Maybe that was a dangerous word to throw around, but if she considered what he'd already done to her, it wasn't unrealistic that she'd love him no matter what.

That didn't mean she could do anything about it.

On a whim, she texted him and asked when they could meet and talk.

He answered immediately, saying he'd reserve them a hotel room tomorrow evening and would she want to meet him there for dinner?

She huffed a laugh, amused. Dinner? Or did he mean sex? He said he'd get her into a bed soon. She wasn't such a fool she wouldn't take him up on it when he offered her the chance.

She confirmed the time they would meet and put her paints and brushes away. Reid needed her time too, and she had a lot of explaining to do.

Alienating him would be stupid. If she was going to break off their relationship, she had to at least do it in a professional manner. She wasn't sure if that's what it would come down to, but she owed him more than she was giving him.

She pressed a light kiss to the half-finished painting and picked up her purse. She'd come straight from her parents' house, and she still wore her heels and black lace dress.

The sun slowly sank behind the horizon, and she walked down a busy sidewalk full of people bar-hopping. A woman bumped into her, and startled, Zia automatically said, "I'm sorry."

"No worries . . . Zia Bishop."

She studied the woman, her face vaguely familiar, but she couldn't place her. She smiled politely, and the woman laughed.

"You don't remember me."

"No, I'm sorry."

"We met at Post 15. I'm Rebecca Gainsborough. Do you remember now?"

"Yes, I'm sorry. How are you?" She didn't like the woman's glinting eyes or the way her mouth twisted into a sneer, but she kept a smile pasted on her face.

"I'm fine, though not as well as I'd be if I was preparing for a showing. Congratulations again, for that. You're sure to be a huge success. Do you have studio space around here?"

She gestured to the high rise behind them. "My agent rented me space. It's full of construction, but the windows let in a lot of light. I'm happy with it."

"That's nice. You do lovely work."

"Thank you." Shivers of apprehension crawled up and down her back, and she said, "I have somewhere I need to be, so please excuse me. Maybe I'll see you at the showing?"

"You can count on it. Bye."

"Have a nice evening." She hurried to the parking garage

where she parked her truck, relieved she could leave the woman behind.

Though there would be leftovers from her father's repast, she ordered Reid's favorite meal from a nearby Italian restaurant and prayed their talk would go smoothly.

She needed something to go right.

Her average wasn't very good so far.

She juggled the takeout boxes and cappuccino cups up the stairs outside the garage that led to the apartment. Her purse bumped against her hip, and fumbling with her keys, she dropped them on the landing.

She set the containers on the step and leaned against the cool siding.

The neighborhood was quiet. Couples inside for the evening eating a late dinner or parents putting their children to bed.

Her mother moved around inside the house, disappearing from her sight to go into a room or around a corner. She hoped her mother had help cleaning up. That Matthew or a couple of her mother's friends had stayed behind. She should have, and it was another thing on a long list that made her feel horrible.

It seemed like lately she couldn't do anything right.

The apartment's door opened, the hinges squeaking faintly. "What are you doing out here?" Reid asked.

"I'm sorry. How did you know I was back?"

"I heard your truck pull up. Are you all right?"

She sagged in relief. He may still be angry, but at least he wasn't giving her the silent treatment.

"I'm okay, just overwhelmed."

"Come inside and we'll talk about it. You brought food? Let

me help you." Propping the door open with his foot, he picked up the cappuccino cups.

"Thanks."

They settled on the couch in the small living room, the plastic containers she brought sitting on the cluttered coffee table in front of them. The spicy scent of her entrée should have made her ravenous, but it only churned the acid in her stomach. She hadn't been eating, and she was going to make herself sick if she didn't start. She didn't have an appetite, but she forced herself to sip her coffee.

Reid wrapped his arm around her, and she sank into his side, resting her head on his chest.

"I'm sorry about today," he said, his lips pressed to the top of her head.

"No, I am. I should have told you."

"It's not that you didn't tell me, honey, it's that you've been carrying this alone. You found out when you went to your appointment?"

She told him what the gynecologist said about her scarred tubes. She'd need to tell her mother and Matthew, and the thought of having to repeat the details made tears creep into her voice. She hadn't had much time to think about it, but because of her father's will, her infertility would be front and center for years to come. She hated that her imperfection as a woman would be laid out for all the world to see.

"Why didn't you say something?" He nudged her away, and she met his eyes. "Haven't I made you happy? We've been together for years and all this time you've seemed happy, but we come to Lake Kenosha and you turn into a different person."

"My father—" she started.

"I know." He held her hand. "But how close to your father were you? You never came home to visit. Not once. And your dad didn't always go with your mother to visit us. I'm not saying you don't have a right to grieve, he was your dad, but I *am* saying I don't think your behavior toward me has anything to do with your father's death."

She bristled. "I'm under a lot of pressure and you have no right to make assumptions. My father's funeral was today. Not six hours ago I found out I was cut out of his will, like a family member he was ashamed to acknowledge. How do you want me to act? Now I have to paint my ass off for this *Fall and Foliage* thing you signed me up for."

His mouth dropped open. "You love to paint. You live to paint. And you can't deny you do your best work when you're sad. Given the circumstances, the paintings you'll create for this showing will be nothing less than spectacular. Why are you blaming me? You went to Post 15, too, if I recall. You could have said no."

"Well, I can't now," she snapped. "I need the money. My father didn't leave me a penny, and my mom's business is doing well, but she can't support me."

"What are you talking about?" he asked, incredulous, raking his fingers through his hair. "You don't need her to support you. You've always done well. We've always been just fine." He braced his elbows on his knees. "Zia, you haven't let me touch you since we've been here, and you can't or won't tell me why. I'm worried about us."

So was she, but she didn't know what to do about it. "I don't want to talk about this anymore. I need to shower and go to bed. It's been a horrible day."

He followed her into the bedroom. "We're not done."

"Yes, we are." She wiggled her feet out of her heels and peeled off her dress. She shouldn't have felt self-conscious being almost naked in front of him, but she did.

No, it wasn't modesty.

It was guilt.

Wearing her bra and panties, she started the shower in the tiny bathroom.

"I love you," Reid insisted, pushing on the door as she tried to close it. "You used to tell me you love me, too."

"I do love you," she said, shoving his shoulder until he backed away.

She closed the door in his face.

But I love Matthew more.

Matthew helped Sylvia and the catering company straighten the empty house, Chloe, of course, disappearing whenever there was work that needed to be done. It galled him she still thought she had the right to live with him, but she was correct on one level. They still had pretenses to maintain, such as they were. Once Zia and Reid went back to LA, he didn't care what she told people and he could kick her out.

Sick of being her cash cow, he welcomed her leaving, and he considered selling his house and moving as well. Everywhere he looked, from then on, he'd see Chloe, and he didn't want to be reminded of the years wasted on a woman he loathed.

The morning after Raymond's funeral, she sat at the kitchen table reading the paper, a mug of coffee near her elbow. Wisely, she hadn't tried to sleep in his bed. There was a fine line between the rough sex she liked and the fury he wanted to take out on her.

Full of contempt he struggled to keep in check, he calmly poured a cup of coffee and sat next to her.

She didn't meet his eyes.

He pulled the note Raymond had written him out of his pocket and let the paper flutter onto the table.

She stiffened.

"Would you like to explain this?" he asked.

"I don't know what you're talking about."

Leaning forward, he said, "Don't give me that shit. You know damned well what this is."

"It's the scribbling of a delusional man. It could mean anything."

"Or . . . it could mean you told him everything. Why would you do that when I've given you whatever you wanted for the past several years? That was our entire agreement. I gave you what you wanted if you kept your mouth shut."

She shook her head in defiance. "I thought he should know what kind of a woman he was married to. What kind of a man claimed to be his best friend. It hurt him, and he acted accordingly."

"You told him to protect him? Christ. Like any judge or jury would believe that. You didn't tell him to lay the truth out there, you told him because you hoped he'd write you into his will, and he did. You knew he wouldn't have left you anything, believing I would take care of you. Why give you his money when you have mine? That was how Raymond thought. You knew he'd cut Sylvia out of his will, and it worked."

"So what if it was a win-win situation for me? Raymond deserved to know the truth. I didn't want him dying thinking he was surrounded by friends and family. He was surrounded by liars and cheaters. Sylvia didn't deserve what little Ray left her, but he still loved her, even after I told him about the letters. What he couldn't wrap his mind around was you sleeping with Zia when she was only eighteen. The photos I showed him made him sick. The icing on the cake was when she sat with him before he passed. Seems she had her own confessions to make and asked for his blessing to be with you. Can you imagine?"

"That's what she told him? Good Lord. How nice for him to have the changes in his will justified."

"You know him too well. He was angry I didn't tell him sooner, but he thanked me for finally revealing the truth. He died peacefully, knowing everyone got what they deserved, and that's all that matters."

He sipped his coffee. "I don't guess he gave it to her? His blessing to be with me?"

Chloe scoffed. "Of course not. He died hating you. You received nothing. He didn't even leave you a pair of cufflinks."

"That's where you're wrong, dear," he chided, pushing away from the kitchen table. He'd thought this through and consulted with Spencer.

"What do you mean? He didn't leave you a goddamned thing. I checked with Spencer to be sure. My brother didn't mention your name in his will at all."

"He had nothing to leave me. Not in the way you're think-ing. I have my half of Bridgewater and all the income and bene-fits that go with it. He couldn't take those away from me, even if you managed to make him hate me. No. He gave his half of Bridgewater to you. Which means *you're mine*."

She tossed her hair over her shoulder. "I don't know what you're talking about. You run Bridgewater. You've been doing it alone since Ray got sick. Keep doing what you're doing and I'll keep doing what I've always done."

He *tsked*. "It's not that simple. You own half of Bridgewater now. I don't make enough off my fifty percent to run a hundred percent of the company. You may have thought you won, but really, you asked Raymond to do something he'd been wanting to do for years."

"And what's that?" Chloe narrowed her eyes.

"Put you to work."

"You're fucking crazy. I'm not working."

Laughing, he said, "Yes, you are. You don't get it. *You own half of Bridgewater Financial.* If you're going to draw an income, then you're going to have to earn it. I can make you work, or I'll claim you abandoned the company and I'll sue you for your half. I thought after Raymond's death I'd be rid of you, but he ensured I'm still going to have to see you every goddamned day. Isn't the world a lovely place?"

"Fuck you," she spat, standing so quickly she bumped into the table, sloshing coffee over Raymond's note.

"You have. For the past seven years. The tables have turned, Chloe, and you only have yourself to blame. I'll see you tomorrow morning at eight o'clock sharp. Don't be late. The banks have been on autopilot for the past couple of weeks, and we have a lot of catching up to do."

In a blur of pink satin robe, she flounced out of the kitchen.

He chuckled. This would be fun. He wondered how long it would last.

Zia looked over her shoulder before opening the door of the Harborview Hotel and Spa. It didn't have a view of a harbor, but the hotel was one of the finest in the city and it didn't surprise her Matthew had chosen it as the place to have their rendezvous.

She'd slipped out of their apartment not long after Reid had gone to Post 15 to talk to Shirley about an issue that had come up. He was still her agent, whether they were having relationship issues or not, and when Shirley called, he said he'd take care of it. Zia had worried all day how she'd meet Matthew, and she'd sagged in relief when Reid left.

She walked through the gold and cream lobby and rode the elevator to the top floor where only the grandest suites were located. Matthew had booked them the presidential suite, and though she couldn't spend the night, she looked forward to the few hours they could be alone.

He must have felt the same because when she knocked, the door flew open, and he jerked her into his arms not giving her a second to even say hello.

"Are you going to let me in? Or are you going to make me stand in the hallway all night?" she asked, laughing, breathless.

"Come in, come in. We can eat now, if you're hungry."

"Not really. I haven't been, you know, but a drink sounds nice."

He cupped the back of her neck and kissed her forehead. "You should eat. I know things have been difficult, but the hardest part is over."

"Is it, though?" she asked. Matthew meant her father's death. She meant the years keeping them apart.

Pouring a glass of wine, he said, "You don't think so?"

She pulled off her trench coat revealing a gauzy summer dress. Labor Day had come and gone, declaring it unfashionable to wear white, but while fall was slowly closing in, it still felt like summer, and she dressed like it, calendar be damned. "I suppose."

He handed her the glass of white which she downed in two gulps. "More, please."

"Sip this one. You've already had one drunken night, no need to have a repeat so soon."

She followed him to a conversation area, and he sat in a chair, another positioned beside him, a table positioned between them. Sipping her wine, she sat on the edge of the empty chair. "Is this the way it's going to be?"

"What do you mean?"

"You over there, me over here."

He set his drink on the small table. "Come here, then," he invited, opening his arms.

Zia tucked herself into his lap. "I needed this."

"I agree. We need each other more than we should."

The pit in her stomach that never seemed to go away intensified. "This isn't the part where you tell me we're never going to see each other again, is it?"

His grip tightened. "No, I've said it enough, but isn't that what you're going to tell me?"

She brushed her lips over his neck, past his jaw, to his lips. She'd missed him so much. Being with him at her father's funeral, at the repast, the reading of the will, it wasn't the same as this. Being able to touch, being able to show him how much she loved him.

Still a little girl trying to play a grownup's game.

Slowly but surely, she was learning the rules, learning how to play. Sneaking around Reid's back was teaching her.

And she was earning As.

"I could never tell you that. You were the one who sent me away. You've been the one living with my aunt for the past seven years."

"That's going to change, Zia. Now that your father's gone, I can stop appeasing him. Had he not gotten sick, I don't know how long I could have kept it up. You saw me at the party, I wasn't doing well. Living a life you weren't meant to live will take a toll on anyone, and it did me. Then Raymond was diagnosed with cancer, you came home, and it seemed like I might finally get back on my feet."

She traced the lines around his tired blue eyes. "Why did you do it, Matthew? No one will tell me why."

"I took one for the team, as you kids say," he said, a slight smile on his lips.

"Stop calling yourself old," she murmured.

"I'm not, but it's what I ended up doing, taking her off Raymond's hands, keeping her out of Sylvia's way. Chloe won't entirely be out of mine. Now that she has a piece of Bridgewater, I'll be seeing her at the office every day."

Imaging her aunt sitting behind a desk, pecking at a computer, she tipped her head back and laughed. "She'll love that. I've never known her to work a day in her life."

"She hasn't, and she's always been very open about spending my money, living off Bridgewater. But let's just say the conversation I had with her this morning was very enlightening."

"I hate thinking about you living with her," she said, resting her chin on his shoulder so he couldn't look into her eyes.

"You have Reid. Do you think I like that after you leave my bed later, you'll sleep in his? Let him make love to you?"

"Then you know how I've felt."

"Life isn't always what we want it to be," he said, cuddling her closer.

"I know."

"You love him," he said.

It wasn't a question.

If she wanted to be a grownup, she had to act like one. Know the rules, play the game, and that meant sometimes telling the truth. Sometimes, not always, but sometimes, and one of those times was now. "Yes. He's been good to me. He gave me a career I can be proud of. He nursed me back to health. When he found me, I was like a broken little bird and he took care of me, in a way I needed."

"Then I'm indebted to him." He stood, cradling her to his chest, and she wrapped her arms around his neck. "I'll always want what's best for you, Little Star, even if that means you're happy with another man."

He hadn't asked her to come here to tell her they'd never see each other again, but he did ask to meet so he could tell her goodbye. Things might have changed, but not enough, or he'd be telling her they could be together.

He wasn't.

She knew he wouldn't.

"Will you make love to me?" she whispered in his ear.

"I'll do whatever you ask," he said, laying her down on the bed.

That was a lie, but for now, she allowed herself to believe it.

He made love to her, slowly, gently, taking her the way he should. Desire had swept them away on the stairs of the hotel and at the beach, but here, in bed, the setting sun glowing through the window, alcohol and arousal fizzing in their blood, he took her, under the covers, whispering words of love he meant but couldn't act upon.

It brought him back to the night he'd taken her virginity. Sweetly, showing her what making love meant, and how a man should feel about a woman while he was doing it.

He pushed into her, not asking about birth control. Her saying they didn't need it took on a whole new meaning, and after, as she laid in his arms, his hand on her belly, he said, "I'm sorry."

She linked their fingers. "There's nothing to be sorry for."

"Reid was angry."

"He wasn't angry I can't have children. He was angry I didn't tell him."

"You didn't tell your mother, either."

"No. I was going to wait. She'd been so worried about Dad, and I didn't want to add to it. I wanted to tell her in private, but then Dad had to do that with his will. It's insane. Spencer knew it was too, it's why he warned us before he started reading. That Dad was of sound mind." She paused. "You were his closest friend. You didn't know?"

"Raymond didn't confide in me, if that's what you're asking."

He spooned her from behind. He didn't want to look at her. She'd know he was keeping things from her.

"Then no one knows why my dad did what he did."

"Your father was a wise man. He's getting Chloe out of the house, forcing her to work for a change. She can gloat all she wants that Raymond didn't leave much to your mother, but it won't be long until she wishes your father to the fiery depths of hell for what he did. I'll make sure of it." He buried his face in her neck, kissing her soft skin. "You're good at changing the subject."

"I have no idea what you mean," she said, but giggled, her lips brushing his arm.

"Will you tell me? What the doctor said?"

As she recounted her appointment, her voice grew quiet and sad. "Do you want children? When you see me now, do you see half a woman?"

"Little Star, will you look at me?"

She turned onto her back, and he bit back a sigh, wiped the tears off her cheeks. Her haunted green eyes cut him to the bone. When would he ever stop making her unhappy?

"Zia, I'm fifty-three years old and don't have children. Do you know why I never had any? Why I never found a woman and started a family?"

"No," she whispered.

"If we ever made our relationship public, you know what people would say, don't you? They'd call you a Lolita, me, a creepy old man. They'd accuse you of having daddy issues, they'd accuse me of using you as the daughter I never had. There would be lots of talk, lots of armchair psychology. Some of it would be true." He propped his head on his hand and brushed the hair away from her face. "I never had children because all along I had you. You've been my life, since your mother let me hold you in the hospital, and as you grew older, I started feeling things a man my age shouldn't feel for a girl your age."

He laid on his back and kept her in his arms, her wet cheek pressed to his skin.

"When you were small, you were my everything, and as the years passed, it began to turn into more than me taking you places your parents didn't have time to go. It turned into me waiting. Waiting for you to be old enough to be with me. To answer your question, I've never wanted children. I've only wanted you. It doesn't matter one bit you can't have babies, Little Star, because you're here, and you're all I need."

She lifted her head and braced herself against his chest. "That was beautiful."

"You're beautiful, Zia, and I love you, very much. I'm sorry. For everything." He tangled his hands in her hair, lifted his head off the pillow, and kissed her.

"There's nothing to be sorry for," she murmured against his lips.

"Yes, there is. Lots of things, too many things, and don't forgive me because you love me. Now, we should eat. You're too thin. Steak and ice cream?"

She grimaced. "How about a salad, and I'll split a piece of cheesecake with you."

"Only if you share my steak with me."

She smiled. "Deal."

He traced the curve of her lips. "Keep that there."

"I'll try."

"Good. I'll help you."

Zia hummed on the way to her studio. She'd missed several of Reid's texts asking if she wanted to meet for dinner. As she walked down the sidewalk, she texted him back, saying she was painting, and she'd be home later.

Dusk didn't give her the best light to paint, but there was no help for it.

Under the fluorescent lights, she finished the painting she'd started of Matthew and her walking the beach at Lake Kenosha.

What he told her lightened her heart. She'd spent her whole life loving him in some way, and it made her happy he felt the same.

She sighed, darkening a cloud in the sky. He was determined they couldn't have a life together, but he couldn't make love to her and tell her he loved her, then tell her to go back to LA after the showing and marry Reid. Couldn't he understand how impossible that would be?

Maybe he was right. Maybe her father really did just want Aunt Chloe to start working, make a name for herself like she and her mother had done. Maybe it didn't have anything to do with anything else, but anyone in the world was better qualified to run half of Bridgewater than Chloe.

Matthew had his work cut out for him, and she didn't envy him at all. It seemed he'd never be able to completely rid his life of Chloe.

Being forced to work . . . Chloe will make all of Bridgewater miserable.

Close to midnight she set aside her brush and rested the canvas against a wall to dry. Two down, as many more as she could finish to go. Now that her father was no longer in pain and had gone on to a better place and the funeral and reading were over, she could concentrate on her collection. If that meant less time with Reid, well, she wouldn't complain.

She wrapped her trench around her to ward off the slight chill and headed toward the hotel's parking garage.

Footfalls sounded behind her, and she sped up, her sandals scratching over the concrete.

"Zia!"

She slowed, her body slackening in relief. Too high strung. On edge. She couldn't simply walk down the sidewalk without thinking someone was out to get her.

"Reid. What are you doing here?"

"Looking for you. You said you were painting, but I stopped by the building and security said you'd gone. You need to start checking your phone more often, sweetheart."

"I'm sorry. I get so caught up, and I'm tired."

"Sylvia offered me a vehicle," he said, reaching for her hand, "but I ordered an Uber, thinking I would catch a ride home with you or maybe talk you into getting a drink."

She froze, her mind scrambling, and he frowned. "What is it? You're acting so strange lately, and it's making me really worried about you." He kissed the top of her head. "I have to admit, it will be a relief to go back to LA."

"I'm worried about my mother. She hasn't been taking any of this well."

"You not getting any sleep isn't helping, either. Come on," he said, tugging on her hand in the direction of the public parking garage.

"I didn't park there today."

"Then where's your truck?"

"I parked at the Harborview. I . . . met Matthew."

"Why did he want to see you?"

"Just to go over a few things, what the will means for my family, like that."

He scowled. "Isn't that the attorney's job?"

"Matthew's been a family friend since before I was born. Just because my father passed away doesn't mean he'll stop." She pulled her hand out of his grip.

"Calm down. I didn't mean anything by it. If you're at the Harborview, let's stop in the bar and have a drink. You need something."

She forced herself to smile. "That sounds good. I'm sorry."

"Don't be . . . but I hope you can start acting more like yourself soon. The Zia I know and love."

She wanted to say maybe her true self was finally coming through. Maybe her true self was when Matthew was holding her in his arms.

But over wine and appetizers and romantic music, she reminded herself she used to love Reid, appreciate him, respect him. She used to love having long, deep conversations with him, used to love sleeping in on Sunday mornings. Used to love their life full of art and parties and glamour.

She used to love it, and they could have that life back, after the showing.

The problem was, she didn't know what she wanted anymore.

Or rather, she did, but Matthew was hell-bent on keeping it from her.

Forget about him.

She brushed her fingers over the necklace he'd given her. If only she could.

Matthew's days were full of listening to Chloe bitch about work and sitting in meetings watching her eyes glaze over.

He missed Zia.

It wasn't that he stayed away from her on purpose. Someone had to run Bridgewater, and it wouldn't be Chloe.

They'd all been wrong when they guessed at Raymond's motivation. It wasn't to punish Sylvia for writing Matthew letters, it wasn't to force Chloe to work.

It was to sentence him, torture him, for every sinful thing he'd ever done. Because he'd rather die the most painful death that man had created than face one more meeting with Chloe, who was doing her best to make everyone hate her.

When anyone asked him why she was taking up valuable space and breathing in precious oxygen, all he could do was shrug and say it's what Raymond wanted.

He never drank at lunch, but he slid into a booth across from Sylvia at a bar and grille not far from Bridgewater and ordered a scotch.

"Bad day?"

Matthew scowled. "I'd never wish Chloe on my worst enemy. That woman . . . a tree stump has more common sense. I have no idea what Raymond was thinking."

He downed his drink and gestured for another.

"Yes, you do, and my husband succeeded in ways no one could've imagined."

"You're telling me."

"Matthew, I'm worried."

He held her hand. "You don't have to be. I'll always take care of you and Zia."

"How can you, when you won't be here?"

Wincing, he said, "Obviously, that's not going to happen now. Chloe could never do my job. Hell, you've run your own business for close to thirty years, but you couldn't, either. Even if I let the board of directors take control, that was all wishful thinking. I could never abandon Bridgewater."

"You could sell it."

"No, I can't. It needs to stay in the family, as a legacy for you, Zia, and her children."

"But—"

"I know, but Spencer said the will didn't stipulate they must be her biological children. She can adopt."

"I wish you, or Chloe . . ." Sylvia rubbed her cheeks.

"Listen to what you're saying. You wish Chloe would have procreated? What fresh hell would that have been? Bridgewater's only a business, but I want to hang on to it for Zia. She's young. Her life could go in a million different directions and I don't want to do anything I'll regret later. Besides, we're running a business people can be proud of. They don't worry about investing with us. They don't open an account and three years later check the balance and find nothing because we took out twenty dollars every month in useless fees. We're offering an honest service, and that would go right down the shitter if we sold it. Ray wanted a bank for the people, by the people, and in all the years we've run Bridgewater, that's what we've given our customers." He gripped her hand. It felt good to remember why he and Raymond opened Bridgewater Financial. It felt good to remind himself there was more at stake than just dealing with Chloe every day. "It's a legacy you and Zia can be proud of, and we'll pass it on to Zia's children. She'll have children somehow, Sylvia. She'll make a lovely mother. As you are."

"Then you're not leaving."

"No. I'm sorry you've worried about it."

She sighed. "I have to admit, you've made me feel better."

"Good. Now, since we're here, you should eat something. You've lost too much weight, like your daughter."

"Have you seen her lately?" She opened the menu.

"The other night for dinner. She told me what her doctor said. It sounds like there are things she can try, medical procedures, so all hope isn't lost if having biological children is something she wants. With Reid." He swallowed. "Or whomever. In the future."

"But not you."

He laughed, but it wasn't out of happiness. "Chloe had her fun, telling Raymond what happened between you and me, and me and Zia, but she hasn't told Zia about the letters, and she will. Chloe's like a cornered animal, wounded. She's going to lash out, and that's the way she'll do it. She's biding her time."

She dropped the heavy, leather-bound menu onto the table. "That's why Raymond did what he did."

"Yes. Chloe thought she won, too, until I told her I had the legal right to make her work. She's not so smug now."

Lifting her wine in toast, she said, "Karma's a bitch."

"It is, but I'm not stupid, Sylvia. Karma will get me, too. The relationship I had with you. Sleeping with Zia before she went to the Art Studio. Living with Chloe for the past seven years. Call me the Bishop gigolo. It doesn't make me look good, does it?"

"The circumstances—"

"Don't mean shit. When I found out Raymond was courting you, I should have stepped aside. I should *never* have touched Zia, no matter how much I loved her. Had I behaved, Chloe never would've had the ammunition to make me do what she wanted. I'm a weak man, and my feelings for you and Zia have fucked me good."

"If we're so terrible, you should go. Let Chloe run Bridgewater into the ground. Let Zia marry Reid, though she doesn't love him. Retire to a beach somewhere and let a little thing wearing a barely-there bikini serve you daiquiris. Don't let us keep you from enjoying the rest of your life." She looked away.

He knocked back the rest of his drink. "I said it fucked me up, I didn't say I regretted it. I love Zia, and you're one of my best friends. I'll always look out for the both of you. Now order your meal. We're part of the working class, and I need to get back to the office before Chloe burns the whole building down."

Meeting his eyes, she said, "You really are a good man."

"Yep. I know. But haven't you heard? Nice guys finish last."

CHAPTER NINE

"You want to plan what?" Zia asked her mother the next morning.

Reid was working, fielding calls and setting up appointments the best he could. The distance was wearing on him, and he already had their plane tickets booked for the day after the showing. It was a late afternoon flight, but still. She was annoyed he didn't consult her, assuming she was in as much hurry to go back to LA as he was. She wasn't, but there was no reason to linger, and she'd kept her feelings to herself.

She had plans to paint all day, but she stopped in to see her mother first. She didn't feel like painting, but like any artist, sometimes she had to work whether she wanted to or not. People depended on her, and her pocketbook depended on them.

"A dinner party. For you and Reid. We haven't properly welcomed you to Lake Kenosha, and him meeting everyone at your dad's repast was unavoidable but not in good taste. He needs a proper introduction."

"Do you know what will happen if we're all in the same room? Besides, he met everyone at Matthew's birthday party."

"This will be more intimate, and you didn't have your showing planned then. We'll announce that, and we can invite that Shapiro woman, and Aimee. You haven't seen her much since you've been back. Matthew, of course. Chloe. Spencer. Tucker. A few others. It'll be nice, and it will show everyone that the Bishops might be down, but we're far from out."

"So that's what it is? A rally cry?"

"It's all over town your father left his half of Bridgewater to Chloe and not to me. She's made sure to tell everyone she knows. So, yes. This dinner is for me as well as for you. I'm not going to lie on the ground like a kicked puppy."

"If that's what you want." She loaded her coffee cup into the dishwasher.

"It isn't, but we can't hide, Zia."

"No, we can't." Her mother was right, but she didn't like being put on display. She was used to it in her professional life, but in her personal life? No thanks. "Fine. Let me know what I can do."

"You can help me plan the menu."

She kissed her mother's cheek. "I'll be over tonight. Until then, I need to paint, or there won't be a showing."

On the walkway, she paused. Through the living room's window, she watched her mother sit on the couch and stare into space.

Her father should have done more for her mother. Married and in love for over twenty-five years, yet her he barely mentioned her in his will.

Suddenly, she was glad her mother insisted on a dinner party. She could corner Spencer and maybe figure out what happened.

Matthew had secrets. Chloe had secrets. Her father had secrets he brought with him to the grave.

She didn't have any secrets. It seemed like everyone was up in her business.

Everyone but Reid.

She cast a glance above the garage, and he stood in the window, looking down at her.

Unease settled in her stomach.

He lifted a hand and she blew him a kiss.

He stepped back, the curtain fluttering into place. Quickly, she jumped into her truck and drove away.

Matthew understood, could even appreciate, why Sylvia decided to host a dinner party, but it didn't stop him from wishing she hadn't. If he had to watch Reid kiss Zia's shoulder one more time, he'd go mad. He understood Reid's intentions, too, could even appreciate them, a man staking his claim, but he didn't have to like it.

Sylvia's guests ambled around the front room, appetizer stations wafting scents of shrimp scampi, mini quiches, and smoked salmon on some kind of cracker. A waiter stood in one corner near a champagne station, serving guests.

They couldn't get enough of the free food . . . or the rumors that were whispered in one ear and came out the mouth of another.

"This isn't so bad, is it?" Sylvia asked, sitting in the chair next to his and holding two low ball glasses and a bottle.

She'd brought the good stuff Raymond hid in his study.

"Not when you're drinking that," he said, accepting the glass she offered him.

"One must when one can." She sipped and shuddered.

"You could stick to champagne."

"Not with this crowd. Here, keep it. We're gonna need it." She shoved the bottle into his lap and walked away, stopping to speak to Zia, Reid, Aimee, and the director of Post 15, Shirley Shapiro.

"Oh, the good stuff," Tucker said, dropping into the seat Sylvia vacated.

"Sylvia brought it over."

"That's my girl," Tucker said, adding a couple fingers to his empty glass. "How are things holding up?"

"If you don't count me wanting to slit Reid's throat, all is well."

"You don't want her, yet you want her. You can't have it both ways."

"It's not that I don't want her, it's that I know I can't have her. Two very different things."

"Hmmm."

"What? You don't think so? Say Zia forgave me the love letters to her mother, and she very well could because she's a true romantic at heart, there's still the fact I'm too old for her. We don't have anything in common besides sex, and that would fizzle out in the day-to-day of a relationship. Come on, you're the one who told me that."

Tucker sipped his drink. "You're right. It's difficult to get past the love conquers all idea, that's all."

"It makes it slightly more bearable that I know it's for the best. Slightly. Besides, I'm enjoying tightening the noose around Chloe's neck. It will ease the burn Zia's gone. She's an absolute disaster and everyone at Bridgewater hates her."

"How long is that going to last?"

"As long as it takes."

"For what?"

"For one of us to kill each other."

Zia tugged the lone sleeve of her asymmetrical green dress. The lace itched her arm, and it irritated her Reid wouldn't stop kissing her shoulder. Ever since she told him she'd had dinner with Matthew, he'd been more possessive than usual and she didn't like it. Even if she and Matthew didn't end up together because he was too stubborn to admit how much he wanted her in his life, her and Reid's relationship was coming to an end. She hoped her professional career didn't suffer, though she'd been approached by other agents offering representation. If they did as well as Reid, she'd be okay.

"We have fifteen minutes until dinner," her mother murmured into her ear.

"Okay."

As a waiter filled her glass at the champagne station, she searched for her father's attorney. As luck would have it, Spencer was right then walking into the room alone. She filled another flute and rushed to his side, startling him.

"Spencer, I was wondering if we could talk private," she asked, handing him a flute.

He sighed and turned away from Matthew and Tucker who, by the look of it, were drinking scotch out of her dad's private collection.

"It won't take long, and my mother said dinner would be served soon."

Glancing at Matthew and Tucker again, he waved his flute in the air. "Lead the way. I have a couple of things I need to speak with you about as well, though I hadn't planned on doing it tonight."

"Thank you."

She led him to her father's study, the same room where the

will had been read only days before. Playing hostess, she poured Spencer a lowball of what Matthew and Tucker were drinking in the drawing room.

Smiling wryly in appreciation and embarrassment, he accepted it and set his untouched champagne on an end table. "I was that transparent, huh? What can I do for you?"

She sank onto one side of a loveseat, set her flute near Spencer's abandoned glass, and tried to dry her palms on the skirt of her dress. "I want to know why my father left Chloe my mom's share of Bridgewater."

Perching on the loveseat's arm opposite her, he raised an eyebrow. "I thought you'd want to talk about your inheritance being dependent on you having children. That doesn't worry you, what with the news you shared with us?"

"Maybe it would if I was poor, or lazy like Chloe, but I do okay on my own. What concerns me is my father's motivations. You were very clear that Dad's mind was sound. So, I want to know, what was he thinking?"

"There's not a lot I can tell you because of client/attorney privileges, but it's safe to say he found out a few things that made him change his mind about the way he'd previously written his wishes."

She straightened her spine. "What in the hell could he have found out that would make him do something like that? He gave Chloe, a woman who hasn't worked a day in her life, half of the largest bank chain in the Midwest. Matthew's been working sixteen-hour days first to recoup hours from when Dad was sick and now to cover for my aunt. He's essentially working two jobs because of my dad."

He drained his glass, twisted the empty crystal in his hand, and stared at the floor.

She slid to the edge of the cushion and prepared to stand. If he was done talking to her, then there wasn't any reason to keep him. "I—"

Abruptly, he stood, settled onto his haunches in front of her, and held her hand. "I've been your family's attorney for a long time, Zia. I attended Ray and Sylvia's wedding ceremony. I went to your baptism, and before that, Matthew and Ray consulted me when they were considering starting Bridgewater. We spent hours upon hours going over this, going over that. I feel like part of the family. It hurt me to do what your father wanted me to do, and I tried to talk him out of it."

"Thank you. That means a lot."

"I can't say any more about Sylvia's inheritance, or lack thereof, but I can tell you he didn't want you and Matthew in a relationship."

She sucked in a breath.

"He heard something, and he swore he wouldn't let it happen. He left his share of Bridgewater to Chloe to make him work, to make him miserable, having to deal with her as a business partner." He paused. "Your father wasn't stupid. He knew Chloe would be useless. He counted on it."

Tears flooded her eyes and her vision blurred.

"By the look of how things are going, he succeeded. He heard something, something that made him think you and Matthew were, or are, lovers. I can't tell you what he heard, or whom he heard it from. I'm doing the best I can, giving you the information you want without betraying Raymond's trust, trust he paid me for."

Who could have told her dad about her and Matthew? Matthew wouldn't have. He'd been the first to tell her they had to keep their love a secret.

But someone had found out and told her dad.

Instead of being happy for her, her father punished her. And Matthew.

And by punishing Matthew, he punished her mother.

This was all her fault.

All those years ago, if she hadn't forced herself onto Matthew in the maze behind this very house, none of this would have happened.

She let the tears drip down her cheeks.

Spencer handed her a tissue. "There's no point in crying about it. It's over and done. The good news is, your father didn't consider the idea you couldn't have your own children. I told Matthew a couple things I wanted to pass along to you about that. Did he?"

She shook her head. She didn't remember him telling her anything. Maybe. Maybe at the hotel after they'd made love, but she'd been so wrapped up, literally and figuratively, in his arms, she couldn't recall what they'd talked about. "I don't know."

"Okay. Mainly, there are ways around it. Raymond made no mention of biological children, and you can marry someone who already has children or you can adopt. If you don't mind me asking, are you and Reid serious? Does he have children?"

"He asked me to marry him, but he doesn't have any kids," she murmured.

"Then perhaps before you go back to LA, you could schedule a meeting with me. He'll want to know his options, Zia. I'm sure at some point he'll want to become a father and he'll be interested in the legalities of the stipend Ray granted you to care for those children."

Zia lowered her head.

Matthew didn't want children.

All he wanted was her.

Someone told her father that.

Before he passed away, she'd justified his decision to

change his will when she confessed she was in love with Matthew.

"Will you excuse me?"

"Of course."

She stumbled into the bathroom connected to her father's study.

Champagne roiled in her stomach.

She closed the door, and with her face buried in her hands, she slid to the floor and cried.

"You don't look very good, are you okay?" Matthew whispered into Zia's ear as the group went into the large dining room for dinner.

He'd watched Zia and Spencer leave the sitting room and walk down the hallway. He assumed they'd gone into the library or Raymond's study but he hadn't a clue what the attorney could have told her that would make her look like this. She'd bitten off all her lipstick and her cheeks were pale. Her eyes were red from crying.

"I'm fine." She squeezed his hand.

That was a good sign, at least.

Sylvia assigned them seats, and he tensed when Chloe sat next to him. Still playing the part in public, he draped his arm around her shoulders.

She smiled, hate flashing in her eyes.

Sylvia sat at the head of the table, Shirley Shapiro to her right as the guest of honor.

Being this was supposed to be a dinner to celebrate Zia's showing at Post 15, Sylvia had been paying special attention to the director of the gallery.

Aimee sat next to Zia, Reid on Zia's other side.

Tucker sat on Matthew's left, and the other guests occupied the remaining spaces: Spencer, a few clients of Sylvia's, two or three supporters of Post 15 who had been invited upon Shirley's recommendation. They were patrons of the art community who would buy one, possibly two, of Zia's works, and they sat across from Reid. While they waited for the catering waiters and waitresses to serve, he started a discussion about the artists in their collections.

At least he was good for something.

The first course was a soup, a clam dish Matthew disliked, and he swirled the creamy grey goop around in his bowl.

"So, tell me, Chloe, how are you liking your position at Bridgewater?" Sylvia asked, not a bitter note in her tone.

Softly, he chuckled at his spoon.

Beside him, Chloe bristled. "It's difficult because I don't have a business degree. I'm starting from scratch, and it's relentless. I haven't been shopping in days. I go home, fall into bed, and it starts all over again. Honestly, Sylvia, if Ray's share had gone to you, I don't know what you would have done. You already owning a business and all."

Sylvia smiled demurely. "Ray was very wise. He knew exactly what he was doing."

Chloe pursed her lips and glared. "Yes. He did."

"Zia, how's your collection coming along?" Shirley asked, holding her spoon halfway to her mouth.

"Very well, actually. I started a theme and all the paintings will have the same feel. I didn't realize how many memories I have that included fall. I'm very excited to show them." She sipped her wine.

He met her eyes across the table knowing he'd remember every one.

Reid clued in to the conversation saying, "I had no idea Zia missed the seasons so much. Sylvia, we'll need to do a better job of visiting. I've seen snow only a handful of times, and that was to go skiing, of course." He kissed the back of Zia's hand.

"Of course. You two are welcome any time," Sylvia said. "Christmas carols don't have the same meaning if you don't have a little snow for the holidays."

Shirley cleared her throat. "Well, I have a tidbit of news, and it's quite terrible. In fact, I thought about not mentioning it at all, but I didn't want anyone asking me later why I didn't say something." She sucked in a breath. "Post 15 was vandalized last night."

"Are you all right?" Zia asked, alarmed.

"I was there, working in my office. The lights went out, but when I went to see what was going on, I was locked inside. My first thought was thieves, naturally. We'd just had a small showing, nothing elaborate because we're putting all our energy into yours, dear, but I heard a crash, and it was at that moment I knew they weren't stealing. They were destroying." Shirley paused, meeting the eyes of everyone at the table. "Every sculpture on display had been smashed into the tiniest bits and pieces, and someone had taken a can of bright orange spray paint to the walls. Atrocious."

"That's a shame," Reid said, leaning back, allowing a waitress to remove his soup bowl and replace it with the main dish: grilled pepper steak and au gratin potatoes. "Did the security cameras catch who it was?"

"No. Whoever it was knew exactly what they were doing. When the lights went out, it was because he cut the power to the entire building. The cameras were useless."

"You have insurance, surely."

"Yes, but to think of all that art. It's such a waste."

"You're lucky you weren't hurt," Zia said, handing the waitress her soup bowl.

"Indeed." Shirley sniffed. "I spent today organizing

cleaning efforts to put the gallery to rights. The owner's using the opportunity to update a few things. He wants the gallery perfect for you."

"Aimee, were you there, too? Are you okay?" Zia asked.

Aimee picked up her fork and steak knife. "No, I wasn't. This happened very late and I'd already gone home. Zia, I didn't tell you that I've decided to go to grad school."

"Oh, Aimee, that's great!"

Matthew cut into his steak and let the conversation scratch at him. A thin edge of tension padded the voices, like a smear of butter hiding a knife's sharp blade.

"Are you up for a run tomorrow?" Tucker asked.

He hadn't had time to run, not for a while, and his body was starting to feel it. "That's a good idea. Thanks."

"Sylvia, the dress you're wearing suits you. Did you find it on clearance?"

He gripped Chloe's thigh under the table, his fingertips gouging into her skin. *Play nice.*

Sylvia finished chewing, swallowed, and said, "Thank you, Chloe. Actually, Aimee, Zia, and I went shopping a couple days ago. We were in Saks, and a representative from Elie Saab was visiting the store. She admired Zia's coloring and insisted on gifting us dresses. Zia told her about the showing and ball and she dressed us for that, as well. It was quite surreal when she told us she owned a Zia Bishop. We walked out with several thousand dollars' worth of complimentary clothes and accessories, and I couldn't have been more stunned. It was a very lucky day, wasn't it, girls?"

"Yes, it was," Zia murmured.

"It was amazing," Aimee agreed, nodding.

"I look forward to seeing them," Chloe said, her eyes narrowed.

He dug his fingertips in deeper, and she tried to jerk her leg out of his grasp.

"I hear you moved out of Matthew's house."

A chill settled over the table, and the guests began looking between Sylvia and Chloe. If they'd attended the dinner to see a catfight, they weren't disappointed.

"I have," Chloe said, her voice smooth. "I'm at the Harborview for now, biding my time. There's a beautiful lake house that recently became available, and I put in a bid. Floor to ceiling windows, split level. It's gorgeous, and now that I have my inheritance, well within my budget. Matthew wants to live closer to Bridgewater, but I say he already lives there."

"What do you mean, closer to Bridgewater?" Zia asked, a frown puckering the smooth skin of her forehead.

"I've been looking at condos downtown," he told the table at large, hoping to dispel some tension. "I'm getting too old to shovel snow and mow grass. A condo would take care of that, and the building I'm looking at has a pool and exercise center. Downtown is the place to be."

"Oh, yes," Shirley gushed. "I live downtown, and I can't get enough of the nightlife. I live in the old Burlington building, and the wooden flooring is to die for. Original!"

He breathed a sigh of relief and let the older woman carry the conversation.

For dessert, Sylvia set up cheesecake stations and after-dinner coffees, once again in the front room. He wanted to duck out, but his conscience wouldn't let him abandon her. He had to admit, he was proud of her for standing up to Chloe, and she did look gorgeous in the black and amber dress she wore.

As the evening wound down, Reid spoke to Sylvia's clients and the art collectors about pieces currently up for auction at Sotheby's, and Sylvia, Tucker, and Spencer stood in the corner sipping Irish coffee.

Chloe looked trapped, speaking with Aimee, Shirley, and Zia, but the few manners Chloe still possessed locked her in place, an insincere smile freezing her mouth.

Taking a cup of coffee with him, Matthew stepped into the backyard, and he walked along the side of the house through the grass, easing through the sunset's shadows. The fresh autumn air alleviated his stress, and his shoulders loosened. He wanted to support Sylvia, but he wished keeping up pretenses wasn't so draining.

"Matthew? Are you out here?"

Zia's low, throaty rasp made him hard, and he swore under his breath. He shouldn't say anything. He should stay quiet and let her go back inside. "I'm over here, Little Star."

He sighed. He had no self-control when it came to her.

"What are you doing out here? It's getting colder and Mom hasn't had the yard sprayed for bugs in a long time."

"They haven't bothered me. Did you need something, sweetheart?"

"Just this."

She stepped into his arms and he set his mug on a patio table Sylvia had yet to put into storage.

"Are you all right?"

"I am now," she said, tucking her head under his chin.

He took his suit jacket off and draped it over her shoulders. "Aren't you cold in that little nothing of a dress?"

"You keep me warm enough."

Wrapping his arms around her, he savored holding her. Her scent, her soft skin. These moments happened so infrequently, but her showing was coming up and soon they would stop altogether.

"Did you really mean what you said? About selling your house?"

"Yes, I did. I don't like the thought of it, but I don't enjoy living there anymore."

"It's where we first made love."

"Another reason, perhaps, to let it go."

She stiffened and he rubbed her back.

"Don't be like that. I don't need a house to remember how you feel, to remember how much I love you." He nudged her away and put a finger under her chin, asking her look at him. "It's only a house. No one can take away how your skin turned to silk under my touch, or how my heart pounded when I first came inside you. I'll always remember how you tasted, your sweet honey on my lips. Nothing, no matter what happens, can erase you from my heart."

Threading his fingers through her curls, he kissed her, gently, his breath fluttering over her cheeks. He didn't say those things to be romantic. He said those things because they were true.

"I grew up in your house, almost as much as I grew up here."

"I know, Zia, but Chloe ruined that house for me. I don't want to live there anymore. I'm sure you can understand."

"She's ruined a lot of things," she said, stepping away. She slid her arms through the sleeves of his jacket and he smiled at the sight. A little girl playing dress-up.

"She has," he said, tilting his head. "Has she done something else?"

"I talked to Spencer before dinner." She drifted toward the maze where the fairy lights sparkled.

"I saw you two leave the sitting room," he said, following her.

She took a deep breath. "I think she told Dad about us."

He forced himself to remain calm. Maybe she didn't know

everything. If he were anything but the coward he was, he'd tell her himself. Right now.

But he couldn't.

Call him a million kinds of fool, but he couldn't do it. Not tonight.

Treading carefully, he asked, "Why do you say that?"

"Because . . . Spencer said my father left his share of Bridgewater to Chloe to punish you . . . because he found out we're sleeping together."

"Spencer told you that directly?" He couldn't believe the attorney would've been that free with information.

"No, but he didn't have to. I practically admitted it when I started crying. Why would Chloe tell Dad? Because she was jealous? And how did she know in the first place?"

"Come here, Little Star," he said, holding his arms open. He hated she'd become so involved in this mess. "None of this is your fault."

Cuddling against his chest, she said, "Yes, it is. I was eighteen and stupid. I didn't care about anyone but myself. You tried to warn me. You said people would talk, and you were right. But you were my father's best friend. Why wouldn't he want me with you? You of all people, he'd know you would take care of me."

"I'm older than you are, Zia, and not by only a handful of years. He would've known a relationship between us would be difficult. I was the adult and should have kept my hands off you, but even back then, I'd loved you for a long time and when you offered yourself to me, I was too weak to say no. If you're intent on taking the blame, then at least let me share it."

"But it *was* Chloe."

He tipped his head back and gazed at the stars that popped against the black canvas of sky. "Yes. It was."

"How did she know? How do you know it was her?"

Leading her to a bench, he said, "She was watching my house the morning after. She has pictures of me kissing you. She has pictures of you with your hand down my pants." That morning felt like yesterday.

She shivered. "What in the hell was she doing outside your house?"

"At your party, she'd invited herself over, but I turned her down. Maybe that night, she saw you leave. Maybe she over-heard you say something to Aimee. I don't know. She's conniving, and in that instance, especially, it served her well."

Standing from the bench, she burst out, "That's why you were fingering her in your office. That's why. She told you if you didn't do what she wanted, she'd tell everyone."

He hung his head. God, when she put it that way, he sounded like such a bastard. "Yes."

"You should have let her." She crossed her arms over her breasts, the sleeves of his suit coat hiding her hands. "You should have just let her, Matthew. Everyone knowing wouldn't have hurt me."

"That's the little girl talking, Zia. You're no longer a little girl."

"It would have hurt you."

"It's more than that. I'm not saying I handled things the right way. I buckled under Chloe's demands and that was cowardly. But you have a wonderful career ahead of you now. You wouldn't have had that if you'd stayed here, and I *know* you wouldn't have left me behind."

She sniffled. "You're right about that. Practically the only way I would've left you was how things happened."

"Come here, sweetheart," he said, patting his knee. "You can blame Chloe for telling Raymond, but telling him cut off her nose to spite her face. She talked big at the table tonight, lake houses, her huge salary, but there isn't a day that goes by that she's not in the ladies' room crying."

"That's something, anyway," she said, settling on his leg.

"Yes, and it's an important something. I'm slowly wearing her down. To what end, I'm not sure. But I'll tell you what I told her. The game has changed. She's not holding the cards anymore."

"I should never have thrown myself at you at my party. Or at yours." She laughed. "God, I'm so stupid and immature."

"Hey, look at me."

She met his eyes and he skimmed a fingertip over her cheek. "You made me a very happy man. No regrets now, huh?"

"Okay."

"We should go inside. We've been out here too long."

They walked across the cool grass toward the house. The rooms were still lit up, but he hoped they missed some of the goodbyes.

"I told him, too."

He stopped just outside the patio door. "You told what to whom?"

"Dad. When I saw him for the last time. I told him I was in love with you and asked for his blessing."

"But, Little Star, you have Reid, and here he is now, not looking very happy, either."

Reid pushed the door open and glowered at them. "What are you doing out here?"

"Just chatting," she said, a hand to his arm. "We're only talking."

"Wearing his jacket?"

"Oh, yeah. I'm sorry. It's chilly out here." She took his suit coat off and handed it to him.

He faced Reid's hostile glare.

"Your mother's looking for you. She's saying goodbye to a few guests," Reid said. "And Aimee's about to leave."

"Thanks. I'll talk to you later, Matthew. Goodnight. Come on, Reid. We can go, too."

"I'll be with you in a second, honey," Reid said, not breaking eye contact with him as Zia walked into the other room.

He leaned against the wall, the back of his head brushing a picture of him and Zia. He knew the picture was of the two of them. Sylvia hung it almost twenty years ago and had never moved it. He raised his eyebrows and waited.

"I'm going to ask you, gentleman to gentleman, to stay away from her."

That was fair.

Reid wasn't stupid, otherwise he'd never have taken Zia's career to the level it was, and pretending nothing was going on would only insult him.

"Just answer me this, then," he said, clutching his coat in his hand, "do you love her?"

"Of course I do." Reid leaned into his face. "Every night she spreads her legs, begging me to make love to her, and I do. I come inside her as she pants my name. She's mine, do you understand?"

He swallowed. "Yes."

"Good. Our flight's the day after the ball. After that, don't think you'll see her again." Reid patted his shoulder. "Good talk."

Reid walked away and he sagged against the wall.

He didn't blame the man. In fact, it surprised him it'd taken Reid this long to tell him to fuck off.

He'd overstepped his bounds. Again.

When it came to Zia, he'd never learn.

CHAPTER TEN

Zia readied a large canvas, the city of Lake Kenosha spread out in front her, glimmering in the morning sunlight. Because the gallery needed time to hang her paintings, she had less than two weeks to finish her collection. The first few she'd done had already been delivered, one being used in the brochures and gallery posters announcing the elegant event.

She had many more to complete, and as she painted, she thought back to the dinner party. Her mother was pleased with the results, and Shirley had called Sylvia the morning after, bubbling with excitement about the fabulous time she'd had.

It made Zia happy her mother had made baby-steps in regaining her equilibrium in her personal and social life. Chloe had also been a help, in a roundabout way, declaring her mother too busy to run half of Bridgewater and confirming that her design business thrived. She wondered what Matthew would've done had her mother inherited like he'd assumed. Her mother knew as much, or as little, about banking as Chloe did.

His announcement he was selling his house saddened her,

and she hoped he took his time putting it on the market. It would be difficult to say goodbye to so many memories.

She combined little dabs of yellow and red, searching for the perfect color to create fire.

A bonfire.

And she needed blue. The center of a fire was blue, hot, and dangerous, like Matthew's eyes.

She'd been ten, and her parents had taken a vacation without her to Paris to celebrate their anniversary. Other children may have been sad to see their parents go, but not her. When her parents went away, it meant she could stay with Matthew.

One night he'd lit a fire in his backyard, and they'd talked late, past her bedtime, while they roasted marshmallows and made s'mores.

She's always cherished those talks. He never spoke to her like the child she'd been, and it thrilled her.

It still did.

She'd fallen asleep in her chair, and he picked her up and carried her inside, his strong arms wrapped around her, her head against his chest.

Reid didn't understand their relationship. That it went deeper than friendship. That it went deeper than love. A feeling more powerful than anything she'd ever encountered bound them together.

She and Reid argued the night of the dinner party, but she supposed it couldn't have been avoided. He was angry. No doubt he felt the electricity between Matthew and her, even though they tried to hide it, albeit, not very well. She followed him inside their apartment, and in a quiet fury, he'd turned on her.

"You smell like him and it makes me sick."

"We're only friends."

She didn't have the strength to fight. Didn't have the inclination, really, to defend herself. He could think what he wanted.

"Fuck buddies is more like it," he muttered, unknotting his tie.

"That's crude. When did you become so vulgar?"

"When I realized the woman I love, the woman I want to marry, is seeing another man behind my back. Is that what you're doing when you say you're painting? Screwing him? He's old, Zia. His dick probably looks like a rotting cucumber. You want that inside you?"

She shoved past him on the way to the bedroom. "You're being an asshole, and I'm not doing this with you."

He caught her arm, yanking her to him, and covered her mouth with his, ramming his tongue between her teeth. "I doubt he can get you off like I can."

"Stop it." She pushed him away and wiped her lips. "I told you, I'm not sleeping with him," she said, jerking out of his grasp.

"Do you think I'm going to believe you when you don't let me touch you once we're in bed? I'm tired of it." He lowered his voice and brushed a curl away from her cheek. "Let me in. Please."

"I can't," she whispered. "I'm under a lot of stress. My father just passed away. Can you . . . give me some time? I know you don't believe it, but I'm grieving."

He cuddled her to him. "Okay. I'm sorry. I'm just getting antsy, that's all. It'll be nice to be back in LA. Back to normal."

"Yeah. I'm sorry, too."

He'd never been violent before, had never raised his voice. He loved her, and he was scared to lose her. She understood. The thought of losing Matthew scared her, too, though that seemed inevitable. Chloe wasn't their only obstacle.

Humming, she painted by feel, by emotion. She painted memories and dreams, guided by her ten-year-old heart.

She finished the painting, tears blinding her.

Two weeks. Two weeks, and then everything would be over.

Drowning in pain and desperation, she drove to Matthew's, her hands gripping the wheel so tightly her knuckles turned white.

Shaking, choking on her misery, she pounded on his door.

He answered, and she fell against his chest.

"Shh. Little Star, I've got you." Covering her face in kisses, he swept her into his arms and carried her to bed.

The only place she felt she belonged. The only place she felt truly loved.

Three days before the showing Zia stood in her studio, chewing on a fingernail. She wanted to paint one more, but she'd run out of time. She had thirteen, and while she never considered the number unlucky, it was a silly superstition of hers to never open a show with an odd number.

Through the thin silk of her blouse, she rubbed her stomach. She hadn't been feeling right the past couple of days. Nauseated. It was only nerves, but she didn't like the constant churn of her stomach that seemed to follow her everywhere she went, no matter what she was doing, no matter what she ate. Wine tasted off, and she sipped lemon Perrier, another reminder of the first night she spent with Matthew.

They hadn't seen much of each other, mostly because she'd locked herself in her studio, needing to paint as much as possible.

It wasn't difficult, the painting. Missing Matthew gave her

plenty of emotion to fuel the brush against the white. She was grateful she didn't have to worry about quality over quantity. Thanks to Matthew, she had both.

The odd number would bother her.

There was no help for it, as earlier in the week Reid had scheduled the usual interviews in the newspapers and the city's magazines and a TV spot on an early morning local network program. That had taken a lot of her time, and her mother, as one last gift, planned a day at the spa for her, Zia, and Aimee.

Thankfully, Reid had calmed down, and attending the dinners thrown in her honor, the past few evenings returned to being tolerable, if not pleasant.

She tried her best to treat him as a friend. It helped, to a degree. It would get them back to California, and if that was the best she could do, so be it.

She needed to bring one more painting to the gallery that night, then she'd be free to meet her mom, Reid, and Matthew downtown. It would be their last family dinner, and her mom insisted. She'd rather go to bed early. Besides, the thought of food didn't appeal.

Sighing, she checked her cell and groaned. Her phone was dead.

Reid always laughed, saying it was her artist's temperament, but it irritated everyone else when they couldn't get a hold of her. Now she couldn't text her mother to let her know she was on the way.

Just as she was reaching for the last painting that had finally dried enough to make the trip without damage, the lights went out.

The city's bright glow cast eerie shadows on the walls.

Her heart pounding, she paused. The dark didn't spook her, but she remembered the story Shirley relayed at dinner of the gallery's vandalism. The lights had gone out then, too, but she knew she was alone. It must be just a fluke. She picked the painting up by the edges, then paused. Did no electricity mean she couldn't use the elevator?

Crap. Now what was she going to do?

The elevator dinged, the high-pitched sound echoing across the floor, and turning to lean the canvas against the window, she heaved a sigh of relief. She wouldn't have to carry the painting down all those flights of stairs. "Reid, thank God. I couldn't text you, my phone's dead—"

A blinding white light cut her off, and pain ripped through her skull.

She staggered, a buzz filling her ears, and she caught her cheek on one of her easels as she fell.

Through the blackness, she heard the faint ding of the elevator and the doors slide open.

Matthew drummed his fingers on the table as Sylvia tried to call Zia for the tenth time. They'd been at the restaurant for half an hour, waiting, though Reid had slipped into his seat only fifteen minutes earlier, claiming traffic.

It could be true, the traffic story, as downtown was always congested, but since their "good talk" at Sylvia's, he'd look for any excuse he could find to dislike the guy.

Tardiness would be a petty thing, but he wasn't above taking it.

"I don't know what you two are so worried about," Reid muttered, gesturing to their server. "I told you she stopped at the gallery to drop off the last painting. She and Shirley are probably chitchatting like women do."

Sylvia narrowed her eyes, but Reid shrugged and smiled.

"You don't need to be upset," he said, patting her arm. "She'll be here."

"I'll call Shirley and remind her that we're waiting on Zia," Sylvia said, already bringing up her contacts list.

"Fine by me," Reid said, knocking back his drink the second their server set it on the table.

We didn't ask your permission, Matthew thought, gritting his teeth.

"Good evening, Shirley, this is Sylvia Bishop. I'm looking for Zia. She's not answering her phone. It goes straight to voice-mail," she murmured.

He waited, jiggling his leg. He knew Zia better than anyone and she'd have a good reason for running late. She wouldn't stay and talk to Shirley when she knew they were waiting.

"What do you mean she didn't show up? Reid said she was supposed to drop off one last painting." She paused. "She didn't stop by. Okay, thank you. I'll let you know when we find her."

He pulled his wallet out of his pocket and dropped a few bills onto the table. He wasn't going to waste time sitting around drinking if no one knew where Zia was.

"No. Reid can drop it off in the morning. No harm done?" she asked, adjusting her purse strap on her shoulder.

Shirley's tinny voice carried through Sylvia's phone. "No harm done at all. Goodnight."

"Goodnight."

Sylvia disconnected the call and shoved her phone into her purse. "You said she was at her studio?"

Reid shrugged. "Yeah, but you're upset over nothing. She probably got caught up in a painting. She was unhappy having thirteen. Maybe her phone's dead, or she has it on silent. Or she's stuck in traffic, like I was. You're so overprotective. It's no wonder why she never wanted to come home to visit."

He stepped forward, but Sylvia held him off, pressing a

hand to his chest. He let her. He didn't need to cause any more drama.

"She's my daughter, and I'm entitled to worry a bit. We'll see you back at the house?"

"If that's what you want. No use sitting here by myself."

"We'll take my truck," he said as they rushed through the restaurant as quickly as they could and still remain polite. "Her studio isn't far from here."

Fortunately, he'd been able to park near the restaurant, and seconds later, he held his truck's door open. She climbed in and buckled her seatbelt. He trotted around the back and settled behind the wheel.

"She really could be painting," Sylvia said, worrying her purse's strap between her fingers. "And Reid's right. She never checks her phone."

"I know. He probably *is* right. About everything. But it doesn't keep me from wanting to bash his face in."

"You're hostile this evening."

"I don't like the guy. And I'm worried."

"She'll be okay. Nothing bad happens in Lake Kenosha. When was the last horrible thing that happened to someone you know?"

"This morning. I had to see Chloe's face at the office."

Sylvia huffed a laugh. "See? You haven't lost your sense of humor."

"I'm trying."

Matthew parked his truck on the street in front the building where Zia painted. Nothing seemed amiss, the sidewalk quiet and the concrete steps empty, and he led Sylvia through security, nodding to the guard sitting on a stool texting on his phone.

When Reid had rented the space, he explained the realtor told him the building was kept open overnight to be cleaned, making it that much more convenient to use as a studio. Zia could paint whenever she wanted.

It did seem like that was a plus for her, who had come to his house very late one evening smelling of tears and paint.

He thanked God Chloe moved into the Harborview. He'd asked her, politely, of course, to leave, and knowing he had the upper hand concerning Bridgewater and her position there, she'd packed in a storm of furious and frustrated tears. She was gone that afternoon.

He'd felt like shit making love to Zia in the bed Chloe had vacated only a few weeks before, but the feeling was nothing new and he'd swallowed back the guilt and shame while Zia cuddled in his arms after a round of hot sex.

The elevator ride seemed longer than usual, the floors ticking by excruciatingly slow. Someone had turned the music off and they stood in silence, blood rushing in his ears.

The doors slid open.

"Will you still want dinner?" he asked.

"I couldn't eat a bite, not now," Sylvia said, following him out of the elevator. "But I'll need a stiff drink. These last few days . . . I have to admit, I'll be happy when the showing and ball are over. I need to get back into my old routine."

He brushed his fingers over the wall, looking for a light switch. The city's bright glow wasn't enough to see by. "Missing Ray?"

"Yes, but having Zia here helps. When she and Reid go back to California, that's when I'll feel it most."

"Yeah." He couldn't add more. The thought of Zia leaving . . . Well, he had four more days with her and he wouldn't ruin them by being sad about the inevitable.

He flipped on the light, the fluorescent bulbs buzzing. His shoulders sagged. "She's not here," he said, but he already knew that. She wouldn't have been painting in the dark.

"I can't believe Reid expected her to paint in this dump. Look at all this junk. He couldn't have rented her a real studio? What kind of agent is he? She could have gotten hurt." Sylvia stepped across the floor toward an easel that had a blank canvas waiting on it. "Maybe she did want to paint one more— God, Matthew, she's over here. Call 911. Hurry."

Clipping his hip on the corner of a crude table made with sawhorses and a large sheet of particle board, he rushed past Sylvia, his heart in his throat.

Zia laid on the unfinished wooden floor, the scent of sawdust, paint, and blood in the air.

He leaned down to roll her onto her back, but Sylvia said, "Don't touch her! Oh, God, my baby." She started crying, her hands fluttering over Zia's body, looking for some way to help and finding none.

"I can't—" he choked, smoothing Zia's hair away from her face. He rested two fingers against her neck. "She's still alive." His hand shaking, he pulled his phone out of his jacket pocket.

Speaking to the 911 operator through clenched teeth to ward off his sobs, he explained where they were. Blood congealed near her hairline, and purple spread down her temple and into her cheek, the skin puffy and swollen. "Oh, Little Star. What happened? Who would do this to you?" he whispered.

"Sir, are you still with me?"

"Yes, I'm sorry."

"I'll stay on the line until the paramedics arrive. They're en route."

"Thank you."

Sylvia cried against his shoulder, but he didn't have the strength to comfort her. He clutched Zia's lifeless hand and gave the dispatch the exact directions to their location to help the paramedics find them as quickly as possible.

He stood helplessly as they rushed onto the floor pushing a gurney, barking orders at him and Sylvia to stay back.

It took all of five minutes for them to whisk her away, an oxygen mask over her face, her skin pale, and he made every bargain known to man and God praying Zia would be okay.

"Let's go," Sylvia said. "I want to be at the hospital. I want to be there in case she needs me."

"Yes," he murmured, confusion and grief clouding his head. How long had she lain there, alone?

The thought of Zia by herself, scared, knowing she couldn't call for help, crushed him.

He was no good for her.

How many times did he have to fail her before he finally gave up?

For good.

Matthew and Sylvia sat in the ER's waiting room, impatiently waiting for word. Reid sat near them—with them, but not—and guilt weighed him down.

It had become them against Reid.

Reid hadn't done anything but love Zia, too, and in that, there was no crime, but try telling that to his heart.

A man dressed in a suit stepped into the waiting room and spoke briefly to a harried nurse at the nurses' station. When she pointed their way, Matthew straightened his back.

A cop.

"I'm looking for Sylvia Bishop?" he asked, glancing at a small notebook.

The detective looked like every cop Matthew had ever met: aged, thoughtful. A good head on his shoulders, if Matthew could guess. He hoped, because he wanted to find out who did this to Zia and make them pay for thinking they could hurt her and get away with it.

"That's me," Sylvia said, standing.

"I'm Detective Donovan," he said, holding out his hand. "I need a few minutes of your time."

"But I can't—"

"Don't worry, Mrs. Bishop. When I spoke to the nurse, she said your daughter wouldn't be allowed visitors for quite some time."

"I . . . okay. Matthew, you'll come get me if you hear anything?"

"Of course."

The detective led Sylvia down the hallway and to small sitting area that had a coffee machine, a coffee table full of magazines, and several plants sitting on end tables and on the floor. Detective Donovan push quarters into the machine and handed Sylvia a cup of coffee.

He turned back to the ER waiting room and cradled his head in his hands. A headache pounded behind his eyes, and he wished he had a drink.

"Thank you, for going to find her."

He glanced at Reid in surprise.

"I really thought she'd gotten caught up painting. She does it so often, I'm used to it, I guess. It never occurred to me she could be hurt."

"It's nothing," he murmured.

He tried to think of something else to say, but he came up blank. Paramedics rushed into the ER pushing two gurneys, and the smell of blood and adrenaline saturated the room, saving him from having to respond further.

"Car accident," one paramedic shouted to a nurse.

The commotion moved down the hallway and the waiting room quieted once again.

"Mr. Harcourt? Can I speak to you for a moment?"

He stood and kissed Sylvia's pale cheek. "There's no news. Are you okay?"

"I'm fine. He's a nice man. He only wants to figure out what happened to Zia."

"Okay."

He followed the detective to the same alcove but declined the offer of coffee. He was already jittery, and caffeine would only exacerbate it.

"How long have you known Zia Bishop?" Detective Donovan asked, sitting on the coffee table instead of a chair or loveseat.

"All her life," he said, sinking onto a chair's armrest.

"And you were expecting to meet her for dinner?"

"Yes."

"Do you have any idea who would want to harm Miss Bishop?"

He shook his head. "I have no idea. She's only in the area because her father passed away recently." He paused. "There was a painting she was supposed to bring to Post 15. She's doing a showing there in a few days. Did Sylvia tell you? Is it still there, in the construction space? If whoever attacked Zia stole it, it'd be worth several thousand dollars. Especially if Zia already signed it. I can't remember, I mean, I didn't think to look—" He rubbed his eyes. His only focus had been on Zia and calling 911.

"That's fine, Mr. Harcourt," Detective Donovan soothed. "Thank you for the information. I'll send a uniform to check. It'd be nice if this was a run-of-the-mill robbery. When something like this happens because of personal reasons, it's more difficult to puzzle out. People take slights in different ways, in varying degrees, and it's never a sure thing how they'll retaliate, if they do. You can't think of anyone who holds a grudge against her? For any reason?"

He parted his lips, but stopped. Considered how much of their dirty laundry needed to be exposed during the detective's investigation. He wanted to help, but if he could save them any more embarrassment, he would.

"Mr. Harcourt? If you know of anyone, even if it's just a suspicion, it can help tremendously. Ruling someone out who has an alibi is closer than not."

He sighed and said, "Zoe's aunt, Chloe Bishop, took a dislike to Zia a long time ago. It's jealousy, really, but out of anyone in Lake Kenosha, she's the only person I can think of. Zia doesn't have enemies, and as I said, she hasn't been in the area for the past few years. She didn't inherit when her father passed away, so the attack couldn't have been about money, unless the painting's gone."

The detective grunted and jotted something in his notebook. "That's unusual, isn't it? Raymond Bishop owned half of Bridgewater Financial. He had plenty of assets to pass to whomever he wished, and you're telling me he cut out his daughter? Completely?"

"Not completely. She'll inherit five million dollars when her firstborn turns twenty-one, but she can't have children. Something Raymond apparently didn't know."

"Huh," Detective Donovan said. "I can't see how any of that has a bearing on what happened tonight, but I appreciate the information." He paused and scribbled another note. "Just out of curiosity, to whom did Mr. Bishop leave his half of Bridgewater to?"

"His sister, Chloe."

"That must have made Chloe Bishop feel good, to inherit over the niece she hates, and her sister-in-law, too."

"It did, but Chloe planned it that way." Matthew blew out

a breath. *In for a penny, in for a pound.* "Before his death, Chloe told Ray Zia and I had slept together when she was only eighteen. And Chloe knows . . . we still are."

Moaning, Zia woke, her tongue glued to the top of her mouth. A vicious pain shot through her head, and the ever-present nausea hadn't gone away.

"It's best if you try not to move," a voice said, somewhere on her left.

She tried to pry her eyelids open. "What happened?"

"I don't have many details, but from what I know, you were attacked. You have a concussion and a gash on your forehead," a nurse wearing blue scrubs said.

"Right."

Knowing she was in the hospital calmed her, and she tried to relax. The scents of cleaner and stale food lingered in the air. She wanted to ask what time it was, but she couldn't make her mouth move. She let her eyelids drift shut and listened to the sound of a TV coming from down the hallway.

"I'll get the doctor. Your family's waiting to see you, but your doctor has to give them the okay, first."

"Hmmmm." Matthew was there. Tension eased out of her body enough she dozed while she waited, and she woke more alert when a cool hand touched hers. The mattress sank as someone sat by her feet.

"Hi, Zia," a woman's gentle voice said.

She couldn't place the voice without opening her eyes, and she did so, slowly, the hospital room coming into soft focus. "Dr. Jennings."

"How are you feeling?"

"My head hurts."

"That tends to happen when someone hits you with a two by four."

Wincing, she tried to swallow. "Can I have a drink of water?"

"Of course, but let's sit you up first. Tell me if it hurts." Dr. Jennings pressed a button on her bed, moved her into a sitting position, and adjusted the pillows under her head. "How's that?"

"I'm okay. Thank you."

A kind nurse had placed a white and grey plastic mug on the rolling tray next to her bed, and the doctor held it to her mouth. Gratefully, she sipped the cool water through the white bendy straw.

"Is that enough?"

"Yes. Thank you." It was all her queasy, empty stomach could tolerate.

"Do you remember what happened? There's a police detective who needs to speak to you when you're able, but we'll let your family see you first."

"I was at my studio," she said, searching through foggy memories. "And the lights went out. I was using the top floor of an office building to paint my collection for the *Fall and Foliage*. I needed to bring a painting to Post 15, but I thought I was stuck up there. I didn't know if the elevators would work when there's no electricity."

"Right. That's a lot of stairs."

"Yes, and I didn't want to drop my painting. But then the elevator doors opened, and I thought it was Reid coming to help me. I can't remember anything after that."

"There's not much to remember," Dr. Jennings said, patting her foot through the thin cream blanket. "Someone hit you on the head, and you scraped your cheek when you fell. The detective said I could tell you if you asked. Mr. Harcourt and your mother called 911 right away."

"Matthew found me?"

"Yes, and your mother. You were supposed to meet them at a restaurant for dinner and they were worried when you didn't show up."

"And Reid." She remembered that part now. She was going to drop her last painting off at Post 15, say a quick hi to Aimee, and then meet everyone at Luna Blanc. "Why are you here? The nurse said my doctor wanted to see me. Aren't you a gynecologist?"

"Yes, I am. How are you feeling?"

"A little better. Queasy. Some painkiller would be nice."

Dr. Jenning's smile was full of sympathy. "You're on as strong of a painkiller as we can give you."

"Oh. It doesn't feel like it's enough," she said, prodding her temple, a bandage taped to her skin. She'd look lovely at the showing and ball.

"It probably isn't. Zia, I don't think you understand why I'm here."

"You're the only doctor I've seen since I've been in Lake Kenosha," she said. "I don't have a primary care physician."

"That's true, but it's not the reason. They did your blood-work and contacted me. You're about eight weeks pregnant."

She covered her belly with her hand, the IV pinching her skin. "I'm what?"

"I did an ultrasound, and you're measuring at about eight weeks. This is good news, isn't it? After your visit?"

She stared out the window where clouds hid the sun and a large flock of birds flew across the sky. It wasn't good news. "The baby's father won't want it," she murmured, tears welling in her eyes.

"How do you know if you haven't told him?"

"We've already had the conversation. He doesn't want kids. He's . . . a lot older than I am, and he said his time for children has passed."

"Maybe if you—"

She shook her head. The motion brought the pain shooting back into her skull and nausea rolled in her stomach. "No. Please, don't tell anyone."

"I won't. Your medical records are protected under law. I can't say anything to your family without your okay, but the other doctors here will know if they look at your chart. I'll call a prescription for prenatal vitamins in to your pharmacy, unless . . ." Dr. Jennings paused. "Unless you think you might not keep it. You don't have long to decide."

Despite the ache in her head, she whipped her gaze to the doctor and glared. "No! This baby's mine."

"Okay. I'll let you rest. You need sleep."

"How long have I been here?"

"Fourteen hours or so. You were brought in last night."

"My showing's the day after tomorrow."

"Under the circumstances, they want keep you until tomorrow to make sure you don't have any side effects from your concussion. Whether you want to attend will depend on how you feel. The baby's fine, perfectly healthy. It has a very strong heartbeat. After seeing your tubes, I never thought this would be a possibility. Not without medical intervention. You're a very lucky woman."

"Thank you."

"Get some rest, and good luck, Zia. Schedule a prenatal visit soon. Either with me, or if you're going home after the showing, a doctor in LA."

"I will. Thank you."

Dr. Jennings walked out of the room, her heels clicking on the tile.

She closed her eyes, her cheeks wet.

Pregnant.

There wasn't any doubt whose baby it was, either.

Matthew didn't want kids, and at the time he told her, she'd thought it romantic. Now it made her want to cry because she suddenly realized what he'd been trying to tell her.

When this baby turned ten, he'd be sixty-four. When their child went to college, Matthew would be over seventy years old.

She could picture them in public, could already hear the murmurs. A man spending time with his daughter and grandchild. What else would they think when the baby would look like both of them?

More tears trickled down her cheeks. He wouldn't want their baby. Wouldn't want the burden of a child when he was thinking about retirement. He was selling his house, looking at condos, wanting an easier way of life. Bottles and diapers and whatever else wasn't an easier way of life. She remembered her parents fighting about her. She wouldn't do that to Matthew.

She wouldn't tell him. She didn't want him to keep her and their baby out of obligation, and he would, too. That's the kind of man he was.

He wanted her to go back to LA with Reid, keep her art career going on the West Coast.

So she would.

He didn't have to know.

She rubbed her belly. She wouldn't show for months. She could keep her pregnancy a secret another few days.

Just make it through the showing and the masquerade. Make it to the airport without falling apart, and then, in LA, she'd break up with Reid, paint her heart out, and have her baby.

She'd live her quiet life and give their child all the love she'd never be able to give to Matthew.

Do the right thing. Start thinking about other people instead of herself.

Maybe she was finally growing up after all.

"Hey, Little Star," Matthew murmured the next time she opened her eyes. Sunlight shined around the edges of the closed blinds.

He sat beside her, holding her hand, his thumb brushing her cheek.

He hadn't shaved, and he looked as he had at his birthday party, his complexion grey, lines gouging his face.

"Hi," she whispered, scrubbing her fingers over his scruff. "You look so sexy."

His low chuckle warmed her. "You must be feeling better."

Besides the ache in her head that had lowered to a dull throb, she felt significantly better than when Dr. Jennings had spoken to her earlier. Dr. Jennings. Right.

She dropped her hand. Couldn't get too close. Well, they were already close, but they couldn't stay close. The smartest thing she could do was use the time she still had in Lake Kenosha to put distance between them. Start saying goodbye. Wasn't that what he'd been doing this whole time? Take the fucking hint. "Are you okay? You look horrible."

Matthew kissed her palm. "You just said I looked sexy."

"You do, but worried, too. I'll be okay."

"We didn't know that, not for a while. Head injuries can be serious, but the doctor said you'll be able to go home in the morning."

Zia swallowed. "That's good."

"Yes. I'm sorry we didn't find you sooner."

"It's my fault for never charging my phone. It's okay. I don't know who would want to hurt me."

"Detective Donovan said your painting was still at the studio, so this was personal, not theft. He asked me the same thing, and sweetheart, the only person I could think of who would want to hurt you is Chloe."

She struggled to sit up, and he wrapped an arm around her. Casually, she leaned out of his embrace. Too close. "Aunt Chloe might hate me, but I don't think she hates me that much. She won, didn't she? When Dad gave her Mom's half of the bank. She won. There wouldn't be a reason to attack me."

"That might be, but he asked for anyone, to start ruling out suspects. You haven't lived here for several years and there was absolutely no one else I could think of. Sylvia thought I was reaching, but she couldn't come up with anyone, either."

"I don't know." She paused. "Can you help me to the bathroom?"

"Do you want me to call a nurse?"

"You've made love to me. Seen all my bits. I think you can walk me to the bathroom."

Matthew huffed a laugh. "Okay."

She did her business and washed her hands, staring at herself in the mirror. She looked banged up, naturally, but her physical appearance only reflected how she felt inside. She lifted her chin. She'd need to be stronger than that. She had someone depending on her now.

Matthew helped her back into bed, covered her legs with the blanket, and pressed a light kiss to her bruised cheek.

"Thanks. Where's Mom and Reid?"

"Reid's at the gallery talking to Shirley. He's been sitting with you, don't think he hasn't been. Your mom had a meeting with a potential client. She's been here, too. If I hadn't said I'd stay, she would've canceled."

She smiled faintly. "Stepping in like you always have."

"You'll always be mine, you know that, don't you, Little Star?"

Maybe he didn't know he was telling her lies, but she did. She didn't belong to him. She didn't belong to anyone. "I know." She brushed her thumb over his lips. "I love you, Matthew."

He cuddled her to his chest. "I love you, too. Scared me."

"Sorry," she whispered, back to the little girl she used to be, her hero protecting her, always.

"Nothing to be sorry for. I hope they find whoever tried to take you away from me."

She couldn't talk about this anymore. "I'm tired. Can I go to sleep?"

"You don't need to ask, sweetheart. I'm going to get a cup of coffee, then I'll sit with you. I don't want you to be alone."

"Thanks."

When she knew he was gone, she let the sobs come. She'd never be able to tell him that it wasn't the person who attacked her who would've taken her from him. It was the little baby growing inside her that would keep her away.

It wasn't fair she had to trade one love for another.

But then, it was only in bedtime stories and dreams where life was fair, and she was too old for both.

Matthew leaned against the wall outside Zia's room and listened to her cry. He wanted to rush to her, hold her in his arms, and demand to know why she was crying. If she was in pain, if there was anything he could do.

But for the past seven years he'd been a coward, hadn't fought for what he wanted. Telling Chloe to go to hell.

Standing up to Raymond, finally admitting he was in love with his best friend's daughter.

Hell, all his life he'd been weak.

That hadn't changed as he stood outside Zia's room, listening to her keening.

When he couldn't take it any longer, he shuffled down the hallway, the coward he'd always been, too scared to ask the questions.

Too scared to know the answers.

CHAPTER ELEVEN

Zia pulled her dress over her head, avoiding the injured side of her face as much as possible. While she dressed, her mother spoke to the nurse, signing her release papers and going over her care instructions.

A light knock made her turn toward the door, and a man dressed in a rumpled suit and scuffed black dress shoes stepped into her room. He reminded her of Matthew, in a way, tired and maybe a little sad. Worn out.

"Can I help you?" she asked, reaching for the wide-toothed comb her mother brought from home, though it didn't matter what her hair looked like. The first thing she was going to do when her mother drove her to the house was shower.

"I'm Detective Donovan," he said, holding up a badge, "from the LKPD. Are you Zia Bishop?"

"Yes, I am. Matthew said you wanted to stop by. You have questions about who would've done this to me." She gestured to the side of her face where her temple and part of her cheek were a deep purple. She'd needed stitches, and a white bandage stood out against her red hair.

"I do. Can I sit down?"

"Yes. I'm sorry."

Detective Donovan sat in the chair Matthew had vacated only hours before when her mother came to take his place. Though she told him he didn't need to, he'd spent the night, his head propped in his hand.

"Do you have any idea who could have done this to you, Miss Bishop?"

"No. And please, call me Zia. I'll be listening to enough of that 'Miss Bishop' business at my showing. I hope you'll come. Tomorrow evening, before the *Fall and Foliage* ball, at Post 15."

"Will you be well enough to attend?"

She shrugged. "It will give me a reason to leave early."

Detective Donovan tapped the side of his nose. "I like the way you think." He slid a small notebook out of his jacket's pocket and scanned a few pages.

She sat on her bed and tried to find the energy to brush her hair.

"I did my share of digging around yesterday and this morning, and I don't like admitting, came up empty. You're sure you can't think of anyone, anyone at all, who would have wanted to do this to you?"

"Isn't there some other way you can find out? The building's security?"

"When the power was cut, it blanked out the security cameras. We're dusting for prints, but it seems unlikely we'll find anything in your studio."

"What do you mean, 'when the power was cut?' Someone did that on purpose? When the lights went out, I thought it was an outage."

"No. Someone found the circuit breaker box in the basement and turned them all off. Maintenance flipped them back on, but whoever did it had plenty of time to attack you and still get away. You ticked someone off."

She stared at her comb, light blue plastic, white teeth. "No. I'm sorry, I truly can't think of anyone. Matthew said he thought Chloe could have done something like this, but I don't see her as the violent type. Conniving and bitchy, yes, but she's too lazy."

"Those are the ones you have to watch out for, but, in this case, you're correct. She has a tight alibi. Mr. Harcourt did tell me something that seemed of interest to the investigation. He mentioned that you two are in a relationship?"

She bit back a bark of laughter. "If that's how you describe sleeping with someone on a semi-regular basis and nothing else, then yeah, I guess you could say that Matthew and I are in a relationship."

"I found that interesting—"

"Did you?"

"—from an investigative standpoint."

She stared and waited.

"You came to Lake Kenosha with Reid Vaughn, correct? Your agent?"

"Yes, that's right, and we're scheduled to fly out the day after the showing. We've been here for quite some time, and he represents other artists who need his attention."

"It's always the innocent ones who don't understand where I'm going," Detective Donovan grumbled. "You're in a relationship with Reid Vaughn, a real one, by the sounds of it, yet you're sleeping with Matthew Harcourt. Where was Mr. Vaughn the night you were attacked?"

"With Matthew and my mother waiting at Luna Blanc. I was going to meet them there. Wasn't he there?"

"He was, but after some questioning, it turns out he was late, and can't, or won't, account for his whereabouts. At least, he said he left your apartment later than he'd liked and was hung up in traffic."

She stood from the bed, the comb clattering to the floor. "He'd never do this to me. Not long ago he asked me to marry him. He loves me."

"He asked you to marry him. So, he's serious about you. What do you think he'd do if he knew you were sleeping with Mr. Harcourt?"

"I don't like where this is going."

"And I don't mean to do this, to you or to your family, but someone attacked you and Reid Vaughn has no alibi and a strong motive."

"My aunt—"

"Chloe Bishop was having dinner at the time of your attack. She has several witnesses and a security camera caught her image when she arrived at the restaurant and when she left. It wasn't her. I'm sorry. There's not going to be an answer to this question anyone likes. We'll try not to make this unpleasant for Mr. Vaughn, but I can't lie to you, Miss Bishop, he's our number one suspect."

She sank onto the bed. She didn't believe Reid had done this to her.

"Zia, are you ready?" Sylvia asked, stepping into the room. "Oh, I'm sorry. Am I interrupting? The doctor said she could go," she said to Detective Donovan. "Matthew's driving the car around now."

"Where's Reid?" Zia asked.

"At the gallery. He's helping Shirley put your showing together. I told him I wanted you to stay at the house. There's no reason why not, and I want to keep an eye on you. Doctor's orders. I made up the guest room for you both."

"Okay."

Detective Donovan nodded at her. Whether he meant it in

goodbye or for her to take her mother's advice and avoid being alone with Reid, she didn't know, but she nodded in reply. He left without saying another word, and with her mother's arm around her, she waited for a nurse to help her into a wheelchair.

At this point, she didn't care who attacked her. She just wanted her showing to be over. She wouldn't relax until she was on a plane, putting as many miles between her and Matthew as possible.

Reid couldn't have done such a thing.

She was naïve and maybe a little stupid, but Reid wouldn't hurt her.

In fact, all she had to do was ask.

"I'm ashamed you have to ask," Reid grumbled, jerking at his bow tie, knotting it tightly at his throat. "First we spend the night with your mother across the hall, like what? She thinks I'm going to finish the job? And now you point-blank ask. Good Lord, Zia, I tell you I love you and that doesn't mean anything anymore, does it? Maybe it never did, and I've been blind. No wait, I haven't been blind. I knew you were sleeping with Harcourt. You were the one who lied about it."

Zia picked up her orange and black butterfly mask and skimmed her finger along the edge. It matched the black and orange dress she'd wear to the showing. Aimee had stopped by earlier and helped her apply butterfly tattoos: one on her shoulder, one above her right breast, a small one on her cheek, and one on her ankle.

Going to the *Fall and Foliage* ball might have been fun if the side of her face didn't feel like it was going to explode, if her stomach wasn't so queasy she thought she was going to throw up, and now this. "I'm sorry. I told Detective Donovan you wouldn't have done it. I defended you. But I want to know why you were late. Why did Matthew say you were acting like an asshole while you waited for me? In LA, if I would have been late and you weren't able to get a hold of me, you would've checked on me yourself." She lifted her chin. "Why did Matthew and my mom look for me? Why didn't you?"

Reid dropped his hands and turned away, grabbing his plain black mask off the table. "Why would I? We've barely spent an hour together in weeks. If we go out, it's with your mother and *Matthew*," he said, sneering, "or a group of people I couldn't give fuck-all about. You didn't want to see me."

She cuddled against him and wrapped her arms around his waist, under his jacket. He stiffened, but after a moment he hugged her to him, and despite everything, she felt safe. "I'm sorry. Let's . . . let's get through tonight, and tomorrow, on the plane, we'll talk. Really talk about everything."

"They may not let me leave town," Reid joked, laughing bitterly.

"I believe you. I believe you, and I'm sorry."

She sobbed against his chest, ruining her makeup, but she didn't care. So much had happened, too much, but tomorrow, she'd put it behind her.

A fresh start. Maybe a new city. A new place to live. Somewhere nearer to the ocean to help her move on. Because God, would she need it.

She quieted and Reid said, "I was late because I got lost. What man wants to admit that? I'm sorry, too. I haven't been very supportive." He kissed the top of her head. "I agree. We'll talk on the plane, figure this out. I really do love you, and my proposal's still on the table. Think about it." Nudging her away he said, "Let's go now. Shirley's put a lot of work into this, and it would break her heart if you were late."

"I need to fix my makeup, then I'll be ready."

"You're already beautiful, but okay."

She reapplied her lipstick and mascara, relieved that what Reid told her made sense. He'd been lost in a city he hadn't visited before.

She believed him.

But that left a chill in her heart because if he didn't do it, and Aunt Chloe didn't do it . . . Then who the hell did?

Matthew tried to stay hidden during the showing, tucking himself behind pillars and columns and little nooks designed to give pieces of art their own spotlight. He didn't want to talk to anyone, and the gallery was full of people who wanted to do exactly that. Quiz him on Bridgewater, how things were going at the office. Women weren't the only ones who gossiped, and he quickly tired of assuring the gentlemen he did business with he could run the company without help.

He'd stopped asking Sylvia's opinion. She had no say, and none of the income would reach her pocketbook. Not ever again.

Raymond had seen to that.

Bridgewater's future belonged to only him. At least, it felt like it.

"Why are you hiding?" Sylvia asked, offering him a fresh drink.

"Why aren't you?" he asked, leaving an empty champagne flute near a vase that cost more than his monthly salary.

"Networking. These are potential clients. Come on, people have been asking about you and it's starting to look bad."

What looked bad was the way Reid wouldn't leave Zia's side, nor did it appear she wanted him to.

She held court in front of one of the largest paintings she'd done for her collection. Ten feet long and eight feet wide, the painting exploded with autumn color. A large pile of leaves filled the canvas, and Matthew couldn't imagine how long it had taken her to paint each leaf, to give each one life. A man's feet, along with a little girl's, kicked at the leaves, and they flew into a rich blue sky.

The sound of her giggle came through the paint, and it brought tears to his eyes. He remembered that day.

He remembered all the days displayed on these canvases. They depicted the most perfect moments of his life when Zia had been a child.

She'd painted his every wish.

"You have a good memory," he said. He didn't have to look at her to know she stood next to him. Her presence would always be with him, would always haunt him. He could be standing in a sea of a million people, and he would know. He would know if she ever stood beside him, without her making a single sound.

"You were good to me. You could have treated me like the little girl I was. Told me to leave you alone, that you had better things to do. But you never did. Not once."

"I've loved you all your life, in some way," he said. He couldn't lie. "I've tried not to. You weren't mine to love. Never have been, really. Never will be."

"I didn't paint these to make you sad. They're my best memories, and they turned into my best work."

He finally met her eyes. The bruise looked worse now than when she was in the hospital, if that was possible. "It doesn't make me sad. I'm humbled, that after all I've done, you would still think of me that way."

She smiled and shrugged. "Sometimes it's better to leave the past in the past."

"Yes, I agree. You're not drinking? Do you want a glass of champagne?"

She brushed a hand over her belly. "No, thank you. Not with the painkillers, you know."

"Right. I'm sorry."

"It's okay. Detective Donovan's here, asking questions. I know you were disappointed when he cleared Chloe."

He sniffed. "It would've solved a lot of problems, but no. Zia, I'd never want anyone you thought you could trust to do that to you. Even Chloe. Once trust is broken, it's hard to get back. I know that firsthand. And for what it's worth, I hope Reid checks out, too."

"He told me he tried to find the restaurant without his GPS and got lost. I believe him."

"Good. That's all that matters. Be careful, Zia. Don't go anywhere alone."

"In this crowd, I don't stand a chance. Reid wants me, I need to go."

She kissed his cheek, and he breathed in her scent of rosewater and the musk that radiated from the perspiration that made her skin sparkle. She had a right to be nervous.

She was a star.

People already filled the ballroom, sipping champagne and chatting excitedly. They'd begun to trickle out of the gallery when word spread all Zia's paintings had sold.

Exhilarated by the unexpected success in Lake Kenosha, Reid glowed, trading handshakes with the patrons of Post 15 who had scrawled several zeroes onto checks that were locked in the safe in Shirley's office.

Shirley fluttered around the ballroom accepting congratulations on the most successful showing of her career. She accepted all the praise, preening, as if she were the sole reason for the evening's triumph.

Zia lingered near the outskirts of the crowd. It was the same ballroom where Matthew had celebrated his birthday. It seemed fitting, somehow, that the first place she'd seen him when she'd returned to Lake Kenosha would also be the last.

Her stomach clenched.

She didn't like the thought of flying while she felt like this, but she couldn't put the trip off. Reid would only accuse her of wanting to stay for Matthew, and she sure as hell didn't want Matthew thinking the same thing, but feeling this nauseated wouldn't be comfortable, even in first class.

Ducking into a back stairwell, Zia leaned against the wall and breathed shallowly through her mouth. She didn't want to throw up. She *really* didn't want to throw up. It was the most disgusting thing in the whole world. She sank onto the stairs, her fingers trailing over the carpet.

Her heart twisted. This was the stairwell where she and Matthew had made love. Whimpering and burying her face in her hands, she realized that her baby had possibly been conceived on these stairs.

The night Matthew announced his engagement to another woman.

Out of everything that happened in the several weeks she'd been back in Lake Kenosha, at least that had gone her way. She'd never been happier than when Chloe moved out of Matthew's house. Now if there was a way to shove her out of Bridgewater . . . But short of Chloe being arrested, like Matthew said, it would sort out a lot of problems, there didn't seem to be any solution.

That was none of her concern. Bridgewater wasn't any of

her concern. It wouldn't be her legacy, no part of it would be passed down to her or her children.

Matthew could handle it. He took every opportunity to tell her how old he was. If he was so adult, he could handle it, and all the trouble Chloe brought with her.

Taking a deep breath, she opened the fire door and let in the sounds of the ball. Elated murmurs layered under the music.

She headed to the bar hoping a glass of ginger ale would settle her stomach, but a tall, thin woman intercepted her. "Zia! Congratulations! It was a beautiful showing, and you sold out, I hear! That's fantastic! Your paintings really are to die for."

The woman wore a black and pink dress, similar in style to hers, and a black mask. Pink ribbons floated to the floor. If she was feeling better, she would've complimented the woman, but nausea rolled in her stomach and sweat beaded her skin. Instead of the bar, she should be looking for a bathroom.

"Thank you," she said through clenched teeth. She sounded like a bitch but she didn't care. She didn't know who this woman was, though her voice sounded vaguely familiar.

"I'm Rebecca, do you remember me? We've met a couple of times now," the woman said, pulling off her mask.

"I'm sorry. I do remember you, but it's so stuffy in here. I was going to the bathroom. I don't feel right," she said, pressing a hand to her stomach.

Rebecca linked their arms. "I know exactly what you mean. In fact, I was about to go up to the roof and get some air. Would you like to join me?"

She hadn't been to the roof before. Being outside under the stars and in the fresh air sounded heavenly, and she allowed Rebecca to lead her out of the ballroom. She'd calm her stomach tell Reid she wanted to go home. Everyone would understand she needed to get some sleep. She'd been annoyed

Reid scheduled their flight so soon after the ball, but now she was grateful.

Putting Lake Kenosha behind her couldn't come soon enough.

Sitting at an empty table in the back of the room, Matthew sipped his drink, clinking the ice cubes at the bottom of the glass. Tired, he wanted to go home and drink himself silly, black out until tomorrow evening, then when he woke up, the worst part would be over.

He didn't have the strength to say goodbye. He'd congratulate her, one more time, then he'd slink away like the asshole he was. He didn't have any fight left to do more than that. It was what he deserved for wasting so much of his life. And Zia's. He hoped she could move on.

"Mr. Harcourt," Detective Donovan said, sitting next to him, a green bottle of Heineken clenched in a fist. "You people sure know how to party."

"You've never been to one of these before?"

"Yeah, once, back in college. My girlfriend's dad struck it rich building malls, and she wanted to go. Hasn't changed much. Meaning, I haven't missed much."

He chuckled. "You're right about that." He nodded at the beer bottle. "They know good booze, though. How's the investigation going?"

Donovan sized him up, not in a hurry to answer. "We cleared Vaughn, if that's what you're after. He used the GPS function on his phone to find the restaurant. It would have been difficult for him to be in two places at once."

"Good," he said, meaning it. "I didn't want it to be him."

"Sure you did," Donovan disagreed good-naturedly. "No

better way to get rid of the competition. But I know what you mean. You love her, but if you can't have her, at least she's with a guy who'll treat her well."

"Something like that," he muttered.

"We did have a crack in the case, though, and I'm looking for a—" he pulled his little notebook out of his jacket pocket— "Rebecca Gainsborough."

"I don't know who that is."

"Apparently, she's an artist Post 15 has featured at one time or another. Someone vandalized the gallery not long ago. Did you hear about that?"

"Yeah. Shirley Shapiro was a guest at a dinner party Zia's mother hosted, and she told us about it. Lots of art destroyed, that kind of thing."

"That's right. Uniforms canvassed the area and found an empty can of orange spray paint in a dumpster. We got a lucky hit off a partial. The print belongs to her. I talked to Ms. Shapiro, and all this hoopla was supposed to be for this Gainsborough woman until Miss Bishop painted her way into the picture, so to speak. Eager to make a name for herself at the gallery, Ms. Shapiro bumped Miss G faster than I can spit, and she didn't take it too well."

"I don't know anything about any of that. Reid Vaughn would be the man to ask if you have questions."

"He and I have spoken, but he didn't have anything to contribute. Doesn't matter. The print's good enough for me, but I wanted to bring her in and question her about Miss Bishop's attack. I have a pretty mean game of 'good cop/bad cop,' and I hope I can get a confession out of her before she knows what hits her and lawyers up. Without a confession, we're back at ground zero because I've got zip on anyone else who has motive."

"Maybe we'll never know."

Donovan scoffed. "I don't like that."

"Neither do I. It's possible Zia's heard something tonight. The only thing people love to do more than drink is gossip. Aimee," he called out as she walked by their table. "Hold on a second. Have you seen Zia?"

Aimee pulled the mask off her face before answering. "Mr. Harcourt, I mean, Matthew. She didn't look very good. I think she has a stomachache. I saw her go into the side hallway with Rebecca. Rebecca Gainsborough. She's an artist who shows at Post 15 sometimes."

He stood, sweating, his heart pounding. "What does she look like?"

"She's wearing a black and pink dress, and she has blonde hair. She's tall. Taller than Zia, and super-skinny."

"Thanks. If you see Zia, will you let her know we're looking for her?"

"Is Rebecca in trouble?" Aimee asked, worrying her mask between her fingers and frowning. "Did she do something?"

"No," Donovan cut in. "I have a question or two about the vandalism at the gallery a few weeks ago. I figured since I'm here and she's here, I could get it out of the way."

Aimee tried to smile, but it trembled on her lips. "She was a little upset Ms. Shapiro wanted Zia to do the showing for the *Fall and Foliage,* and I heard Rebecca yelling the day Ms. Shapiro told her, but I don't think . . . I mean, I really don't think . . ."

Her voice faded as he led Donovan away from the table.

Zia took a deep breath of the cool fall air and pressed a hand to her stomach. If this was the way the next seven months were going to go, she didn't look forward to it. Fatigue weighed on her and she craved sleep. She'd need to schedule an appointment with an obstetrician as soon as she landed at LAX. Morning sickness was natural, but this kind of nausea was too much. What was the point of calling it morning sickness if it lasted all day?

"It's gorgeous up here," Rebecca said, stepping across the rooftop.

The city lights spread out in front them, twinkling. Zia swallowed back the need to throw up. It didn't help, and she sank into an outdoor loveseat. "Why isn't it open? The bar, I mean?"

"The hotel closes it during winter months starting in October. In case bad weather comes early. These couple of weeks are my favorite time to be up here. It's not that cold, and I like the quiet."

"Yes, I can see how you'd like spending time up here," she said, leaning her head against the cushion. She had no desire to make conversation, but Rebecca seemed determined to talk. She closed her eyes and listened to Rebecca's voice hum in her ear like an annoying mosquito.

"The showing went well," Rebecca said, staring over the city. "I had a showing for the *Fall and Foliage* a couple years ago. It didn't go nearly as well as yours. This year was supposed to be my redemption. I've been working so hard, and I'm studying under Bailey Sky. She's wonderful."

"Oh, what has she been teaching you?" she asked, unimpressed. She'd heard of Bailey Sky. She'd been accused of producing forgeries, though no one could make the charges stick. Bailey Sky was a brilliant artist in her own right, but once accused of forgery, there was no shaking the reputation.

"Technique, mostly." Rebecca shrugged. "She says I have a difficult time translating light onto the canvas. I'm getting better, and tonight was supposed to be a comeback of sorts. I've been working on my collection for months."

"Sorry I threw a wrench into your plans," she said, not sorry at all. Sweat beaded on her skin though a cool breeze blew, ruffling her dress. "There's always next year."

"Maybe."

"I need to go back downstairs and find Reid. I'm not feeling well, and I want to go home."

"Oh, Zia. You're leaving tomorrow. Come here and look at the city. You won't be seeing it for a while, will you?"

She sighed. She needed to go, but though it saddened her to admit it, she wouldn't be coming back to Lake Kenosha. She'd be dealing with enough pain trying to forget Matthew while looking into their child's eyes.

Swallowing down the bitter taste of bile, she dragged herself off the loveseat and stood at the edge of the roof near Rebecca, their arms brushing. "It's beautiful, and I'll miss it."

"Yes, you will, you bitch," Rebecca snapped, grabbing a fistful of her hair.

Pain shot through her temple, her stitches pulling. She stumbled on her heels, her stomach doing a quick roll.

"What the hell is wrong with you?" she shrieked, grappling at Rebecca's arm.

"This showing was supposed to be mine. You ruined it. Ruined it," Rebecca screamed, yanking her hair. They leaned precariously over the ledge, but she couldn't move. "Shirley promised she'd put all the power of Post 15 behind me, but once you came along, I didn't matter anymore. Precious Zia Bishop, *artiste extraordinaire*. Like you're so great, you and your stupid fall paintings. They look like you did a bunch of paint by number kits. What do you do? Buy them in bulk from the hobby store?"

"Were you the one who attacked me?" she asked, gasping in pain.

"Yes, and I should've hit you harder. Stupid woman, painting by yourself in a construction site. What kind of agent is he, that he didn't rent you a real studio? Fucking moron. People fawning all over you two, it makes me sick."

Rebecca wasn't the only one who was sick.

The woman twisted her fingers in Zia's hair, and she cried out. The skin around her stitches felt like it'd caught fire, and pain sizzled along the side of her face.

The door to the stairwell slammed open, and Detective Donovan and Matthew charged through. The detective drew his weapon and shouted, "Let her go and put your hands where I can see them."

She met Matthew's panicked eyes.

"Fuck you," Rebecca barked.

Her stomach had had enough.

Rebecca shoved her, and she stumbled, nearly losing her balance, her hand grazing the concrete balustrade.

She wretched, spraying vomit all over Rebecca's sparkly black stilettos.

CHAPTER TWELVE

Zia sat in the hotel's lobby, sucking on a peppermint she took out of the bowl on the registration desk, Reid's jacket wrapped around her.

Everyone kept trying to persuade her to drink to calm her nerves, but she pushed every glass away. Shivering in shock, she tried to answer Detective Donovan's questions, but it was coming up on midnight and she could tolerate only so much more of Matthew's disapproving glare.

"I think that about does it," Detective Donovan said to her relief, slipping his pen into the inside pocket of his tuxedo jacket. "I appreciate your patience, Miss Bishop, and I'm sorry we didn't find her sooner."

"I just want to go home." And by home, she meant anywhere that wasn't Lake Kenosha.

"Come on," Reid said, hugging her close. "Let's go. Sylvia, you're riding with us?"

"Yes. Thank you. I'm ready."

"I haven't given Zia my gift," Chloe called across the lobby, her heels clicking against the marble. Wearing an emerald green dress, her hair done in an elegant updo, her aunt demanded attention, and beside her, Detective Donovan whistled low under his breath.

She glanced at Matthew and frowned. He'd gone ghostly pale.

Gripping Reid's jacket around her, she stood and inched toward the lobby doors. She didn't want to hear what Chloe had to say. Nothing could be worse than carrying a child whose father didn't want to be one.

Chloe stopped in front of her, her eyes maliciously bright, her smile insincere. "I'm so glad I caught you," she said, clasping a stack of envelopes in her hands.

"I was busy, you know, while someone tried to kill me," she said, her lip curling in disgust and nausea. Throwing up all over Rebecca had probably saved her life, but, unfortunately, it hadn't helped her stomach calm down.

"That would've been a shame," Chloe said, not comprehending, or ignoring, her sarcasm. "I wanted to give you these."

Reluctantly, she reached out to take them.

Her mother whimpered.

"Mom, are you okay?" she asked.

"Chloe, do you have to do this? Can't you leave it alone? You already won," Matthew said, standing, his voice sounding so forlorn she almost went to him.

"It will never be enough. Take them," she ordered, pushing the envelopes into her hands.

"What are they? I don't understand. Letters? From who? To whom?" She ruffled through the corners without seeing them.

She didn't care.

"From Matthew, to your mother."

She shook her head. "They've been friends for years. Aunt Chloe, this is ridiculous. I'm not feeling well and I have a flight tomorrow. I don't give a fuck if Matthew writes letters to everyone in Lake Kenosha."

Chloe lifted an eyebrow. "Telling them he loves them? That he misses them more than anyone?"

"I'm sorry?" she said, her vision swirling.

Reid steadied her, and she turned to her mother who was . . . crying. There was only one other time she'd seen her mother cry, and that was at her father's funeral.

"Mom?"

"When I was at university, your mother and I had a long-distance love affair. We wrote to each other for a handful of years while she dated your dad," Matthew said, his eyes never leaving her face.

Matthew had been in love with her mother. Zia found that . . . oddly . . . sweet.

And once again, who the fuck cared?

By the way everyone was looking at her, apparently, *she* was supposed to care.

She leaned heavily against Reid as things clicked into place.

The secret.

This was the secret. The one secret everyone had kept hidden because if her father found out, it would have torn her family apart. Not to mention Matthew and her father's friendship.

What would have become of Bridgewater?

"Did you . . . did you sleep with her?" she asked Matthew.

"No. We only wrote to each other. I was homesick, and your mom—"

"I missed him, Zia. The three of us had always been such good friends, then Matthew went to school and your dad began courting me, and I . . . I didn't know. I was so torn. But your dad was here and Matthew wasn't, and I've never regretted the choice I made. I loved your father very much, until the day he died."

"How did Aunt Chloe find them?"

"I stored them in an old steamer trunk the movers accidentally gave her while I was at a job. They delivered the wrong one."

"You kept them."

"Yes."

"Did you keep yours?" she asked Matthew. "The ones my mother wrote to you?"

"No."

"Aunt Chloe told Dad everything before he died. That's why he changed his will."

"He had a right to know, Zia. He had a right to know he'd been living with a conniving bitch and the man he considered his closest friend was a cheater who wrote love letters to his fiancée right up until the night of their wedding."

She glared. "Don't go all high and mighty, Chloe. You blackmailed Matthew into a relationship. That's why . . ." Gasping, she covered her mouth. "That's why Matthew started dating you. Because you had the letters *and* you were spying on us the morning after my party. You threatened to tell Dad everything, and oh, God. What would my father have thought if he knew Matthew had had a love affair with his wife and slept with his daughter on the night of her high school graduation."

"I should have—"

"Save it," she snapped at Matthew.

Honestly, she didn't care about what Matthew had done. She didn't care about the letters, and it surprised her that everyone expected her to. It had been a long time ago, and she couldn't throw stones. She didn't blame her mother for being confused. It wasn't like she'd been able to resist Matthew's charms. She'd eagerly handed him her heart over and over again only so he could break it.

But she did realize Chloe had handed her an opportunity.

Because in all this, she couldn't forget about the baby.

Now that everything was out in the open, secrets scattered like shattered glass across the floor, she and Matthew could be together. Nothing was holding them back. Not Chloe and her threats. Not her father. Not her mother. Not even Reid.

But while Matthew had made it sound beautiful, romantic, she couldn't forget the core of what he'd told her that evening at the hotel. He didn't want children, and despite all the lies he told her, she believed deep down in her heart that wasn't one of them. At fifty-three, he didn't want their baby, and she wouldn't tell him.

She'd use the situation to break it off completely.

Be the grownup everyone wanted her to be, expected her to be.

She kissed her mother's tear-soaked cheek, wetting her lips. "You lied to me when I asked you about the rumors, but I don't blame you." She pressed the letters into Sylvia's trembling hands and met Matthew's eyes. Flinging his words back at him, she said, "I've loved you all my life, in some way, but I never want to see you again. Please, if you care about me at all, leave me alone."

Holding her head high, she walked out of the lobby and onto the city sidewalk, and, oh God, out of Matthew's life forever.

Zia wandered the apartment above the garage while Reid packed their things in the guest bedroom at the house. The flight made her nervous and she hoped to sleep through most of it, if she could. He hadn't said much after they left the hotel the night before, holding her close and keeping his lips pressed to the top of her head. Rebecca's attack weighed more heavily on his mind than her family's secrets, and she loved him for that.

Idly, she opened doors, closed them, skimmed her fingertips along textured walls, the surface of an empty dresser in the second bedroom.

She checked the closet for anything she might have hung up that she wanted to keep, as she'd be true to her word. She wouldn't come back to Lake Kenosha ever again.

The painting she'd hidden there several years ago leaned against the back wall, and she sank to the floor, tears dripping down her cheeks.

Matthew's blue eyes peered at her, a lock of his black hair flopping over his forehead, a slight smile on his beautiful mouth. Wide shoulders, strong arms, his hands, gentle but firm.

She rested her head against the doorjamb. He'd taken her with so much love that night, no man had ever compared.

"There's your daddy, little one," she whispered, rubbing her belly. "How I want to remember him."

"Zia," Sylvia called, "We're almost ready to go."

"I'll be right there." On impulse, she lifted the painting out of the closet. She couldn't keep it with her, but . . .

"Will you give this to Matthew?" she asked, carrying the painting into the small living room. "I painted it before I left for the Art Studio. I painted it to . . . to . . ." She set the painting on a kitchen chair and wiped her face. It hurt too much to talk.

"I will, if that's what you want."

"Yes. I'd like him to have it, so he knows how much he's meant to me."

Her mother sighed. "Zia . . . I don't know much about what's going on between you two, but if you're leaving, if you're not giving him a chance because of me—"

"That's not it. You know I don't hold what you and Matthew had against you. Your friendship and what came out of it was special and I would never resent either of you that. I have very much loved having him be a part of my life, and I only blame Chloe and her jealousy for causing us the problems we've had to deal with. But he's older than I am, by a lot, and it's something he can't let go of. He wanted the out, so I gave it to him. End of story."

"He's always been so noble," Sylvia said, sinking onto a chair next to the painting. "When he told me he was going to do whatever Chloe wanted to keep our secret . . . every year that went by, my heart cracked a little more because of what he was giving up for our family."

"It wasn't his place," she said through gritted teeth. "So what if Chloe would've told Dad everything? If he would've been that angry, you would have gotten more in a divorce settlement." She pressed the heels of her hands into her eyes. "I can't talk about it anymore. We all need to deal with the choices we've made. He doesn't want to be with me so I took the burden of our breakup onto myself. He's given us so much, it was the least I could do."

"Are you sure—"

"Mom, will you listen? *He doesn't want me.* He thinks he's too old for me, and maybe he is. I want children. I want a family. He said he doesn't. You know women who try to use babies to trap men only do more damage. Leave it alone."

"You're not telling me you're pregnant, are you?"

"No." It hurt to lie to her mother, but there had been enough secrets and she couldn't ask her mother to keep something as important as a baby from Matthew. She'd crack before twenty-four hours were up. "But one day I'd like to be, or try to be, or if that's not possible, I'd like to adopt, and Matthew doesn't want kids. He's been very clear. Give him the painting like I asked, okay, Mom?"

"Okay. I . . ."

"Leave things be. Dad's gone. Chloe had her fun but she's paying for it now. Let Matthew do with her what he will. You have your business, I have my painting. Everything worked out how it should. Dad was right after all."

"You're right," Sylvia said, sighing, "but I wish things could have turned out differently."

She hugged her mother, long and hard. She didn't know when she'd see her mother again. Not for a very long time if she had a choice. "Matthew and I love each other, but sometimes love isn't enough. Let's go now. I want to go home."

"Your home used to be here. I'm going to miss you, my baby girl," Sylvia said, cupping her face between her palms.

"I'm going to miss you, too, but Lake Kenosha hasn't been my home for a long time and it won't be, ever again."

Zia placed her hand in Reid's as their plane taxied down the runway. She'd need to do something about him, but for now, she took the comfort he offered because it was all she had.

"I want out."

Matthew scowled and looked away from his computer screen. "You want to go out? Then go. Why are you asking me?"

He hadn't been able to stop her from coming in late, taking a three-hour lunch, then leaving early, but he'd been keeping track of her hours and how little she worked. Soon he'd compile enough evidence to sue her for her half. Hell would freeze over before he kept allowing her to draw the kind of income she claimed to be entitled to while contributing nothing in return.

The days of him being her doormat were over.

It took losing Zia to learn how to defend himself.

He'd known it would happen. Had wanted it. But he hadn't realized how much it would hurt. The seven years he'd lived under Chloe's thumb had numbed him and he'd grown used to Zia's absence. Knowing he was doing the right thing had made it bearable.

But this, *this*.

Chloe stomped her foot though her boot made no sound on the carpeting. "I want out. Of this company, out of this city, out of this state. I want out."

"You're fucking crazy. You put all of us through hell, and for what? Jealousy. Revenge. You got what you wanted. Raymond changed his will for you. *For you*. Now you don't want it? How many lives did you destroy because of your vindictiveness? You can give me the old song and dance that Raymond deserved to know the truth, but what it amounted to was you being unhappy with your own life. You can leave, but you can't escape yourself."

"Then you'll buy me out?"

Eyes narrowed, he stared at her and then picked up the phone. "Belinda, will you send Jayson up from legal, please? Thank you." He hung up the receiver.

"What are you doing that for?" she asked.

Tapping a pen on his blotter, he said, "Because I don't trust you. Any agreement we come to today will be signed and locked. You'll never be able to change your mind, is that clear?"

She sat in a chair in front of his desk and lifted her chin. "Yes."

He studied her. Her hair was perfect, her makeup impeccable. The Chanel suit she bought hoping it would make her fit in, in a place she didn't belong. "Just tell me why you did it. Cut the crap and tell me why. Raymond adored you. He took care of you without complaint. Zia never did anything to you, and Sylvia had always been a very generous sister-in-law. What did you have against any of them?"

"It wasn't them. It was you. All I ever wanted since the day you and Ray became friends, was you. Yet there you were, kissing Sylvia's ass, and later when Zia came along, Lord Jesus on high, you'd think a goddess had been born. You never looked at me. Even though you were there by force, the seven years we were together, I was happy."

He scoffed. "You weren't happy because we were together. You were happy because you'd taken me away from Sylvia and Zia. There's a difference. You may say you wanted me, but I know better."

Someone knocked on his door, and he called, "Come in. Jayson, Miss Bishop has decided to leave us."

Sitting at the conference table in his office, for the next two hours, they negotiated.

He refused to back down on the meager sum he was willing to pay Chloe to buy her half. She still had the inheritance Raymond left her and what her ex-husbands had given her in their divorces. She was wealthy without him paying her a dime.

They called in his personal assistant as a witness to sign the contract, and after she and Jayson had gone and he and Chloe were alone, he shook her hand. "What will you do?"

"The offer on the lake house fell through and I bought a condo in St. Petersburg. When we were kids, our parents took Ray and me there on vacation. The beach will be nice, and I might find another husband since we didn't work out. I'm not going to say I'm sorry because I'm not. And I'm not going to say I'll miss this place because I won't."

"Well, darling, that makes two of us. I'm not going to miss you, either. *Bon voyage,* and all that. Good luck, Chloe."

Silently, she stepped into the hallway and closed the door, and he prayed to God he'd never have to see her again.

He leaned back in his chair in the office of the business that was completely and totally his.

He tried to find peace in the fact that Zia was where she belonged. In LA creating her art, perhaps engaged to a man who deserved her.

Convincing himself things had worked out in the long run would require more than a bottle of lemon Perrier. He'd go home, while the house was still his, and count his blessings over numerous glasses of scotch.

Because he did have some.

Even if he didn't feel like he did.

CHAPTER THIRTEEN

Matthew stopped by Sylvia's once a week to check on her, and on Christmas Day they ate a small dinner, exchanged inexpensive gifts, and avoided talking about Zia.

He spent New Year's Eve alone, and on New Year's Day like everyone else he knew, he made New Year's resolutions and flipped through self-help books looking for answers as to why his life had turned out so terribly.

The only problem was, he was the same person as the year before, and he knew of only one way to make his life how he wanted it to be.

He'd never be happy without Zia.

One snowy evening he looked in on Sylvia, and she invited him in to have a drink and a meal. He liked the visits as much as he hated them. Sylvia would always be a good friend, but the house reminded him of Zia.

"How's the world of banking?" she asked as they settled in front of the fireplace sipping after-dinner drinks.

"Better, now that Chloe's gone, but there's still a lot of work and I've been headhunting for someone who can lighten the load. I need someone who shares our values and ethics, and I'm looking more in the nonprofit sector instead of stealing someone from a different financial institution. Raymond and I founded Bridgewater to give people a bank they could trust and rely on. I don't want that to change, and I don't think Ray would want it to, either, despite hating me at the end." He leaned his elbows on his knees and stared into the fire. "I redid my will and left everything to Zia. Bridgewater is hers. It always has been."

"Matthew, I . . ."

"Have you heard from her?"

"She calls every couple weeks. Tells me she's okay and hangs up. I want to go out there but she doesn't want me to. I can't force her to let me visit, but I'm worried."

"She'll be okay, and she's got Reid."

Sylvia bit her lip. "The day she left, she gave me something to give you, but I didn't. I don't know why."

She slipped out her chair and walked through the living room entryway, and Matthew sipped his scotch and waited.

"Zia said she painted this the night before she went to the Art Studio. Until I looked at it, I don't think I realized how much you love each other."

The man in the painting looked like him, but not. A younger version, happier. Not so world-weary. Seven years and a lot of pain separated him from the man on the canvas.

She captured how he'd looked, in bed, leaning over her, love bright in his eyes. His Little Star. He'd taken much more than her virginity that night. He'd taken her innocence, her sense of wonder, and he'd twisted them with lies and deceit. He'd turned her love into hate, and he didn't think he'd ever be able to reverse it.

"I don't want it. It will only be a reminder of what I lost."

"You should take it. She wanted you to have it."

"To punish me, maybe. To taunt me. That night should never have happened."

"If Chloe wouldn't have done what she did," Sylvia asked, thoughtfully staring into her wineglass, "do you think you two would have made it?"

He barked out a laugh. "What kind of question is that? Of course not. She was fresh out of high school. She needed to explore, experiment, find her talent. She never would've become what she is without me sending her away. There were nicer ways to go about it, but it still would have broken her heart."

"And yours."

"She might have been eighteen, but she was a little girl. I was the adult, and I did what I had to do."

"She's older now, and you let her walk away."

"Like I did you."

Sylvia set her wineglass on the side table and knelt by his feet. "You didn't let me walk away. I chose. Don't you think after our letters and Ray and I going on our dates, I would've known whom I wanted to spend the rest of my life with? It was a difficult choice, but if I had wanted you, I would've said so. You think you're weak because you lost me, but that's not true. You think you're weak because you let Chloe screw you, and screw you over, but that's not true, either. I told Zia you were one of the noblest men I know. You lived through seven years of hell to keep Ray from finding out about us. That's not weak. I will be indebted to you for the rest of my life."

"You don't need to thank me for that." He held her hand and rubbed his thumb over her knuckles.

"Yes, I do. Do you know what Zia said when I told her that?"

"I can't imagine," he said smiling, thinking of his Little Star in all her spit and fire.

"She said we should've let him find out. That I would have gotten a fairer deal in a divorce. She's right, you know. We both let Chloe win. Not just you. I did, too. I'm sorry I didn't say anything to Ray. I should have owned it. I shouldn't have let you go through what you did alone."

He dropped her hand and drained his glass. "I need to go."

"Will you look in on her?"

"What? You want me to fly to LA? I'm trying to get Zia out of my heart. If I saw her, I'd only miss her more."

"I want you to see her. I want you two to talk, one last time."

He placed both hands on her shoulders and looked straight into her bright green eyes. "I still love her. More than I could ever put into words. If she, by some miracle, could forgive me . . . are you saying you'd give me your blessing to be with her?"

She rose on her knees and cradled his face in her hands. "I'm telling you, as your friend, as a woman who has admired your strength, not only in the choices you've made in your personal life, but in the way you've handled Bridgewater since Ray got sick, that there is no one on this earth I'd choose who would be better for my daughter. She's a flame, my Zia, you said it yourself. Bright, like a blaze on the head of a match, but you are her candle, Matthew. You need her, to shine, but she needs you too, to rekindle her spirit when life gets to be too much and she burns out."

Her words were pretty, but reality wasn't a poem. "She can't have a career here."

"No, she can't. Post 15 was the best she could do. But, you don't need to stay in Minnesota to run Bridgewater, do you?"

He opened his mouth to say yes, yes, he did, but his heart started thrumming with possibility, with realization. "No.

Whomever I hire can run it with my help, wherever I am, but Sylvia, what about you?"

She fluttered her hand through the air. "I'll be fine. I have my company, and this house . . . Raymond and I were together for a long time. I need to find myself again. I've been a wife and a mother, but now I want to be . . . me. I have a million books to read and TV shows to watch. Maybe I'll adopt a dog to keep me company on cold winter nights. You'll visit, won't you? You and Zia? And I'll visit you."

"If you promise not to call me your son-in-law."

She huffed a laugh. "I could never think of you as my son-in-law, but you'll always be my friend. You deserve to be happy. Go get her."

"Thank you," he said. "For everything."

"Treat Zia well, and I'll call it even."

On a day dawning bright and cold, he flew into a thunderstorm and a temperature of fifty-five. Standing in the rain on a stoop that belonged to a small house near the beach, Matthew knocked on Zia's door, dread and joy mixing in equal measure in his heart. He wanted to see her, his Little Star, but knew full well she could tell him to go to hell.

"She's not home," an elderly woman said, peering around the front door of the house next to Zia's.

"Do you know when she'll be back?" he asked, intending to wait. He'd come too far to back out now.

"No, but I can tell you where she is. A gallery downtown, getting ready for a showing, she said. Do you want the address?"

"Yes, thank you."

Using his phone's GPS, he drove to a posh section of Santa Barbara and parked near the gallery.

He trudged through the downpour, thinking up excuses that would explain why he was there. Her mother wanted to make sure she was all right. He wanted to tell her in person he'd bought out Chloe and Bridgewater belonged solely to him. That he needed a vacation and he was in the neighborhood. He grimaced. Like she'd believe that.

Opening the glass door, he spotted her the moment he stepped inside. Zia stood with her back to him, directing a woman adjusting a spotlight. Canvases covered the walls, dark, twisty, nightmarish, and full of misery. "These are different for you," he said, and she turned around.

Her hands cradled her swollen belly, and he staggered backward, his heart breaking. He was too late.

"Ingrid, will you give me a second?" she asked.

"Of course." The woman scurried off the ladder and rushed down a hallway.

"Matthew, what are you doing here?" she asked, her face growing pale. Her hands shook against the baby she carried.

"I came to . . . congratulate you, it seems. You and Reid decided to start a family. I'm happy for you. But I thought you couldn't get pregnant?" His voice was calm and he praised himself for it.

"I . . . a miracle baby is what my doctor calls it."

"It?"

She smiled faintly. "I haven't found out if it's a boy or a girl. I want it to be a surprise."

"You haven't told your mother. She's going to want to know."

"I'll tell her, but I . . . I didn't want *you* to know."

His mouth dried. It had come to this. "I'm sorry. I don't mean to cause problems between you and your mother. All I ever wanted was for you to be happy. I know you don't believe that, not after everything I've done, but you don't have to worry about Sylvia passing along news of you and Reid and your child. As long as you're happy, that's all that matters to me." His eyes devoured her, one last time. She wore a black scarf in her hair and an emerald green sweater to ward off the chill. A clingy black dress hugged her belly.

She looked like the artist she was, earthy and carefree, and he envied Reid his life and the family she would give him.

He shoved his hands into the pockets of his slacks, reluctant to leave. He didn't want to, not yet, because he'd never see her again. Instead, he gazed at the paintings. The storm clouds, the red slashes, the black. "These don't look very happy. This one," he said, pointing to a redheaded woman standing on a cliff, crying, while the ocean churned below her.

She stood next to him. "What I said was true. I paint how I feel, and my feelings for you have given me my best work."

He made her unhappy.

His heart plummet to his feet. Hearing her say it, he knew he wouldn't get a second chance. "I should go. I wanted . . . well, it doesn't matter now. Good luck to you, Zia." He kissed her forehead.

He was reaching for the door's handle when she called his name.

When he turned, his eyes were glassy with tears, and Zia called herself all kinds of fool for stopping him. She should have let him go. She could have told him goodbye, watched him walk into the rain. But he'd come for her, and that had to mean something, didn't it?

"Will you sit with me for a minute?" she asked, tilting her

head toward a bench that faced a landscape ten feet high and fifteen feet long that she'd painted during the worst of her morning sickness. A prairie where the storm churned dark and the tall grass shrank back in fear. It's how she'd felt, too sick to hold a brush, but she'd forced herself, knowing that in her extreme nausea her body was creating something she couldn't live without.

He sat next to her on the black wrought iron bench, and she breathed in his scent: travel, cologne, and something that was only Matthew. She'd missed this man, and she owed it to herself, to her baby, to make absolutely certain he didn't want them.

Zia rubbed her belly, large soothing circles, and the baby kicked under her palm.

"I bought Chloe out," Matthew said, leaning against the back of the bench, his eyes closed. "She didn't want Bridgewater. Everything she did to us, to you, was for nothing. I bought her out for pennies on the dollar. It's ridiculous really, how much pain she caused for so little."

She held his hand, and he gripped it without opening his eyes. It was difficult for him to look at her, and she swallowed the lump of fear in her throat. "I guess I should say I'm sorry, but there's nothing to be sorry for, is there? Bridgewater's better off without her."

"She's in Florida, scouting for a new husband," he said, shaking his head. "I left Bridgewater to you, in my will. I'll run it for you until my death."

"You're not going to die," she said, trying to keep her voice light.

"Sooner than you, Little Star."

She stared at their hands, hers so small in his, resting on his thigh. "Your age has never bothered me. I've never been afraid of the years between us. You've always said it would be too difficult for us to be together, and when you hear something enough, you believe it."

"It's what I've always thought. Not for myself, but for you. I didn't want you to be stuck with an old man like me, and you're not. You have Reid, a man more suited."

"Reid and I broke up when we came back from Lake Kenosha," she said. His eyes widened in surprised and hope prickled her skin.

"But the baby—"

"Is part of the reason. The baby isn't Reid's, Matthew. It's yours."

He paused. "Are you sure? You and Reid were sleeping together. He . . . he confirmed it."

She scoffed, not surprised Reid had lashed out at Mathew when she wasn't around to hear it. "If he said anything, it was because he was jealous and angry. We shared a bed, but while we were in Lake Kenosha, I didn't let him touch me like that. I couldn't. Even after seven years, I knew I was still in love with you." She paused and brushed her fingers over the necklace Matthew had given her. "I think the baby was conceived the night of your birthday party." Due of the timing when she ran out of her birth control pills and didn't refill her prescription, she was certain of it.

He stared at the painting, didn't look at her, and pain tore at her heart. She wasn't enough. She and the baby weren't enough to change his mind.

"Why didn't you tell me?"

She laughed, and it was full of bitterness. "Why would I? You said you didn't want children, that you were too old to have a family. It finally sank in when my gynecologist told me in the hospital that I was pregnant. I can do basic math. When this child is ten, you'll be sixty-three. When he or she goes to college, you'll be over seventy years old. I left because you said that's not a life you wanted and I believed you. I didn't care about the letters, Matthew. They were just a convenient excuse."

He turned sideways on the bench and reached out but let his hands drop into his lap. Tentatively, he reached out again, his hands hovering over her belly. "Can I?"

"Yes, of course."

He rested his hands against her bump, and she laid her hands on the tops of his. The baby kicked as if in greeting, and he chuckled.

"Would you take an old man like me?" he asked, sniffling as the baby kicked under their hands, their fingers laced together, like real parents, waiting for the arrival of their child.

"Matthew, will you look at me?"

He raised his head and met her eyes.

Her breath caught at the love shimmering in the sheen of tears. "For all my life, all I have ever wanted is you. When I see you, I don't see an age. When I look at you, I see a man who is brave and strong, who takes care of the people and things that mean something to him. I want to mean something to you. I want you to love me, without qualifications, without excuses or reasons to hold back. Love me, and our baby. That's all I want."

He framed the sides of her face in his hands and kissed her softly, the tip of his tongue grazing her lips. "I do love you, Zia. I'm sorry. For everything. Anything I have ever done that's hurt you I've only done to protect you."

"I know, but all that's over now. We have many, many years ahead of us. We've wasted so much time." She cuddled into his side and pressed her cheek to his chest. His presence comforted her, and she relaxed into his embrace as he wrapped his arms around her. "I love you so much."

"I love you, too. Let's go home." He sounded tired, but for once, not sad and defeated.

That sounded good, but . . . "Where's that going to be?" she asked.

"I'll need to go back and forth for a while, until I can find someone who can take my place at Bridgewater. Maybe I'll open a branch here, what do you think?"

"You're not going to miss Lake Kenosha if we live here?" she asked, letting him help her off the bench.

"Your art needs you to be here, and if you need to be here, then that's where I'll be, too. I don't want to miss another second of our life together, Zia. No matter what I told you, or how many times I said it, I want to be a father and I'll love our baby as much as I love you."

They stepped into the sun, the clouds parting, the raindrops misting away.

He held the car door open, and she sat, resting her hands on their baby. As he settled behind the wheel, she stared at him. She'd thought, up until the second he walked into the gallery, that she'd be alone. No other man could give her what she wanted, what she needed.

He kissed the back of her hand and smiled.

So many years behind them, full of pain, betrayal, lies, and regret.

Now she had many years ahead of her with this man, the father of her baby, and she looked forward to every single one.

Do you like billionaire romance? Sign up for my newsletter and receive a free standalone novel, an ugly-duckling billionaire romance, *My Biggest Mistake*. There you'll be the first to know of sales, new releases, and what I'm working on. Don't miss out! Go to www.vmrheault.com/subscribe.

ALSO BY VANIA RHEAULT

Don't Run Away

(Tower City Romance Trilogy Book One)

Chasing You

(Tower City Romance Trilogy Book Two)

Running Scared

(Tower City Romance Trilogy Book Three)

The Finish Line

(Tower City Romance Trilogy Book Four,

Bonus Novella)

Wherever He Goes

(A Steamy Forced Proximity Standalone)

The Years Between Us

(A Steamy Age-Gap Standalone)

All of Nothing

(A Steamy Enemies to Lovers Standalone)

His Frozen Heart

(A Rocky Point Wedding Book One)

His Frozen Dreams

(A Rocky Point Wedding Book Two)

Her Frozen Memories

(A Rocky Point Wedding Book Three)

Her Frozen Promises

(A Rocky Point Wedding Book Four)

As VM Rheault

Captivated by Her (Cedar Hill Duet Book One)

Addicted to Her (Cedar Hill Duet Book Two)

Rescue Me

Give & Take (The Lost & Found Trilogy Book One)

Lost & Found (The Lost & Found Trilogy Book Two)

Safe & Sound (The Lost & Found Trilogy Book Three)

Faking Forever

Twisted Alibis (Ghost Town Trilogy Book One)

Twisted Lullabies (Ghost Town Trilogy Book Two)

Twisted Lies (Ghost Town Trilogy Book Three)

A Heartache for Christmas

Cruel Fate (King's Crossing Book One)

Cruel Hearts (King's Crossing Book Two)

Cruel Dreams (King's Crossing Book Three)

Shattered Fate (King's Crossing Book Four)

Shattered Hearts (King's Crossing Book Five)

Shattered Dreams (King's Crossing Book Six)

ABOUT THE AUTHOR

Vania Rheault has lived in Minnesota all her life. In 2003, she graduated with a BA in English with a concentration in creative writing from Minnesota State University, Moorhead. When she's not writing, she's sleeping, working her day job, or going to movie night with her sister.
Find her at vmrheault.com